LONE JACK TRAIL

BOOKS BY OWEN LAUKKANEN

WINSLOW AND BURKE NOVELS

Deception Cove

Lone Jack Trail

STEVENS AND WINDERMERE NOVELS

The Professionals

Criminal Enterprise

Kill Fee

The Stolen Ones

The Watcher in the Wall

The Forgotten Girls

STAND-ALONE

Gale Force

The Wild

LONE
JACK
TRAIL

OWEN
LAUKKANEN

MULHOLLAND BOOKS

LITTLE, BROWN AND COMPANY

New York Boston London

Mulholland Books / Little, Brown and Company
Hachette Book Group
1290 Avenue of the Americas, New York, NY 10104
mulhollandbooks.com

First Edition: August 2020

Mulholland Books is an imprint of Little, Brown and Company, a division of Hachette Book Group, Inc. The Mulholland Books name and logo are trademarks of Hachette Book Group, Inc.

The publisher is not responsible for websites (or their content) that are not owned by the publisher.

The Hachette Speakers Bureau provides a wide range of authors for speaking events. To find out more, go to hachettespeakersbureau.com or call (866) 376-6591.

ISBN 978-0-316-44875-8
LCCN 2020934682

10 9 8 7 6 5 4 3 2 1

LSC-C

Printed in the United States of America

In loving memory of my grandmother, Mummi,
whose strength and quiet resilience
remain an inspiration.

LONE JACK TRAIL

PROLOGUE

What remained of "Bad" Boyd washed up on the beach at Shipwreck Point on a pretty morning in the middle of May, three days after anyone in Deception Cove last saw him alive. Those three days away hadn't been kind to Boyd, and neither had the Pacific Ocean; the crabs had taken to the body by the time Cable Proudfoot and his grandson stumbled across it, nibbling away at what was left of Boyd's once-famous good looks.

Cable spotted the body before his grandson did, and for a split second that stretched to a couple of minutes, he debated with himself whether to just turn the kid around and walk in the other direction, down the mile or so of empty, windswept shoreline until the corpse was out of sight, pretend like he hadn't seen it, and spend the day digging for clams and exploring the tide pools, searching for sand dollars as planned. He didn't get to spend much time with his daughter's boy, not now that they'd moved to Port Angeles, and Cable was hoping to make the most of it: the first beach day after a long, dreary winter, then Tim Turpin's signature fried halibut and chips at Spinnaker's in Deception Cove, and maybe an ice cream cone from the dairy bar back on the reservation in Neah Bay. Heck, he'd been looking forward to this day since the rains started, last November.

But the grandson was seven, and the grandfather nearly seventy, and it didn't take the kid long to grow bored with the rock crab he'd

3

captured by the tide line, to look up and hurry after Grand-pop, catch up with him and follow his eyes twenty yards ahead to the wet, stinking mound of seaweed and torn clothes and ruined flesh, surrounded by waves of hardy flies and tenacious crabs and even a few lingering seagulls—the whole tableau unmistakable, even to an old man and a little boy, as anything but human remains.

The boy saw the body. The boy began to cry. The boy *knew,* and Cable kissed any notion of fish and chips and ice cream goodbye.

Cable put the boy in the back seat of his truck and tried to speak calm and reassuring things as they drove away from the beach. There was no point in calling the police; cell service was spotty out here, on the cusp of the Olympic Mountains amid towering, second-growth timber. It would take just as long to find a signal as it would to drive the highway back to Deception Cove and inform the deputies in person.

The road wound through the trees and along the shoreline, and Cable drove the speed limit. There was no sense in hurrying; the body would stay dead, and the tide wouldn't rise high enough to claim it back again for hours. Soon, the forest widened into open space, and then he passed the gas station and Hank Moss's motel, and he turned north, down the hill on Main Street toward the ocean again and town, the boy in the back seat saying nothing, watching the world pass by his window, swinging his legs and humming softly to himself.

The Makah County sheriff's detachment in Deception Cove sat in a squat, one-story building at the foot of Main Street, overlooking the government wharf and the little harbor beyond, the open strait beyond that, and Canada beyond all. Main Street was quiet, and there were a couple of vehicles parked in front of the detachment, a Makah County SUV and a black, two-door Chevy Blazer. Cable parked beside the Blazer and rolled down the windows partway for the boy, told him he'd be right back and don't try and wander off anywhere.

A young Makah man in a deputy's uniform that might still have had the tags on it sat at the desk inside the detachment doors; Cable recognized him as Lily Monk's boy, Paul, and wondered at how the child had grown up so fast. Although maybe Paul hadn't quite fully grown yet. The rookie deputy blanched as Cable explained the situation, barely waiting for Cable to finish before he craned his neck toward the rear of the detachment and called out Jess Winslow's name. Cable watched Jess come out of a private office in the back and figured it was probably better that she take a look at the body anyway, figured Paul Monk could probably use a little more breaking in before he had to deal with this kind of thing.

Jess looked healthier than the last time he'd seen her, before all the trouble with Deputy Kirby Harwood and his buddies. She'd put on some weight, like she'd finally remembered to eat something now and then, and she didn't look quite so pale, so haunted in the eyes. She listened to Cable, squared her shoulders and nodded, dug in her pocket for her keys, and told Monk to call the county coroner and tell her to meet Jess at Shipwreck Point. Monk picked up the phone as Cable turned to walk out to the vehicles and his grandson, and Jess looked back toward the private office and gave a whistle. Shortly, Cable heard a chain jangle and some kind of shake, and then the black-and-white dog ambled out of the office, sixty-odd pounds of pit mix and muscle, stretching and blinking like she'd just woken up from a nap.

"Come on, Lucy," Jess called, and the dog shook herself one more time and walked over lazily. Jess clipped a lead on her and told her she was good, and then she straightened and met Cable's eyes. "We'll follow you out there, okay?"

———————

Cable watched the deputy in the rearview mirror of his truck as he led her county cruiser back out toward Shipwreck Point. He'd forgotten about Lucy the dog, some kind of rescue, a "companion animal," he'd heard, prescribed by the VA docs to help Jess deal with what she'd been through overseas. Cable looked at the dog—tongue lolling out the passenger window, enjoying the sunshine and the spring air—and wondered if he ought to have driven the extra few miles into Neah Bay, talked to the sheriff himself, wondered if another body might not send Jess Winslow back to the dark places, whatever she'd endured as a Marine that had scarred her so bad.

But he remembered how she'd been in the middle of the trouble with Deputy Kirby Harwood, how the dog had been there too. If she'd come through that strong enough that the new sheriff saw fit to deputize her, well, hell, maybe that dog was just her good buddy at this point and not some kind of mental-health necessity.

The parking lot at Shipwreck Point was still deserted, and Cable parked his truck where he'd parked it before, killed the engine, and climbed out and stood beside his door and watched as Jess pulled the cruiser in beside him. She got out of the cruiser, and the dog tried to follow, but Jess closed the door first, circled around to Cable's side, and Cable pointed through the trees and back east toward Deception Cove.

"A couple hundred yards that way," he told her. "You can't miss it. If it's all right with you, I'll stay here with my grandson."

Jess looked past him at the boy in his car seat in the back of the truck, and her mouth twitched and she nodded.

"You'll tell the coroner where to find me when she gets here?" she said.

"I will," Cable said. "Are you going to need me to give a statement?"

She shrugged. "Not sure yet." Then she looked out through the trees and toward the water. "You get any sense who it might be?"

"Didn't get close enough to tell," Cable said. "I didn't really want the boy to see any more than he already had."

"Yeah, okay." Jess started down the trail toward the beach. "I guess we'll find out soon enough, anyhow."

Cable waited, listening to the sound of the breakers crashing onto the beach and across the black jagged rocks that bordered the sand, and the wind in the trees and the gulls and a raven overhead. After a while he opened the back door of the truck and let the boy out of his car seat, and together they stood in a patch of sunlight and smiled at the dog in the passenger seat of the cruiser.

Jess returned, slogging up through the sand to the dusty parking lot with a grim look on her face.

"Maybe sit the kid down in the truck again, Cable," she said. "I'm going to need to take your statement after all."

The boy, once freed, would not go back easily until mollified with a book and a hunk of a candy bar. Then Cable returned to the front of the truck, where Jess waited with weary eyes.

"That's Brock Boyd down there," she told him, and she shook her head slightly and kind of smiled, though the smile was hollow and there was no humor in her words. "And judging by the hole in his head, Cable, I'd say he's been shot."

ONE

Two weeks earlier

Jess Winslow reached for the handlebar above the passenger seat, the truck rocking off-camber on the uneven road, its engine growling as it tackled the grade, its tires scrabbling for traction in the mud. In the driver's seat beside her, Makah County Sheriff Aaron Hart kept his foot on the gas pedal and both hands on the wheel, guiding the big Super Duty pickup into a maze of old growth along the barest hint of a road, the truck hardly slowing for corners, the headlights piercing darkness.

There wasn't any choice but to go fast, not tonight. Not on an operation like this one. Word tended to spread rapidly in Makah County, and when the sheriff and his deputies set out on a raid, it wasn't long before the whole situation was public knowledge in every bar and back room between Deception Cove and Neah Bay. Sooner or later, word would find its way to the men in Hart's crosshairs.

The new sheriff wasn't the most popular man in Makah County, not among a fair chunk of the population. Hart was a transplant, not a native—an emergency call-up from neighboring Clallam County, come to keep order after Jess Winslow and Mason Burke had killed or put to capture Kirby Harwood and every other one of Deception Cove's sheriff's deputies, the collapse of law and order prompting Makah's aging sheriff, Kirk Wheeler, to retire himself to his fishing boat in Neah Bay.

Under Wheeler and his corrupt deputy Harwood, Makah had grown into something of a haven for cooks and crooks and the otherwise criminally minded, but no more. Aaron Hart wasn't old, and he wasn't corrupt, and in the months since he'd taken the badge, he'd made it his mission to clean up the county — and when it came to Deception Cove, he relied on Jess more and more.

Hart was headquartered in Neah Bay, the county seat, at the very edge of the Olympic Peninsula and the continental United States. Only twenty miles of blacktop separated Neah Bay from Deception, but the towns might have existed on opposite sides of the globe.

Neah Bay was somewhat prosperous, a few thousand people in town and on the reservation next door, a healthy tourist economy, sport fishers and hikers and those come to gawk at the artifacts in the Native museum. The lighthouse at Cape Flattery was a good little hike, and some shipping companies paid to keep a tugboat and crew on standby in the harbor, year-round, in case of maritime emergency. Neah Bay wasn't Seattle, or even Port Angeles, but it was a full-fledged town, anyway. You could see a future there, if you looked hard enough.

Deception, though, was something else. It had once been a vibrant place, lively, prosperous, fueled by salmon and halibut and the money the banks loaned to the men who could catch the fish. Then the fish had stopped coming and the banks quit lending money, and the town had surrendered to a long, inexorable atrophy, those who couldn't afford to leave forced to eke out what existences they could as the rainforest gradually reclaimed its land. Deception Cove was a ghost town, full of the desperate and the slowly dying; it was no accident that Kirby Harwood and his friends had seen opportunity for malfeasance here.

Harwood was gone, though. Aaron Hart was the law now, and Jess Winslow beside him. And nights like tonight were just part of the cleanup.

Hart kept the truck rolling, clearing back-road miles as quick as he dared in the dark, the highway and the lights of Deception long gone behind them, no moon in the sky and only a handful of winking stars visible through the rainforest canopy.

The radio crackled between Jess and the sheriff, and she reached for it, answered, let Hart concentrate on the wheel and the road and the trees that reached out like fingers, scraping harsh and grating against the side of the county truck.

"Winslow," Jess said.

"Gillies," came the response. "We're in position."

Hart raised an open hand in Jess's direction, five fingers pointed skyward. The truck slowed.

"Five minutes," Jess told Gillies. "Wait for our signal."

Off to Jess's right, the land in its vague silhouette rose beside the road, the first of the low hills south of Deception that would grow into mountains if you followed them far enough. The road gained altitude as it hugged the hillside, and Hart slowed the truck further as they crested a small rise. Jess could see in the distance now, through the trees, the lights of a small single-wide trailer, the compound where local rumor said a man named Collier cooked methamphetamine.

Hart killed the headlights, let his foot off the gas, and as the truck rolled forward through the trees, Jess closed her eyes and felt those first familiar stirrings, an electric concoction of both fear and adrenaline to which she'd grown accustomed and maybe even addicted during her time overseas.

She'd completed two tours of duty with the Marine Corps in

Afghanistan and started a third, most of it lodged in some woe-begone northern valley as a member of a Female Engagement Team, brought in to liaise with local women, coax out information that might not have been forthcoming had there been only men on the ground.

It was rewarding work, but it was only half the story; team members were frontline Marines, like the men, expected to patrol and engage the enemy just like anyone else. Jess had never shied from the violence, and in the end she'd grown to embrace it. She'd seen action, and she'd killed her share of the enemy.

She'd seen her friends killed too. Good friends. And it had changed her. Enough that she hadn't completed that third tour. She'd come home to bury her husband only to find herself with a medical discharge and a standing appointment with a VA doc in Port Angeles. With prescriptions for medications that made her feel numb, with nightmares and guilt and a pervasive, all-encompassing sense of hopelessness that she might have let overwhelm her.

With Lucy.

And now, with a man named Mason Burke, who'd served fifteen years for murder, who loved Lucy as much as she did, and who probably loved Jess too. Who'd be sitting awake somewhere back in Deception with Lucy, waiting on her, worrying, hoping she'd make it home.

At her best, Jess Winslow had been an excellent soldier. She'd lived for moments like this. The adrenaline. The action—decisive and final, no room for ambiguity. The violence.

It was everything else that she couldn't comprehend. But she was working on that, with Burke's help. With Lucy's.

Sheriff Hart stopped the truck. Jess reached for her sidearm, checked the action, as Hart did the same. Then she nodded to Hart, and Hart nodded back, toward the radio.

You make the call.

With her free hand, Jess picked up the handset. Then she keyed the transmitter and exhaled, long and slow, to steady her breathing. Spoke to Deputy Tyner Gillies, somewhere out there in the woods, on the other side of Collier's trailer.

"Go get him," she told her colleague. "We've got your back."

TWO

Sometimes Mason Burke dreamed he was still on the island. Still in the rainforest, tangled in deadfall and thick, mossy underbrush, listening to the waves crash against rock somewhere in the distance, the feel of the shotgun alien in his grip as he struggled through the woods toward Jess and the dog.

He'd spent fifteen years in prison and he rarely dreamed about his cell anymore. Nowadays when Burke slept, he dreamed of more recent violence.

Of the stillness of the forest and the staccato report of gunfire, somewhere nearby but impossible to locate. Of the feeling of help-lessness, and of fear, for Jess and for Lucy and, indeed, for himself.

He dreamed of the faces of the men, those he'd killed or wanted to, and he felt guilt and remorse and knew one day he'd be judged for what he'd done. Though he knew also that he'd have done it the same, given the chance to try again, that the men he'd killed had been evil and had meant to harm Jess.

He knew this, but he dreamed of their faces anyway. And he woke with their names on his lips and his body drenched with sweat, reaching for Jess and for Lucy to see that they were all right.

When he dreamed of the island, it scared him, that what he'd done there lingered in his mind. That he still didn't quite feel safe, whether awake or asleep, as though he'd left something on that island that would come back and demand a reckoning.

As though he'd awakened something he'd thought lay long dormant, as though he wasn't the man he'd believed he'd become.

As though he was still the teenaged boy who'd stood trial for murder, who'd surrendered one decade of his life and another five years besides.

As though he was still a killer, and would always be.

It was nearly dawn when Lucy stirred on the floor beside Mason, stood and stretched and yawned, scratched her ear so the tags on her collar jingled, then padded to the galley door and whined, softly, to be let out.

Mason realized he'd fallen asleep, rubbing his eyes and swinging his legs out from the little dining settee. He'd left the lights on, hadn't even bothered to make up the bed. Hadn't planned to sleep much overnight, not with Jess out on a raid, but hell if he hadn't passed out anyways, face in the book he'd been trying to read, still wearing yesterday's jeans.

Hell if he couldn't still hear the gunfire in his ears. The sound of Jess's voice as she called to him, desperate, through the forest.

Lucy whined again, and now Mason could hear the footsteps outside that had roused her, moving steadily up the wharf, boots on treated lumber and the groan of tie-up lines and the lap of tiny waves as the neighboring boats shifted on their moorings.

"Yeah, girl, okay," he told Lucy as the dog shifted again, the footsteps coming closer. "Let's just make sure it's her before we roll out the red carpet."

The footsteps stopped, and Mason peered out through the galley window, straining his eyes through yellow sodium light, and reaching, semiconsciously, for the aluminum Slugger he kept in lieu of a gun.

He and Jess had killed men on that island, and those men had families. Makah County was a small place. Mason Burke was still an outsider.

The boat rocked on its lines, swaying in toward the wharf as someone pulled themselves aboard at the stern. Mason gripped the bat tighter and stayed in the galley's shadows, waiting. He'd rented this boat, *Nootka,* from Joe Clifford's people, a cheap place to stay in exchange for Mason keeping the rig afloat and helping out with the odd carpentry job around town.

Clifford was rebuilding Jess Winslow's old house, rendered unlivable by Kirby Harwood et al., and Mason pitched in where he could there and wherever else Joe needed him. It would do to learn a skill if he was going to stick around here; fifteen years in lockup hadn't taught him much but how to fight—and then, how to avoid it.

They were living apart, Mason and Jess, while the house was being built, Mason on this fishing boat and Jess up at Hank Moss's motel by the highway. Still, they saw each other almost every day, ate dinners together, and mostly shared the same bed. As far as what they would do when the house was completed, well, they hadn't come to that decision yet, had more or less avoided looking too far into the future ever since Mason had stepped off the bus home to Michigan and back into her arms again.

He hoped there'd be room in Jess's new house for him someday. But Mason figured he knew better than to push the issue before Jess was ready to talk.

Lucy panted at the door, her tail wagging furiously, though that didn't bring Mason any peace. The dog was a rescue, bred for fighting in some backwoods hell in Michigan, but as far as Mason knew, she'd been hauled out of that place and into his own life before she'd ever fought a round, and he was thankful for it.

Sixty-odd pounds and brawny, some kind of pit mix, she looked the part of a guard dog. But Mason had worked hard at training the violence right out of her, and by and large, he'd succeeded. Lucy was a gentle creature, more likely to smother you in sloppy kisses than bite you, the most dangerous part of her, her bullwhip tail— at least until somebody threatened Jess.

Someone whistled outside, a few soft bars of "Ramblin' Man," and that was the sign Mason had been waiting for. He set down the baseball bat and stepped out of the shadows and over to the galley door. Nudged it open to let Lucy slip out, just as Jess set her duffel bag down on the fish hatch behind the wheelhouse.

Instantly, the dog was all over Jess, tail wagging and tongue everywhere, leaping up to lick her face as though it had been months since last contact, when by Mason's calculation they'd said their farewells no more than twelve hours ago. But maybe Lucy could sense when Jess was putting herself in danger; she'd whined and paced by the door most of the night, staring balefully at Mason as though it was *his* fault that she wasn't allowed on the raid.

"Oh, I missed you, girl," Jess was saying, bending over to scratch behind Lucy's ears. "I missed you, yes, I did."

She was still dressed for the raid: tactical pants and a Kevlar vest over a dark sweater, her long hair tied back in a ponytail, and Mason could see fatigue in the way she hoisted her duffel bag again and brought it toward where he stood in the cabin doorway.

"I thought you'd be asleep," she said.

"I was," he replied. "The dog heard you coming."

She leaned in to kiss him, and then she stepped back again and looked him over, skeptical. "You're still wearing the same clothes as the last time I saw you, Burke."

"I didn't say I *wanted* to sleep," he said, stepping aside so she could walk into the galley. "But I slept all the same."

He followed her into the cabin, where she stood at the captain's chair to unbuckle her vest and pull out the elastic from her hair. She was beautiful, and he was glad to see her, and glad she was all right.

"How did it go?" he asked, and she shrugged and half sat on the captain's chair and leaned down to untie her boots.

"We got Collier," she said. "Plenty of product."

"That's good," he said.

She didn't look up. "Yeah."

Mason studied her, watched her unlace her boots for a beat. He worried about Jess on nights like tonight, wondered if it was still maybe a little bit early for Sheriff Hart to be sending her off into the really nitty-gritty stuff.

But Makah County was starved for good deputies, and Jess had passed the exam, same as Tyner Gillies and the rest, and the VA doc in Port Angeles had given her his blessing. Who was Mason to second-guess?

"You feel okay out there?" he asked.

Jess kicked off her boots. Leaned back and ran her hands through her hair, blew out a long breath. "I felt fine," she said. "Felt good. Felt like I maybe finally know what I'm doing."

"That's good," Mason said.

"Yeah." Jess pulled the sweater over her head. Then she nodded toward the settee. "You going to make up a bed for us, Burke, or what?"

The bed took some doing to fit together just right, being as it was just the dining table removed from its stanchions and notched in between the bench seats of the settee. Burke set to work on it as

Jess rummaged around in a locker for a bottle. Poured two fingers each of Old Grand-Dad and slipped off the rest of her fighting kit; she handed him his glass and reached for his belt buckle.

"You're overdressed," she said. "Hell, Burke, you're a mess. You had all night to get ready for me."

He sipped the bourbon and let her work on the buttons on his shirt. "You're absolutely right," he said. "I'm sorry."

"Yeah, we'll see." She pulled the shirt over his head, exposing broad shoulders and plenty of muscle; even out of prison, Burke stuck to his jailhouse workout routine, and the carpentry job didn't hurt. "We'll see how sorry you are."

She was amped up, still wired; she could feel it. The adrenaline from the raid was still coursing through her body, searching for an outlet, and Burke was going to have to deal with it. Not that he'd mind, she figured.

It hadn't even been much of a raid, all things considered. Textbook. Nothing like the raids she'd pulled before, *over there*. She'd come back amped from those raids too, and no outlet, at least until her friend Afia died. After that, Jess was as numb after the killing as she had been before, no matter how many rounds she fired in between.

But this was different, and Jess knew it, as she pushed Burke back onto the fishing boat's crummy galley bed and Lucy made her usual break for the privacy of the fo'c'sle. *Burke* was different. It wasn't just the release of tension drawing Jess to the man who was now pulling her down on top of him; it was fear, too, that one day she'd find some way to lose him, same as she'd lost her best friend, and her husband.

This was a celebration of life, and Burke seemed to know it too. He held her close and tight and firm, and his lips barely left her skin, as hers never left his. Her fatigue seemed to disappear. Burke rose up to meet her, and Jess leaned down and pulled him closer, and the boat rocked on the water beneath them and tugged on its lines, and neither of them cared at all.

Afterward, they lay silent on their backs in the dark, their fingers entwined, both laughing as Lucy slunk back up from the fo'c'sle to resume her position curled up beside the bed.

"Thanks for watching my dog," Jess said. She nudged Burke a little, so he knew she was teasing, but it wasn't necessary. The dog belonged to Jess, but she was Burke's too, and Jess didn't ever plan to make Lucy choose between them.

"You might have to start paying me for it," Burke replied. "I've been asking around. Dog sitting's a lucrative business."

Now she elbowed him harder. "You're compensated just fine."

"Is that what this is? Compensation?"

Jess hesitated, the smile fading from her lips. She knew Burke was joking, but there was a kernel of truth to the question, besides, and Jess knew he had cause to ask it.

She'd been avoiding the question, and others like it, pretty well since Burke stepped off the bus back to Michigan and decided he liked the idea she'd proposed to him, that he stick around Makah County a little longer and they'd maybe give romance a try.

It wasn't that she didn't love Burke. It was just that she'd been married before, to Ty, her high school sweetheart, felt these same feelings, love and infatuation and blind, unbridled optimism. Her closest non-romantic relationship had felt familiar too, her best friend Afia, and in the end, both Afia and Ty had died, and died violently, and somewhere inside, Jess knew that she was partly to blame.

She wasn't sure she was ready to risk being hurt again. Though she knew, if anyone, she would risk it for Burke.

But Burke hadn't asked her to risk anything yet, not outright. So they danced around the topic and forded the awkward silences and tried to pretend like there was nothing they were leaving unsaid.

Tried to pretend like that new house of Jess's wouldn't be finished, sooner or later, and that when it was done, those questions they weren't asking wouldn't be harder to ignore.

Beside her, Burke said nothing, and he didn't sigh or pout like another man might have done; he seemed to understand what she was thinking, and she knew he would give her all the time in the world if she asked for it.

Jess rolled over and snuggled up against him, threw her arm over the expanse of his chest and pressed herself as close as she could to the warmth of his body.

"I'm sorry," she said.

Burke pulled her closer. "No need to be sorry," he said. "No need at all." And she took him at his word, closed her eyes, and let herself relax, drift off toward sleep, though she sensed how Burke lay there, staring up at the ceiling as the first hint of daylight appeared in the cabin windows, and she knew he was awake and would likely stay that way now, and she knew, too, that she couldn't dodge the hard questions forever, whether Burke was asking or not.

THREE

It was nearly a week after the Collier raid when Mason Burke first laid eyes on the man who would wind up dead on Ship-wreck Point.

Mason dropped in on Chase Ogilvy's marine supply store on Main Street, downtown Deception, hoping Ogilvy's three messy aisles might spare him a drive to Port Angeles. He carried a shopping list, courtesy of Joe Clifford, and he'd brought a young guy named Rengo along with him. Clifford needed a good tarp and a new drill bit for the work on Jess's place, and Chris Rengo needed work; Mason figured the kid might as well help out a bit, stay out of trouble.

Trouble was where Mason and Jess had found Rengo four or five months back, at the ass end of a rough logging road, guarding a collection of trailers and assorted trash that had once belonged to Jess's late husband. Rengo fancied himself a cook, though whether he'd actually produced any methamphetamine of his own, Mason couldn't be sure. The kid was bone skinny and carried himself like the guys Mason had known in prison—young and probably good-hearted, overwhelmed by circumstance, determined not to be prey in an ecosystem stocked with predators.

Mostly, kids like Rengo didn't make it inside. They caved to the men who were bigger, rougher, older, and if they were lucky, they lived long enough to become hard themselves, brittle and truly dangerous. If they were unlucky, they broke before they had the chance.

Lucy liked Rengo, anyway. And Rengo liked Lucy, looked at her like a kid would, all pretense of toughness disappeared from his eyes. Watching the two of them together, Mason had decided he couldn't just leave Rengo to fend for himself in the forest. Figured he might as well try and make a difference in the young man's life, step in at a time when nobody had done the same for him.

To date, Rengo hadn't proved to be much of a builder. But he showed up every morning, and he worked hard and didn't talk back to Joe Clifford or Mason, and Mason was starting to realize he liked having the kid around. He didn't have many friends in Deception Cove, and Rengo—ten, twelve years his junior, rash and excitable to Mason's prison-honed calm—was one of the few who'd even bothered to make an effort so far.

Anyway, it turned out Chase Ogilvy had plenty of tarps, but he didn't have the drill bit, and Mason was dragging Rengo away from the rifles displayed behind the counter, already dreading the hour-plus return trip to the lumberyard in Port Angeles, when Brock Boyd rolled past the store in a chromed-out Cadillac SUV, and even Rengo looked up from the Remingtons to stare.

"Holy shit," the younger man said. "Boyd's back."

"You know that guy?" Mason asked as he followed Rengo out to Jess's old Chevy Blazer. "Whoever's driving that rig?"

Rengo stared down Main Street to where the Cadillac was backing into a parking space outside Rosemary Marshall's nameless diner, and the neighboring Cobalt Pub.

"That looks like Bad Boyd's truck to me," Rengo said, and he started down the sidewalk. "Let's go see."

The kid was halfway to the Cadillac by the time Mason got the tarps stashed in the back of the Blazer, and Mason glanced at his watch as he climbed into the driver's seat, not wanting to waste any more of a good workday with Jess's place still many weeks from completion.

He coasted down the block toward where the Cadillac was parked and pulled around the far side of the SUV to find Rengo engaged in an animated, one-sided conversation with a man who might well have been a movie idol.

He was tall and broad shouldered and handsome, his straw-colored hair worn longer than was typical in Deception, the kind of haircut that probably cost fifty dollars and came with a free scalp massage. The man wore a fitted leather motorcycle jacket, looked brand-new, and those jeans people bought to make it look like they'd been working, though Mason could tell that this guy, in those jeans, was no carpenter.

In fact, Mason might indeed have mistaken the man for an actor or something, some kind of real celebrity, were it not for the thin white scar down the side of his cheek, and the clear and obvious fact that his nose had been broken, likely multiple times.

Mason rolled down the Blazer's window. "Rengo," he called. "We've got places to be."

Rengo waved him off. "Come on out here a sec, Burke," he replied. "Want you to meet someone."

The man, whoever he was, looked markedly less thrilled to have come across Rengo than vice versa. He looked down at the kid with undisguised impatience, and there was an air about him that suggested this whole situation wasn't unfamiliar.

Mason sighed and killed the engine, climbed out of the truck as Rengo stepped back from the newcomer, beaming and gesturing like he was auctioning a prize horse.

"Mason Burke, meet Bad Boyd," the kid said. "Closest thing our shit-ass town ever had to a bona fide celebrity."

So there: he *was* famous, and as Mason came closer, he pegged Boyd for a pro athlete. He was taller than Mason, for one thing— and that was no small feat. Built out too. And he carried himself in a certain way: precise, economical. No wasted movement as he stepped forward, hand outstretched, a politician's smile every- where but his eyes.

"Pleased to meet you, Mr. Burke," Boyd said, and his grip was firm. He looked Mason in the eye, and Mason met his gaze and held it, as tough as that was. He'd spent almost half his life in a place where eye contact was a challenge, an invitation to fight, and even now, six months out of prison, he was still trying to teach himself a new code.

"Burke was in prison too," Rengo said, catching both men off guard. Boyd dropped the handshake; his smile flickered a little, and there was something underneath, a glimpse of the real man behind the facade.

"Murder," Rengo said, grinning at Boyd. "First degree, right, Burke?"

Now it was Mason's turn to feel like the specimen on display. He started, "Kid—"

"Where'd you do your time?" Boyd asked, interrupting. "Wasn't Coyote Ridge, was it? I'd remember you."

Mason hesitated. *The integrity of the upright guides them,* he thought, *but the unfaithful are destroyed by their duplicity.*

He'd resolved when he came out of prison that he'd be open and honest about his life when he talked about it, take responsibility for what he'd done and own up to the punishment he'd endured. He forced himself to take ownership, even when it was hard.

But this? This sounded like *bragging.*

"I was back in Michigan," he told Boyd. "Upstate. The Chippewa pen."

Boyd nodded. "How long?"

"Fifteen years," Mason told him, and Boyd whistled. "Been out about six months now."

"Well, hell," Boyd said, grinning. "Compared to you, Burke, I'm just a baby. Served three and a half and I about lost my mind."

"It's tough," Mason agreed.

They let that sit for a beat, Boyd still nodding and smiling and sizing Mason up, Rengo grinning like a fool between the two of them, and finally Mason figured he might as well ask, figured Boyd was waiting for it, figured this was what conversation between ex-cons was supposed to look like.

Figured it wasn't much different from the way conversation was like on the inside.

"What'd you go in for?" he asked, and Boyd smiled wider.

"Hell, it was nothing like murder," he said. "It was just a little bit of dogfighting."

"He's a hockey player," Rengo said as Mason drove, tight-lipped, up Main Street toward the highway. "*Was* a hockey player, anyway, until the dog stuff happened."

The dog stuff.

Mason didn't say anything. Didn't trust himself to speak, didn't know what he would say, but it wouldn't be pleasant. He'd seen how Lucy'd looked, the day the lady from the rescue agency brought her into the prison for training; the dog had been terrified, pitiful, too scared to come out of her cage, even.

It was men like Boyd who had done that, instilled the fear in her, and Mason had worked hard to cure Lucy of it. To hear the rescue lady tell it, Lucy had been one of the lucky ones; they'd found dogs in that fighting ring that had been treated so savagely there'd been no choice but to put them down.

Dog stuff, Mason thought. *Just a little bit of dogfighting.*

"He was a damn good hockey player too. Scored eighty points in the show one year, plus he could *fight*." Rengo was rambling, happy, watching trees pass by the window without a goddamn clue. "A guy like that—tough guy, good hands—hell, he could have been a Hall of Famer. And then . . ."

Rengo trailed off, clucked his teeth like it was some kind of tragedy, and Mason busied himself concentrating on the road. Hoped the kid would run out his spiel and shut up for a change, put Bad Brock Boyd in the rearview.

The kid seemed to catch his expression. "Aw, hell, Burke," he said. "It's not like that; you don't have to worry. Boyd wouldn't do anything to Lucy."

Mason kept driving. Winding two-lane road, the Pacific Ocean visible in glimpses through the forest, the truck's engine revving coming out of the corners.

He focused on the road, on the turns of the highway. On the feel of the steering wheel in his hands.

"You're right," he said finally. "He won't."

FOUR

Mason was alone the second time he met Boyd. No Rengo, no Lucy. A rainy day, and Joe Clifford's wonky back starting to ail him, so they'd agreed to take an off day at the jobsite and just rest and relax some. Jess was at work, with Lucy riding shotgun in a Makah County cruiser, so Mason more or less had the day to himself.

He'd eaten breakfast at Rosemary's, two eggs over easy, sausage and hash browns, a cup of black coffee, in the corner booth. Then he'd browsed for a while in Chase Ogilvy's marine supply store, shot the breeze about the weather and the Mariners and the state of Joe Clifford's boat. And Mason had wandered around town awhile, thought of dropping in on Hank Moss at the motel, just to say hello. Besides Rengo, Hank was about the only friend Mason had in Deception; the rest of the town seemed to still regard him as an outsider at best, and at worst, as the man who'd helped murder three of Deception's sons.

Mason figured the average citizen probably saw him as a convicted killer from back east who'd somehow sunk his hooks into the town's decorated war hero, but either way, he'd grown used to eating his meals alone, to the slow sidelong glances in his direction, the hushed voices. To the people who saw him coming and quickly crossed the street.

He was alone in Deception, more or less, but as long as Mason Burke had Jess Winslow, and Lucy, he figured he'd be just fine.

He wound up back at the *Nootka,* curled up on the settee with the stove running and a book in his hand, rain spattering against the wheelhouse window and the harbor outside a monochrome of gray sky and black water and faded reds and blues. He tried to read but couldn't fully focus, caught himself looking up every page or so, thinking the dog should be snoozing at his feet somewhere, but of course the dog was with Jess and Mason was alone, so he spent the afternoon alternately reading and watching the rain.

Until he heard the footsteps on the wharf outside.

There wasn't much of a fishing fleet in Deception Cove anymore, certainly not many boats that were operational, and visitors down Mason's stretch of dock were rare. He set down his book and listened—heavy boot steps on wet lumber—and he slid off the settee and reached for the baseball bat, just in case, slipped on his boots, and pushed open the top half of the Dutch door in back of the wheelhouse to see who was coming, and why.

The visitor was Brock Boyd. The hockey player was dressed for the weather, his motorcycle jacket replaced by a fancy hiker's raincoat in electric orange. Mason watched Boyd scan the dock, read the name on the stern of Joe Clifford's boat, and look up toward the wheelhouse. Watched him see Mason and smile, raise his hand in greeting. "Burke," he said. "They told me I'd find you here."

"Guess they were right," Mason replied. "What can I do for you, Mr. Boyd?"

The too-friendly smile only widened. "Brock, please," he said. "Hell, call me Boyd if it suits you. Was wondering if you might want to go up to the Cobalt, drink a beer together. Trade war stories, kind of thing."

Mason shook his head. "I don't think so."

"You busy?" Boyd asked. "Some other time, then. Hell, maybe

you've got a bottle on that boat of yours, save us the trip up the dock."

Mason realized he was still holding tight to the bat. "That's not going to work for me," he told Boyd. "Not here or the Cobalt, I'm afraid."

Boyd studied him, from out in the rain on that dock in his expensive designer raingear, eyeing Mason like he wasn't sure what to make of him, his smile fading slightly, and the rain wreaking havoc on his haircut.

"Some other time, then," he said again. "Listen, Burke, I'd really like to talk. Maybe you've heard, but I'm not the most popular man in this town, not anymore, and I doubt very much that you are either. Seems to me we could both use a friend."

Mason forced himself to hold the man's gaze. Wished he could see another way out of this but figured he was better off cutting Boyd loose right here and now instead of letting this fester.

"I won't ever be your friend, Boyd," he told the dogfighter. "I don't mean any offense, but that's just how it is."

Boyd opened his mouth to reply. Closed it again. He blinked.

"You're shutting *me* down?" he said finally. "What am I, not rough enough for you, Burke? Because I'll tell you, I never killed anybody, but—"

"It's the dogfighting," Mason replied. "I don't think you and I could ever find common ground, not if you're the type to find sport in that kind of thing."

Boyd stared at him, still partway smiling, incredulous. And Mason figured there was no point in prolonging the conversation any further.

"No offense," he told Boyd. "But I reckon I've said all I need to. Good luck, Mr. Boyd."

He leaned out, took the top half of the Dutch door, and closed it. Set the bat against the bottom half and kicked off his boots, returning to the settee. Picked up his book and opened it to his page, stared at the words but didn't read anything, not until he'd heard Bad Boyd's boots beat a tattoo on the wharf boards, the dogfighter retreating to dry land again.

———

"You couldn't just pretend to be nice to him, Burke?" Jess asked later, propped up on her elbow in bed—her bed, this time— watching Burke's face as he relayed the story.

Burke shook his head. "I just don't like him," he told her. "I don't like what he stands for, or what he's done in his life. There's no point in pretending otherwise."

Jess exhaled, rolled onto her back. Looked up at the ceiling— Hank Moss's best room, and still the odd stain up there. Hank had offered her a sweetheart deal on the room, so she'd taken it; she liked Hank, for one thing, and she liked having a space of her own, somewhere she and Lucy could be alone if she wanted, where she could work on the exercises the VA doc had assigned her, mindfulness stuff to go along with the therapy, some way to move on from Afghanistan—and move on from Afia, specifically.

Whatever Burke thought about their separate living arrangements, he didn't complain, and Jess knew he wouldn't. He'd have gone back to Michigan if he believed it was best for her and the dog.

Instead, he was here in her bed, his powerful body stretched out beneath a tangle of sheets, one strong arm wrapped around her, pulling her close enough that she could feel his heart beating, steady, in his chest.

"Seems like you know a lot about the guy for someone who

never struck me as a hockey fan," Jess said, lifting her head slightly to study Burke's face. "How'd you get caught up so fast?"

Burke let out his breath. "Rengo introduced us the other day," he said. "Seemed mighty proud of the both of us, how we'd both spent time inside."

Jess laughed. *"Rengo,"* she said. As far as she was concerned, it was one of Burke's best qualities, how he'd more or less adopted the kid, found him something to do, brought him out of the woods and into some semblance of civilized life.

Burke had never had that kind of help, Jess knew, and she knew, too, how it was important to him that he give back to someone what he'd learned in prison. She knew he hoped to help kids like Rengo, kids like he'd been, hoped to guide them away from the choices he'd made.

She liked Rengo too, skinny and scrawny and fierce and good-hearted. She suspected that Burke got nearly as much from their time together as the kid did.

But Burke wasn't laughing. And Jess knew Burke was right, knew he couldn't pretend to get along with Boyd. He wasn't the type to blow smoke up anyone's ass; he valued honesty above just about anything, and she admired him for it, but damn him, there were times when a little white lie wouldn't hurt.

"Well, he's not Kirby Harwood," Jess told him. "Could be he's just trying to rebuild his life and do better, just like you, Burke. You ever think about that?"

Burke thought about it. Then he grumbled. "I just wish he'd go about doing it in some other town," he said.

Jess laughed. Leaned up and kissed his lips, the line of his jaw.

"Well, you're going to have to learn to coexist," she told him. "This far out in the hinterlands, that's just how it works sometimes."

FIVE

Mason kept his distance in the days after that awkward encounter on the wharf, caught sight of Brock Boyd's big Cadillac truck in town now and then, saw that luxurious blond haircut leaving the Cobalt Pub or maybe pumping gas at the ARCO up by Hank Moss's motel, but it was nearly a week before the men exchanged words again.

And this time, it was something less cordial.

It happened outside Spinnaker's, the gluten-free, organic gourmet restaurant that Tim Turpin was running out of the old customs house over the water. Mason had never seen the place before Tim got hold of it, but he could see how the restaurateur had made the space his own. The restaurant was situated on pilings set out over the harbor, its double-high picture windows looking out onto the wharf and the Strait of Juan de Fuca beyond, the interior all reclaimed timber and iron, saw blades and fishing lures tacked up on the walls for decoration.

Tim catered to tourists, mainly, especially in the summer months; in the winter, he dropped his prices fifteen percent and just managed to keep the lights on. People in Deception figured Tim had to have money coming in from elsewhere—he was said to have been an investment banker back east, in a previous life—but nobody seemed to care one way or the other, as long as the restaurant kept serving Tim's signature gluten-free fried halibut and chips.

It was the combination of off-season low prices and Joe Clifford being fed up with the BLTs over at Rosemary's that brought Mason and Rengo to Spinnaker's that afternoon. Another beautiful day, sunny but crisp, a chill wind blowing in from over the water. Work was proceeding nicely on Jess's new place; the first floor was framed up and ready for walls, and Joe seemed to think that if the weather held out, he could have the place mostly finished by Labor Day.

The weather might not hold out, of course; from what Mason had seen, it rained in Deception Cove more or less every day ending in *y,* and though the locals swore they saw more sun than not in the summertime months, Mason figured he'd have to experience the phenomenon for himself before he believed them.

He had not only Rengo with him but Lucy too. Jess was working nights this week, running patrol in a county cruiser, sleeping all day. The dog could nap just as well on the jobsite as in Jess's motel room, so he took Lucy along with him, let her roam Jess's property, supervise, get her own feel for her new home.

He parked the Blazer at the foot of the pier that led out to Spinnaker's, let Lucy out of the back seat to sniff around the docks and have a pee while Rengo lit a cigarette, then led her up toward the restaurant's front doors and looped her lead around a guardrail just out front. Rengo flicked his cigarette over the rail into the water in the boat basin beneath, and the two men went inside, ordered three orders of fish and chips to go, and made small talk with Tim Turpin as they waited, gazing at the white-capped water way out in the channel and breathing in the smell of fish frying in the kitchen behind them.

Mason was halfway out the restaurant's door, paper bag in hand and stomach growling, when he caught sight of Boyd's flashy Cadillac parked up the pier by the Blazer.

He felt something when he saw the truck, an unpleasant electricity that wasn't quite fear but anticipated confrontation, a feeling he recalled from days on the yard, a sense that something wasn't quite right, an impending violence. And the feeling only got worse when he found Boyd outside too, down on his haunches and his hands on Lucy.

He was play-wrestling her, batting her around a little bit, the dog wagging her tail but more confused than engaged, from what Mason could see. Lucy looked up and saw him and her tail wagged harder, recognition, but Boyd didn't notice, kept kind of slapping her around.

"You want to step away from her," Mason said, and if he hadn't been holding lunch, he might have helped with the process.

Boyd looked up, grinned when he saw Mason, Rengo behind. "Oh hell," he said. "Howdy, Burke. This your dog?"

"Sure is," Mason said. "And I'd prefer if you kept clear of her."

Boyd looked from Mason to Lucy and back again. Mason held his eyes firm on the man, and this time it wasn't difficult to keep his gaze.

"I'm not going to fight her, Burke, if that's what you're worried about," Boyd said. He still hadn't moved.

Mason said, "I know you're not. But I'll ask you to walk away anyway."

Boyd didn't answer right away. He stood, slowly, looked Mason up and down. "You know, you're awfully high-and-mighty for someone who's killed a man," he said. "Don't make off like your shit doesn't stink just as bad as mine, Burke."

"Maybe it does," Mason replied. "But that doesn't mean I want to smell yours around this dog." The electricity was humming now, same as it did back in the Chippewa pen, where somebody looked at someone else wrong and some minor offense turned to bloodshed. Mason knew Boyd must be feeling it too, his own callback. Knew there was nothing in either man's history that was going to prevent them from brawling.

But Mason tried, anyway. For Jess's sake, and Lucy's. And for his own, for the sake of the man he'd worked hard to become, inside the prison and after he'd walked out of it. "I don't want trouble," he told Boyd. "Just stay away from the dog, is all."

Boyd didn't respond. Mason turned, handed Rengo the paper bag full of Tim Turpin's fish and chips. Reached around Boyd, giving the other man a wide berth, made to start untying Lucy's lead from the guardrail.

And then Boyd hit him.

It was a sucker punch, awkward, given the way they were standing. Boyd swinging with a left-hand haymaker, either thinking Mason was making a move or trying to catch him off guard. Either way, the punch connected, and after that, it didn't matter.

Mason had tried to behave himself in Chippewa. He'd known that any fight behind bars would damn him in the eyes of the people who mattered, the people who'd cast judgment on his ability to reintegrate with the rest of the world. He'd avoided confrontation, aimed for diplomacy.

But sometimes a fight was unavoidable. Sometimes you reached a point where you stood up for yourself or the whole block knew you were soft, and once they knew you were soft, they'd come after you, all of them.

Instinct took over. Survival. You fought to defend yourself, so you wouldn't have to fight again later. And as Brock Boyd's million-dollar fist connected with Mason's jaw, he knew the kind of fight he was in, knew he'd have to prove something to Boyd now, or the dogfighter wouldn't ever give him peace.

He rolled away from Boyd's punch. Came up throwing fists of his own.

SIX

"Holy hell, Burke, what happened to you?"

Jess caught sight of Burke's eye about the moment she stepped inside the *Nootka*'s wheelhouse. He stood over the stove, cooking some kind of dinner—and to his credit, it smelled pretty good—but he couldn't hide the shiner, or the bruise on his jaw and the way he favored his right arm. Heck, looking closer, she could see the cuts on his knuckles, and she paused in the doorway. Stared.

Burke looked up from the stove, gave her a rueful smile. "I guess you'll hear about it all when you get to work later," he said. "I think it was Tim Turpin finally called the law."

"You—" She frowned. Shook her head, couldn't quite process. "You got in a *fight?*"

"It was Brock Boyd," he said. "He found Lucy."

Jess glanced up toward the wheel, where Lucy lay curled by the stairs to the fo'c'sle. Jess made eye contact, and the dog's tail thumped, but she didn't stand, and for a moment, Jess thought—

"He didn't—"

"No," Burke said, reading her face. "He seemed like he just wanted to wrestle with her. But I didn't want him anywhere around her, and I told him."

"And then you fought him."

He looked up at her, his expression earnest. "He threw a punch at me," he told her. "Jess, I know it was wrong. I should have found some way to turn the other cheek, and I know it."

She didn't say anything. She'd never known Burke to fight without reason. Even on the island, with Harwood and the others, Burke had pushed her hard for some kind of peaceful resolution. He would stand up for himself; she knew that. But he hadn't seemed to Jess like the kind of man who saw any point to a fistfight, like he recognized how ridiculous the whole circus must be, grown men who couldn't solve their problems with words.

"He swung first," Burke said. "I know that doesn't matter, but it was one of those things. He's been in jail for a spell himself."

Jess supposed it did matter, *should* matter, logically. And she'd heard about Bad Boyd, knew what he'd done to those dogs; she'd seen pictures, the ring in the barn out back, the kennels. She'd heard stories of what the law had found when they'd dug up Boyd's property. And she'd heard some of the testimony too, what Boyd and his buddies had forced the dogs to do, what they did to the weak dogs, the ones who didn't or couldn't fight.

She knew Lucy had been rescued from the same kind of situation, and she knew Burke knew it too, and she couldn't fault him for standing up for the dog.

But still. She felt queasy inside, just a bit, as though he'd just told her he'd been flirting with Darla Grey down at the Cobalt.

Burke bent down and dug into a locker under the sink, where Jess knew he kept the bowls. But he sighed, and when he stood tall again, his hands were empty.

"I'm embarrassed, Jess," he told her. "I saw Boyd as a convict instead of a man, and I let my instinct get the better of me, and I'm sorry."

"You don't need to apologize," she said. "Not to me."

He studied her face like he could tell how she was feeling, like he could see himself through her eyes and knew he'd come up wanting, perhaps for the first time since they'd met each other.

The silence stretched, and it was the kind of silence where normally Lucy would save them by snoring or farting or just rolling over and looking silly and giving them an excuse to smile and laugh together, but even the dog stayed still, and there was no exit, no escape.

"Soup's on," Burke said finally, gesturing to the stove. "You hungry?"

The food smelled delicious, damn it, some kind of Mexican stew recipe he'd picked up from God knows where, but Jess found she'd just about lost her appetite. "I ought to get to work," she told him. "Gillies will be wondering where I am already."

Burke pursed his lips. Then he nodded.

"Yeah," he said. "Okay."

"I'll see you tomorrow," Jess said. She snapped her fingers. "C'mon, Luce," she called, and the dog sat up, stretching and yawning, and dutifully padded out past Burke to where Jess stood at the door.

"Be safe tonight," Burke said.

"I will," Jess replied, and she wanted to say more, but there was something between them now, something alien, something that hadn't existed before. And Jess clipped Lucy's lead to her collar and led the dog out and was conscious of Burke's eyes on her, watching them go, and she wanted to stop and turn and go back to him, tell him it was okay and how they'd get through this together.

But she knew that if she turned back, she'd see only the shiner on Burke's face and the scars on his knuckles, the way he winced as he moved, and she knew she would watch him and wonder if maybe she'd been reading him wrong, if she maybe didn't know him as well as she'd thought.

It wasn't three days later that she was staring down at Bad Boyd's body on the shore at Shipwreck Point.

SEVEN

Ironically, for all the time Jess had spent in a war zone, the first corpse she ever saw was right here in Deception, just a few miles down the shore from Shipwreck Point. She was a teenager, going steady with Ty Winslow, and he'd taken her out on his little troller for a sunset pleasure cruise, a jog up the coast a ways to a spot where he dropped crab traps, where he swore those Dungeness came up as big as dinner plates.

They'd figured out pretty quick that something was the matter, that old hauler on the back of Ty's boat straining like nobody's business to lift the trap from the water, and Ty had made a joke about how the trap must be stuffed right full of crab, and he hoped Jess was hungry.

But he glanced at the hauler and how the line was drawn taut and he frowned, and Jess knew it wasn't a surplus of crab that was holding the trap down.

"Must be caught on something down there," Ty said, scratching his head. "Tide carried it under a rock or something."

But that wasn't right either.

In the end, it took both of them pulling, plus the hauler behind them, to drag the trap up from the bottom, and she screamed when she looked over the side and saw the face in the tangle of line, bloated and pale, looming out of the darkness like something from a nightmare.

They tied off the line and let the trap dangle there in the water, and Ty took Jess into the wheelhouse and poured her a cup of coffee from the pot on the galley stove, splashed plenty of bourbon in there too, wrapped her up in a blanket, and got the Coast Guard on the radio. And they stayed in the galley, looking out at the sunset, until the little Coast Guard Zodiac motored into the bay, and then Ty went out and talked and Jess stayed put and poured a little more bourbon into the dregs of her coffee.

He was a guy named Blind Ulrich; Ty had fished with his nephews once or twice. As best anyone could tell, he'd been poaching crab from Ty's trap when the line tangled around him as he threw the trap back, dragged him down sixty feet to the bottom. The Coast Guard found Ulrich's boat on the rocks the next morning, a big YETI cooler filled with prime crab.

"Served the bastard right," Ty said, grinning, when he found out. "Some kind of cosmic justice, what with him stealing our crab like that."

Jess hadn't seen much of Blind Ulrich's body, but she'd seen enough to remember. And for a while, she imagined that every body she saw would linger in her head the way Ulrich's had.

Then she'd joined the Marines, and that whole notion had quickly come to seem quaintly naive.

She remembered the unusual deaths, of course. Men shot or blown up in ways she hadn't imagined before. She remembered the first man she thought she'd killed—an insurgent with a Kalashnikov rifle, thirty yards away, him or her—and she remembered, of course, how her friends had died, how broken and waxy and artificial they looked, once they were gone.

She remembered, all right. Friends like Afia, tortured and

mutilated, she couldn't forget. Not even with Lucy and Burke and a twice-weekly trip to the VA doc, Wiebe.

And of course Jess remembered Ty. She hadn't seen his body, not firsthand; she'd been overseas on her third tour when he drowned, but she'd still forced the old sheriff, Kirk Wheeler, to show her pictures anyway, just so she'd know what it looked like.

She supposed, in some way, she'd been testing herself. To see if she cared at all, if she still had the capacity to care.

She'd felt nothing when she looked at the pictures. Nothing but a burning desire to get back to Afghanistan and kill Haji some more.

But that, the VA had told her, was out of the question.

Ty had drowned. Blind Ulrich had drowned. Brock Boyd had come from the water, but he hadn't drowned.

Boyd lay on the coarse sand beside seaweed and jetsam, kelp tangled in that lustrous hair of his, the bullet hole in the middle of his forehead neat and tidy and bloodless; it almost looked natural. It didn't much look like a suicide, either, from the placement of the wound; Jess figured there had to be easier ways to shoot yourself in the head, but she supposed she and the sheriff would have to wait for the county coroner's opinion to be sure.

At any rate, Boyd's eyes were half closed, and if you looked only at his eyes, you'd have thought he looked peaceful, at rest below the tide line and oblivious to the clouds of flies that had gathered around him.

But the rest of Boyd's body was in pretty bad shape. He'd spent time in the water, that much was obvious; his clothes were ragged from rock and wave, and maybe from creatures too. Certainly the crabs had already discovered him. What exposed flesh Jess could see had been torn away, chewed on, whatever else.

She'd seen many bodies before, but she could not recall ever seeing a man in this state, where the violence that had ended his life formed only a prelude to the indignities visited upon the body in the immediate afterward.

Looking down on the ruined remains of Boyd's once-movie-star-handsome face, Jess thought of Cable Proudfoot and his grandson, wondered how much the little boy had seen. Would Boyd stick in the boy's mind the way Blind Ulrich had stuck in hers?

She hadn't known Boyd, but she could tell already that his body would be one *she* remembered, anyway, no matter how hard she tried to push it out of her mind.

EIGHT

The investigation of Boyd's death brought an energy to Makah County that Jess couldn't recall ever feeling before.

"Guess we're going to have to knuckle down on this, Winslow," Sheriff Hart told her as they walked out of the county coroner's office following Boyd's autopsy. "This part of the world ain't exactly a murder capital."

The finding: homicide by gunshot wound, .38 caliber, the toxicology report pending. Bad Boyd had been murdered, and neither the sheriff nor his deputy had any immediate suspects— or, indeed, any idea how he'd come to wash up on Shipwreck Point with the tide.

The coroner's office sat adjacent to the Indian Health Center in Neah Bay, the Makah County seat. It was a low, modest building, a single story with faded aluminum siding. Neah Bay rostered only about a couple thousand people; the county proper, less than ten thousand. The coroner wasn't exactly the busiest woman in town, and she rarely had to rule on a homicide.

Today, though, her parking lot was full, mostly TV news reporters dragging producers and panel vans behind them, and beyond them a collection of bystanders and looky-loos gathered from all over the county to hear tell of what had happened to Makah's brightest star.

Brock Boyd's story was well told in these parts; even Jess had heard it plenty, and she'd been halfway around the world for most of the really juicy bits. Part Makah and part not, he'd found his way to a pair of skates—legend claimed—before he could walk, was filling the nets at the Neah Bay community ice rink by the time he was four. He'd dragged the Makah Screaming Eagles to consecutive regional championships as a teenager, then bolted for the big time just as soon as he was able.

For a while, Jess remembered, the whole county had shut down whenever Boyd had a game on television, and the people around here weren't even particularly interested in hockey. They just liked the idea that a person could make it out of here, find fortune and glory despite the odds stacked against them.

And a lot of them, Jess suspected, appreciated how Boyd had made it with his fists.

Bad Boyd was a fighter as much as he was a hockey player, consistently treading the margins between fair play and foul. But that wasn't such a bad thing to his fans in Makah County or to the coaches who'd scouted him; hockey rewarded toughness, and if Boyd was prone to the occasional cheap shot, so be it. He scored plenty, and scared plenty too.

A reporter stepped out of the scrum as Jess and Hart exited the coroner's office. Jess didn't recognize her, surmised she must have come from afar—Seattle, probably, or even farther. Maybe she was even one of those national reporters—ESPN or something. Boyd's death was getting plenty of coverage, it being the culmination of an epic, drawn-out, tabloid-rag downfall.

"Sheriff Hart," the reporter called. "Can you give us an update as to the cause of Boyd's death? Is there any truth to the rumor that this was a murder?"

Hart's gait hitched a little—not noticeable to the reporter but glaring to Jess, beside him. She realized the sheriff was probably feeling a little overwhelmed himself; this kind of thing didn't happen much in Clallam County either, and certainly not with this kind of attention.

"No comment," Hart told the reporter. "We'll set up a press conference when we have something to share."

"Do you have any suspects? Could this be connected to Boyd's earlier legal troubles?"

Hart forced a smile, nudged his way past the reporter. "No comment," he said again. "Thank you."

Hart cleared a path through the crowd to where they'd parked; he'd driven his Super Duty three blocks from headquarters, while Jess had taken a county cruiser into Neah Bay from Deception. The reporters followed, and so did some of the gawkers, lingering just within earshot, waiting to hear what the law planned to do.

Hart shooed them away. Then he gave Jess a tired smile. "We're going to need to put a face to this thing," he said. "Soon."

Jess nodded. "Yeah."

"I guess you never worked a case like this before."

She smiled; Hart knew she hadn't. "No, sir."

"Better let me handle the heavy stuff," the sheriff said. "You and Gillies just work your connections in town. Ask around about Boyd, figure out what he was into. Who he ran with, that kind of thing."

"Yes, sir."

"Mostly, these things clear up quick. It's usually pretty obvious from the outset. Usually someone close, someone holding a grudge."

Jess nodded. "I'll ask around."

"Keep me posted," Hart said. "I'll do the same. Any luck, we can get this thing cleared in a couple of days."

They said their goodbyes, climbed into their vehicles, and Jess followed Hart out of the lot and as far as the detachment, where he signaled and pulled into the lot, waving to her out the window, and she continued up toward the highway.

She hadn't said anything to Hart about the scars on Burke's hands, she realized, the fight outside Spinnaker's. She wondered if she'd forgotten, or if she simply hadn't wanted to tell.

It didn't matter. The sheriff would find out, sooner or later; there weren't many secrets in Makah County. And Jess imagined there would be more than a few people in Deception who'd heard of the fight, and Boyd's murder, and think the outsider from back east with his history of violence must have been the one who pulled the trigger. Heck, she might have thought it herself if she didn't know Mason Burke like she did.

Jess hoped Hart was right, that they could clear the case quickly. Otherwise, she knew, things were liable to get sticky for Burke, and damn fast.

NINE

One day, officially, into the first murder investigation of Deputy Jess Winslow's career—though so far it didn't seem to Jess as though much had been accomplished. She and Tyner Gillies played it how Hart had instructed: let the sheriff handle the procedural stuff; concentrate on just listening to the vibe in Deception Cove, picking up on the rumors that traveled in whispers, blooming as fast as moss in the rainforest.

Gillies wasn't as green as Jess, but he wasn't exactly a lifelong lawman yet either. He'd worked a couple of years with Sheriff Wheeler in Neah Bay, been moved over to Deception after Aaron Hart took over. Gillies was a few years older than Jess, late twenties, short and well muscled, clean-shaven and close-cropped, and always—*always*—by the book. She'd written him off as your typical law-enforcement meathead, at least until he'd opened his mouth.

Gillies was smart, seemed passionate about his job, and he played well with others. He was competent at his work, and Jess had never heard him complain about anything; through two and a half tours in Afghanistan, she'd come to value both qualities more than just about anything else. She liked Gillies and was glad she'd been paired with him, even if they weren't making much progress yet on the Boyd investigation.

Some said it was an animal-rights activist who'd killed the

former hockey player; some said an old lover, or the husband or boyfriend thereof. Bad Boyd had left more than a few broken hearts in his wake, and he'd broken his share of Makah County homes to boot.

Jess still hadn't told Hart about Burke. She hadn't seen Burke the night before, after the autopsy; she'd made up some story about not feeling well and took to her bed early, lay awake all night. The way Burke had responded, Jess was pretty sure he knew she was telling a lie, but he hadn't pressed the issue. They'd been cool to each other since the day he'd fought Boyd, and she could tell he was waiting on her, probably hoping if they gave it enough time that she might forget it had happened.

Jess wasn't sure what to make of Burke fighting Boyd, and what it meant for their relationship. Maybe Burke was like her: he couldn't escape his violence, no matter how hard he tried or what good he meant to do. She wondered if that meant they would never find peace together, if she wouldn't have to worry about doing something to lose Burke because he might up and lose himself first.

Hart called Jess at the end of that first day, summoned her to meet him out on location down the road from Deception, east toward the county line. And so Jess left the town in Gillies's hands, told him to radio her if anything got out of hand, and she saddled up in her cruiser and drove out to the highway, figuring she knew where Hart was leading her.

Boyd's house sat a couple of miles out of Deception, off a nondescript turnoff from the highway, with a mailbox and an old gate with a shiny new lock. A gravel road wound down through the trees toward the ocean; Jess had never driven down it before, but she'd seen pictures of the house that waited at the end.

The place was probably worth more than every other house in Deception combined. Some kind of architectural marvel, old-growth timber and stone and steel, cantilevered out over the rock bluffs that bordered the ocean. The *Post-Intelligencer* had sent a reporter out from Seattle after Boyd had it built, some kind of Sunday supplement, human-interest piece, and though the *PI* wasn't exactly in wide circulation this far out from the city, approximately every living soul in Makah County had read that particular article, even Jess.

She knew people who'd cruised past it too, on the water side, though by all accounts the house was built to blend into the forest. It apparently didn't look like much from thirty feet below the bluffs; inside, though, from the pictures, the place was a palace.

Hart's county Super Duty pickup was waiting at the bottom of the gravel, a wide, paved driveway leading to a three-car garage. The kennels and the barn where the dogs had been set to fighting were just up the gravel road, past the house, tucked into the trees and almost invisible if you didn't know where to look. Jess figured that was probably the idea. The house had sat empty while Boyd was in prison, a property manager checking in now and then, a rent-a-cop security guy patrolling the grounds. Seemed a shame to let a place like this go unlived in, but Boyd hadn't been married, and he'd earned his time away.

The forecast had called for rain again, but it was holding off as Jess parked beside Hart and stepped out onto the concrete. The sky was gray, and the wind blew clouds fast and low over the treetops, whitecaps on the water just visible around the side of the house. From this angle, the house was all garage and bare, windowless concrete. Jess surmised that the real architectural stuff probably looked out over the water.

"Hell of a place, isn't it?" Hart said, his hands in his pockets, studying the building as if he were her realtor, poised to explain about the three and a half baths. "Figured we ought to take a look around, seeing as how we don't have much else to work with."

Jess thought of Burke. Chased the thought from her mind as Hart unlocked the door that sat like an afterthought beside the three wide garage bays.

"Hold up a sec," he told her, digging in his pocket, and he came out with two pairs of blue latex gloves. Handed her a pair and slipped on the other. "Media will have our asses if we contaminate a crime scene."

The house smelled faintly of that pervasive dampness even the finest houses in the county weren't completely immune to. The scent of cigar smoke lingered in the air too, sickly sweet and obnoxious, and Jess pictured Boyd here, king of his castle, a thousand years removed from the prison cell that had housed him before this.

He'd kept this house, even after the trial, the scandal. He must have felt untouchable here.

The house began with a mudroom, a narrow hallway, and then it opened into something spectacular. Jess had seen the pictures, but the view still took her breath away. An open-concept living area spanned the width of the house. Double-height ceilings, the walls to the north made entirely of glass, a panoramic view of the water. A massive fireplace built from river rock, a pristine kitchen that may well have been bigger than Jess's old one-bedroom home. Great slabs of granite and huge beams of timber, lavish, butter-soft leather furniture. Hunting trophies on the walls that weren't windows, hockey trophies too.

Hart looked around, whistled. "Guess I should have been a hockey player."

At first glance, the house looked as perfect and unlived-in as it had in those newspaper photos, as though everything within view had been meticulously staged to a state of impossible perfection.

Jess and Hart stepped cautiously through the living room. Made note of the small signs that Boyd had in fact lived here: an off-kilter rug; the remains of that pungent cigar, lying dead in an ashtray; the charred wood in the fireplace. Looked in on Boyd's bedroom—palatial, a king bed, made up, if sloppily—and saw nothing, necessarily, that rang any alarms.

"What are you thinking happened?" Jess asked. "I mean, it's obvious that Boyd didn't die on that beach, right?"

Hart nodded. Forensic technicians from Clallam County had been called up to Shipwreck Point just as soon as Jess had reported the gunshot wound in the middle of Boyd's forehead. Prevailing wisdom at the scene—and Boyd's position below the high-tide mark—said he'd been shot elsewhere, dumped into the sea. Said it was Cable Proudfoot's misfortune that the body had happened to wash up at Shipwreck, just in time to ruin the day at the beach with his grandson.

Jess knew there was no reason not to believe the forensics people. But their thinking prompted the question: If Bad Boyd wasn't shot where he'd been found, then where had it happened?

"Hell," Hart said, scratching his head. "I was really kind of hoping we'd come in here and find brass and bloodstains, maybe a note."

They returned to the living room. Late afternoon now, the light starting to fade, a gradual, inexorable dimming of the gray into black. The view through the north windows remained spectacular, ocean framed by rock and trees, but it was a cold kind of beauty, and Jess felt a sudden urge to relight the fire, bring some warmth and light to this stark, lonely house.

Instead, she went over to the kitchen, which appeared, by and large, to have never been used. She adjusted her gloves and peeked into the refrigerator, found beer and milk and a bottle of wine, nothing else.

No dishes in the drying rack or the dishwasher. Where did Boyd eat? Some sundries in the cupboards, canned soup and crackers, an impressive collection of hard liquor. *A bachelor,* Jess thought. *Through and through.*

She'd about given up on finding anything useful, was about to walk back out to Hart and hope he'd suggest they go back to town soon, maybe grab a bite or at least find someplace with a heater, when impulse moved her back to the sink and the little door underneath it.

There she found what she expected: Boyd may have been a millionaire, and an ex-con besides, but he still kept his trash in the predictable spot, and from the state of the bin, he hadn't hit the dump in a while.

Upon cursory examination, Jess saw that most of the bin was filled with old takeout containers, thus answering the question of how Boyd nourished himself. Rosemary's diner, Spinnaker's, that Chinese joint in Clallam Bay: all well represented. But it wasn't the takeout trash that caught Jess's attention. It was the broken wineglass on top.

She'd had a good set of wineglasses, once. A wedding gift from Ty's cousins, they might have been the blue-light special at the Super K, but they were nicer than anything Jess had ever owned before. Over the years, though, they'd all broken, victims of care-lessness and attrition, though by the time she'd thrown out the last one, she'd come home from Afghanistan, Ty was dead, and her tastes had started to turn toward the harder stuff—bourbon, most of the time, but she hadn't been picky.

This wineglass in Boyd's garbage was far nicer than her ill-fated wedding collection. It was broken all the same, sheared off at the stem, the base probably somewhere deeper amid the remains of Boyd's last order of chow mein. It lay there, discarded, hardly more noteworthy than the soggy cardboard and damp paper on which it rested—except for the telltale stain on its rim.

Jess shifted the garbage bin. Knelt closer and saw the imprint, unmistakable, a faded rose color.

Lipstick.

TEN

Elsewhere in Makah County, a cell phone was ringing. It was a burner phone, prepaid, purchased with cash in Port Angeles. It hadn't been purchased for this call, necessarily, but the phone's owner didn't mind. The phone was for making money, and this call fit that description.

The owner did not introduce himself when he answered. Anyone who had this number knew who he was. He cleared his throat, and someone reached for the remote control, muted the television, signaled to the other men to be quiet. The room around him went silent, and the man who owned the burner phone answered it.

"Yeah."

"I'm scared." The woman on the other end of the line had met the man only a handful of times, most of them decades before. "I don't know what to do with myself, I'm so scared."

The woman's voice was hushed, barely more than a whisper. The man could hear the fear in her voice and the urgency, and the knowledge that something had been set in motion that could never be undone.

"They found his body," she said. "I saw it on the news. I thought you said it would never turn up."

With his free hand, the man lit a cigarette and inhaled a long drag. "I said it mightn't," he said. "I never promised."

The woman said, "I just don't know what to do."

"You do nothing," the man told her. "You do how we talked about. Go about your business and forget it ever happened. Let us handle the rest."

"You'll make sure they don't find me?" she said.

"You keep your mouth shut, you're going to be fine," the man said. "We have as much to lose as you do if this goes south, remember?"

The woman seemed to contemplate this. She was silent a long time, and the man, restless, walked to the window and looked out at the road, watched dusk sap the last light of day, hiding the houses opposite, and the forest beyond, in deep shadow. Finally, he heard the woman's breath hitch.

"Okay," she said.

"We'll get it handled," the man told her. "Don't worry."

He waited until he heard the click so he knew the woman had ended the call. Then he set down the phone, aware that the other men were watching him intently from the couches and chairs arrayed around the little room.

The man ignored them. He studied the phone for a long while, thinking.

ELEVEN

Three days now since the autopsy. Sheriff Hart and Jess and Tyner Gillies were turning the county over, looking for the person whose lipstick they'd found on that discarded wineglass. Asking everyone they could whether Brock Boyd had a girlfriend, someone who might know something.

"Could be we're barking up the wrong tree," Gillies suggested. "Could be Boyd was just a guy who liked wearing lipstick."

They'd considered the possibility, however unlikely. But Boyd's master bedroom betrayed no such predilection. Nor did a deep dive into the rest of his belongings. He owned no women's beauty products, no women's clothes. A search of his laptop revealed his tastes aligned pretty close with those of your average heterosexual American man. In truth, the only signs whatsoever of a woman's presence in the home were the lipstick stain on the wineglass and a smudged, partial fingerprint that didn't belong to Brock Boyd or anyone else in the database.

To this point, however, the mystery woman hadn't shown her face. And whoever she was, nobody was willing to talk to Jess or Gillies or Hart about her.

Then the call came in to Hart's voicemail. The tip was anonymous. A gravel-rough voice, indistinct and unrecognizable. The sheriff played it for Jess in his office.

"Mason Burke killed Boyd."

Four words. Nothing more.

For a short while, the sheriff and his deputies set aside Brock Boyd's love life.

––––––––––

They had plans for dinner. At least Mason hoped they did, relations between him and Jess being somewhat strained since she'd found out about the fight, nearly a week ago. She'd straight-up blown him off the night after she'd found Boyd's body, told him some line about not feeling so good, the lie as transparent as the beer Troy Phelps was pouring at the Cobalt these days.

Not that Mason supposed he could blame Jess. He hadn't meant to fight with Boyd, and he knew he'd made a mistake. Knew he'd slipped up, just a little, back to the man he'd had to be in the Chippewa pen, where no matter how much you wanted to stay peaceful, sometimes you had to fight to survive.

He hadn't needed to fight Bad Boyd. A part of him, though, had wanted to, and he was ashamed of it now. He could see how he'd fallen in Jess's estimation. He hoped that tonight, their standing date night out at the Chinese place in neighboring Clallam Bay, he could start to rebuild her trust.

He finished up the workday at Jess's new house, dropped Rengo in town, and drove Lucy and the Blazer up to Hank Moss's motel, where he used Jess's spare room key to let himself in and clean up. The *Nootka* had a makeshift showerhead mounted above the toilet, but it was weak, in a tiny little room, and it tended to drain the boat's meager water supply. Mason tried to shower at the motel instead, as often as he could.

So he showered, shaved, and cleaned up in the bathroom filled with Jess's fancy soaps and beauty supplies, dressed in a fresh pair of blue jeans and a button-down shirt, gave Lucy her dinner, and then turned on the TV and settled in to wait for Jess to come home.

He'd never been much of a sports fan but found himself watching hockey, the East Coast game ending and a game in Los Angeles getting underway, puck drop for the latter at 7 p.m., Jess already running behind. Mason watched the TV with Lucy sprawled out on the bed beside him, and he rubbed her belly and thought about Brock Boyd some more.

Jess wasn't saying much about the investigation, though Mason could understand why, it being about the biggest crime Makah County had seen since, well, Kirby Harwood. The funny thing was, even Rengo was tight-lipped about it, and Rengo hardly ever shut up. Boyd's murder had put a shock through Deception, from what Mason could tell. He wondered how Jess and the new sheriff were getting on.

The late hockey game was well into the second period by the time Jess showed up, the lights of her Makah County cruiser raking the window, painting beams on the wall opposite the bed. Mason listened to her car door slam, heard her fumble for her keys and unlock the room, watched the door swing open, and then there she was.

She saw him and stopped. Blinked. Beside Mason, Lucy's tail thumped on the bed, and the dog stood and stretched and jumped down and went over to Jess, nuzzled at her hands where they hung down at her thighs.

"Everything all right?" Mason asked Jess. She hadn't moved from the doorway. "Tonight's our night, right? The Golden Palace?"

Jess blinked again. Nodded, slow. "Yeah," she said. "Right."

He watched her come into the room, set her bag down, and start to unbutton her coat. She stopped midway through, hesitated. Looked around the room like it was somewhere she'd never seen before.

Mason heard alarm bells in his head. Wondered if she was having a flashback, some kind of trigger sending her brain back to Afghanistan.

The episodes had gotten better since she'd returned to Dr. Wiebe in Port Angeles. But Mason knew those memories must still be lurking down there, under the surface, and he figured it was going to take more than a few months of talking to get Jess to the point where she wasn't bothered anymore.

"You okay?" He hit the TV remote and swung his legs off the bed. Stood. "Listen, if tonight's no good, we can stay here instead. I'll rustle up some food from the diner."

She still hadn't moved, and he made to walk over to her, planning to hug her or hold her or at least help her with her coat. But when he stepped toward her, she flinched a little, like she didn't know him.

"Hey," he said. "What's going on?"

"Tell me about that fight you had with Boyd," Jess said. "Down at Spinnaker's."

She wasn't looking at him. She was looking at the floor about five feet away from her, toward the bathroom. There was something in her voice like she'd been carrying the question around with her the whole day.

"I guess I told you most of it already," Mason said. "I come out the restaurant and he was petting the dog. I told him to stop, and he didn't like it so much. We scrapped some but it was nothing big."

"Tim Turpin called Gillies at the detachment about it," Jess said slowly. "Must have looked pretty big from where he was standing."

Mason shrugged. "Boyd's a big guy—*was* a big guy. So'm I. Tim's—well, you know."

Tim Turpin was not a big man. Nor was he the kind of guy, Mason supposed, who'd seen many fights in his life.

"That the last time you saw Boyd?" Jess asked.

Mason stared at her. Wondered if he'd misheard her, if he was misreading the subtext behind her question. "Look, what's going on here?" he replied. "Where's all this coming from, anyway?"

"The night he disappeared: Where were you?" She still couldn't look him in the eye. "You got someone can account for your whereabouts?"

"What is this, Jess, an interrogation? Are you thinking I had something to do with—"

"Where were you, Burke? That's all I'm asking."

He let out a long breath. Sat back down on the bed and studied her. He supposed he ought to have known this was coming, though he'd have expected it to be Sheriff Hart who asked the questions, not Jess.

"I was on the boat," he told her. "You had the night shift. Me and Lucy ate dinner, and I guess we turned in early."

Jess didn't say anything. Didn't react.

"Nobody to vouch for my whereabouts," he said. "No alibi."

Still nothing. Mason watched Jess and felt numb, the weight of what she was asking like a stone on his chest.

Finally Jess shifted. "Hart got an anonymous phone call," she said. "Said you did it. Killed Boyd."

Mason barked out a laugh, incredulous, and Jess's eyes flashed with life as she spun to face him. "You fought him, Burke. The day he probably died. And as best I could tell, it looked like he kicked your ass."

He felt it then, a cold kind of fear, the knowledge of just how alone he was out here in Deception, an outsider. How much more alone he would be without Jess. "You want to arrest me, Jess?" he asked, standing. "Are you seriously thinking I did this?"

"Burke, no." She brought her hand up, rubbed her face. "I don't know. It's just—Hart wants answers."

"He send you to bring me in?"

Jess shook her head. "I didn't know you'd be here. Our plans—I forgot."

Mason stared at her a beat. "So what do you want to do?" he asked finally. "I'll go down and see Hart if you want, tell him—"

"*No,*" she said quickly. He could see she was scared too. "You stay away from the sheriff, Burke, if you don't have an alibi. Keep your head down until this blows over."

"I didn't kill him, Jess," he said. "I've got nothing to hide."

Jess said nothing. She couldn't quite look at him. Was she scared for his sake or her own? Could she really believe he'd have done something like this?

He waited, and Jess still didn't say anything.

"I didn't kill him," he said again, but the words sounded weak and insignificant on his lips, a flimsy barrier against the storm he knew must be coming for him.

———

Jess lay awake long after Burke was gone. Beside her, Lucy stretched out and snored and chased imaginary squirrels. Jess stared up at the stain on the ceiling and listened to the odd car pass by on the highway outside, and wondered what in the hell she was thinking.

Dinner hadn't happened, obviously. They'd agreed, half-heartedly, to take a rain check, and Burke had excused himself shortly thereafter, looking at Jess with a kind of urgency in his eyes that scared her, a plea for something she couldn't quite bring herself to grant him.

Truth be told, Jess knew some shady anonymous phone call was no good reason to start measuring Burke for handcuffs and a prison jumpsuit. There were people in Deception who didn't like Burke, saw him as a threat who'd come through and caused violence, who'd contributed to the deaths of three good Makah County boys and put a fourth in prison for the next two or three decades. Burke had enemies, and in a county as small as Makah, people talked. Rumors spread.

Still, though. Burke *had* fought with Brock Boyd on the day he'd been murdered. And it wasn't like Burke was a stranger to violence. He'd killed for her before, on Dixie Island. Was it so impossible that he would kill for Lucy too?

Jess couldn't wrap her head around it. But if *she* was even considering the question, Jess knew damn well and clear that the rest of Makah must be too.

Including Sheriff Hart.

TWELVE

Mason remembered the murder, every second. As far as he could tell, there was no way he would ever forget.

───────

It was supposed to be a robbery; that's how Dev had pitched it. Hell, at the outset it wasn't supposed to be anything — another night getting fucked up and chasing girls, Dev with a lead on a couple of sisters he swore would be down for a party.

Mason had swiped the keys to his mom's rust-bucket Oldsmobile, peeled out around dusk before she could notice. Hauled ass across town to the house Dev was staying in, somebody's couch on a glassed-in back porch. Dev was twenty-one, twenty-two; he'd been on his own for five years, maybe longer. As far as eighteen-year-old Mason was concerned, he was about the coolest person in the world.

Dev climbed into the passenger seat, jacket clutched tight around him. Reached inside that jacket as Mason pulled away from the curb. Fumbled with something.

"You want to have some fucking fun tonight?" he asked, and Mason nodded, sure, not seeing whatever Dev had stashed in his coat but knowing he wasn't ever going to say no, whatever it was.

"I mean," Dev said, "like some real fucking fun."

"Yeah, man," Mason told him. "Hell yeah."

Dev nodded. "Good. Let's hit up that liquor store right there."

Mason had never seen the pistol before, not until Dev pulled it out of his jacket. They were parked in front of the store, engine running, and Dev showed Mason the gun and grinned across the car at him, his eyes already bleary from whatever he'd smoked at the house, his breath rancid.

"Gonna scare the shit out of a motherfucker," he told Mason. "Just you wait."

Mason had known at the time that this was fucked up. That he should be saying something, doing something, anything. Finding a reason to keep Dev from going into that liquor store.

But you try saying no to your only friend in the world.

Mason was eighteen and angry, and more than angry, he was lonely, his dad gone, his mom hopped up on Jesus. A high school burnout with no friends but Dev, no life but that which Dev shared with him, no choice but to go along with Dev's schemes.

No opportunity but right here, this car. That gun.

He kept his mouth shut.

The clerk's name was Faraz Karim. Mason didn't know that at the time, and he'd wager that Dev didn't either. Karim was just a guy who happened to draw the night shift, some unlucky bastard with a kid waiting at home.

It must have been only minutes, waiting out in that Oldsmobile, but to Mason, it felt like forever. He kept the radio cranked high and he sipped Steel Reserve and he waited, and the longer he waited, the more certain he was that something had gone wrong. The look in Dev's eyes as he'd handled the pistol. The unsteady lurch as he'd reached for the car door.

The funny thing was, Mason never heard the shots. Didn't really have a clear idea what had happened until the police hauled him in and showed him the security tape. Dev's story was, Karim reached for something under the counter, made a move. Dev's story was self-defense.

The story on the tape was more like Dev shot him, cold-blooded. Karim *with his hands up, talking fast, terrified. Dev talking back, waving the gun like a gangster, arm outstretched and tilted to the side. The security tape showed how Karim kept his hands high right up to the moment when Dev pulled the trigger.*

The security tape showed how Dev was a murderer. An old man across the street put the Olds at the scene, picked Mason out of a lineup, and that made Mason a murderer too. In the eyes of the law, anyway, and in his own mind as well.

———

He'd had fifteen years to think about what had happened. Fifteen years to remember Faraz Karim, to try to picture the clerk's little boy. To think about how they'd taken a man away from his son.

Dev had doubled down on the violence and the anger, and he'd died in a prison fight not long into his sentence. But Mason had chosen the other path. He'd taken responsibility; tried, as best he could, to live within the prison's rules. He'd walked out of that cell into a cold Michigan morning believing the violence was behind him.

But it wasn't.

He'd killed again, and this time directly. He'd killed to protect Jess and Lucy, pulled a trigger and watched a man fall. That the man had injured him too hardly made it better. That the man would have killed Jess was worth something, sure, but it didn't change the facts.

Mason Burke had been responsible for ending two lives. He'd once believed the man he'd been, the man who'd helped murder Faraz Karim, had wasted to nothing in the Chippewa state pen, believed he'd come out a decent, law-abiding man.

But the violence was still inside him. The death of a man named

Joy had proved it. The knowledge kept Mason awake nights; he could still see Joy's eyes, almost five months later.

If we say we have no sin, we deceive ourselves, and the truth is not in us.

Maybe the violence would stay with him forever, follow him around as faithfully as Lucy. Mason wondered if there was any use trying to shy away from it.

THIRTEEN

The morning after the canceled dinner, Jess sat in her Blazer in Spinnaker's parking lot, watching the quiet restaurant and the open water behind it for a solid half hour, wondering what she was doing and if she even had a choice.

Tim had barely unlocked the front door and was setting tables along the far wall of the dining room when Jess walked into the restaurant at 11 a.m. on the pin. A bell tinkled overhead to announce her arrival, and Tim was barely more than a silhouette as he looked back at her and stood straight and came over, wiping his hands on his apron and smiling a good morning to her.

"Jess," he said. "Welcome. Eating by yourself this morning?"

She smiled at him, rueful. Tried to calm the nerves that threatened to set her whole body to shaking, thought semiconsciously how crazy it was she could walk into an enemy village or an outlaw compound without hardly any jitters at all, but ask her to walk into a hometown seafood restaurant and she was more scared than a fox in a snare.

"I wish I was just here to eat, Tim," she told the restaurateur, and she watched how his smile faded and an understanding came over his expression, and she surmised that he'd been waiting for her to come to him, waiting for the questions he must have known she would ask.

Tim flipped the OPEN sign to CLOSED and they took a table by the windows, overlooking the strait and the breakwater and the boats moored in the basin just feet from the restaurant's pilings. Tim poured two cups of coffee, handed one to Jess, and kept one for himself. He sat down opposite her and searched her eyes with his own, and his expression was something of pity, and Jess hated him for it.

"I just need to know," she told Tim. "How bad was that fight?"

Tim winced, and she knew he was seeing her as Mason Burke's partner and not as Sheriff Hart's deputy, and she knew also that Tim *liked* Burke, that the men got along, and that this mustn't be easy for him either.

"It was bad," he said finally. "It was—I mean, Jess, those men really went after each other. I had to call Miguel out of the back to get in between them, and even then..." He blew out a long breath. "If Tyner Gillies hadn't showed up when he did, I was afraid they might have killed each other right then and there."

As opposed to killing each other later, she thought.

Jess looked out over the water. She could see the *Nootka* in the boat basin beneath the restaurant, and though she knew Burke wasn't there—he was working with Joe Clifford, building *her* house—she still felt his eyes on her, watching her betray him.

"I haven't told the sheriff yet," she told Tim. "Gillies said he'd leave it to me. I've just been—" She met his eyes. "I've been hoping there's some other answer."

"Do you think Mason could have killed him?" Tim asked.

"You saw them fighting," she replied. "What do you think?"

Tim sucked his teeth and turned to stare out the window. He didn't reply for a long while. "It was bad, Jess," he said finally. "Those men didn't like each other; I can tell you that."

FOURTEEN

"How well do you know this guy, anyway?"

The sheriff sat perched on the edge of Jess's desk at the detachment, flipping through a thick file she knew belonged to Burke. The sheriff had set out for Deception, that file in hand, as soon as she'd called him, and Jess figured he'd probably been up most of the night memorizing its contents.

The detachment was quiet. Gillies was sleeping off last night's shift, and Paul Monk was home sick with some kind of head cold, he claimed, though it sounded to Jess like your run-of-the-mill hangover. Even the last few reporters had wandered away, grown bored with the lack of progress on the case, the whole story already gone stale.

That left Jess and the sheriff to hash out the Burke problem. And now she'd gone and told Hart about the fight, and Jess knew that must make Burke the prime suspect.

"Burke's a good man," she told Hart. "You know about the murder they convicted him for, the circumstances. Robbery gone wrong; his friend pulled the trigger."

Hart nodded. Regarded her thoughtfully. "Still makes him a murderer in the eyes of the law."

"It does, and Burke owns that," she said. "You go ahead and ask him yourself, Sheriff. He'll tell you he did his part to kill that man and that he served his time for it solid, without any complaint."

She could still feel the nerves alive inside her, wondered how the sheriff couldn't tell she was shaking. Wondered what she was doing defending Burke, what she was doing betraying him.

"Fifteen years," Hart said.

"Yes, sir. And the first thing he did, the moment he came out, was to make sure his dog was okay."

Hart knew the story about Kirby Harwood, of course. But Jess figured he might not be so well versed in how Burke came to be involved, which was to say, how he'd found out that Harwood had taken Lucy from Jess, how the deputy had planned to destroy the dog.

He'd come out here, twenty-five hundred miles from his home, to save his dog. And he'd stayed because he'd seen how Jess was in trouble.

"You know, Sheriff," Jess said, "Harwood and his pals wanted to kill me. They'd have done it if Burke hadn't been there to help." She looked up at Hart, met his eyes. "Hell, it was self-defense, anyway. He nearly died on that island."

Hart held her gaze a short while. Then he turned back to the file. "Be that as it may," he said, "that fight he had out at Spinnaker's was more or less the last time anybody saw Boyd alive."

"Don't forget about the woman," Jess said. "That lipstick stain on Boyd's wineglass."

"Right," Hart said. "The lipstick." He closed the file. Let out a long sigh. "Been days now, Jess, and still no sign of that woman, whoever she is. Look, maybe she had something to do with this; maybe she didn't. But your man Burke, he's got blood on his hands, literally. I think it's about time we brought him in."

She felt her breath hitch, and she started, wondered if Hart noticed. The way he was studying her, she could tell that he had.

"Just to ask him some questions," he told her. "Get his story on the record. Put a few more pieces together, that kind of thing."

She said, "Yes, sir."

He studied her another beat.

"You have the makings of a damn fine deputy," he said, "and I'd hate to lose you on this case. But if you don't think you can handle this, Jess, you ought to recuse yourself now. There's no shame in sitting it out."

Jess knew Hart was right. Knew if this were anywhere else—a bigger county, the city—there'd be no question: she'd be on the sidelines. But this was Makah County. Everybody knew everybody, and Hart's staff was limited already. No way was she taking herself out of the game, not the biggest case the county had seen since—well, since Harwood.

What the hell would I do with myself, she thought, *if they took this from me now too?*

She'd been a soldier, and now she wasn't allowed anymore. And while policing wasn't exactly like the Marine Corps, there were enough similarities—the structure, the discipline, the reliance on your friends amid the ever-present threat of violence—that she'd grown, in this short time, to feel she needed the work. The badge and the gun, the sense of purpose.

What would you do, she wondered, *if you couldn't do this anymore?*

"I swore an oath, Sheriff," she told Hart. "If Burke did it, I'll put him in cuffs myself. I just don't think he could have done it, and I want to see he gets a fair shake, is all."

"He'll get a shake," Hart replied. "This isn't Kirby Harwood's county anymore."

"No, sir."

And you have Mason Burke to thank for it, she thought.

Hart pursed his lips, looked around the detachment.

"Right," he said finally. "I guess we'll bring this guy in."

FIFTEEN

In the end, it wasn't Jess who brought Mason in for questioning, and Mason figured both he and Jess ought to be thankful for that.

He'd been expecting it, ever since Jess had dropped the line about the anonymous tip. Aaron Hart seemed like too good a sheriff to let that sit open for too long, and Mason knew Jess well enough to know she wouldn't stand in Hart's way. That she couldn't, not without risking her job. Sooner or later, the law was going to want to talk to Mason about Bad Boyd. All Mason figured he could do was keep his head down and be ready.

Hart showed up at Joe Clifford's jobsite, Jess's house-in-progress, early on a Tuesday afternoon and the weather just turning to rain again. Mason and Rengo hauling lumber from Joe Clifford's truck, Joe working inside the house somewhere, the sound of a nail gun punctuating the stillness.

Lucy'd found shelter from the rain in the remains of Jess's tool-shed, where Rengo had laid out a blanket and a water dish under the flimsy roof. The dog stayed there most of the day when power tools were in use, and particularly when the weather was bad.

The sheriff brought one of his own deputies, a Neah Bay guy named Derry, tall and uncomfortable in pants just a little too short, his hand resting on his holster and his eyes darting between Mason and Rengo, like all he'd been briefed about was that Mason had killed people, and he might do it again.

Hart, by contrast, was far more relaxed. The sheriff kept his hands in his pockets and his tone conversational, studied the frame of Jess's house as though he had nothing better to do than stand out in the drizzle and talk construction with the locals.

"Coming along, isn't she?" Hart said. At the sound of his voice, Rengo found somewhere better to be, disappeared inside the house, and after a moment or two the nail gun stopped punching, and Mason could hear Rengo's voice, fast and indistinct.

"Yes, sir," Mason replied. "Starting to almost look like a decent place to live."

"You planning on moving in too?" Hart asked. "When it's done, I mean. You all talked about that yet?"

Mason shook his head. "Not yet," he said. "I have my own place for now, figure we'll keep it that way in the short term."

"That's right," Hart said. "You're staying down there in the harbor."

"Yes, sir."

Hart didn't say anything for a time, just looked the house over some more. Then, finally, he took his hands from his pockets and hitched up his trousers.

"Well, son," he said, and there was almost a hint of regret in his voice, "I suspect you know why I'm here."

———

Hart took him to Neah Bay, the headquarters. Mason wondered if that was for Jess's sake. Wondered how much she knew about what was happening here.

He wondered if she believed he could have killed Bad Boyd, or if she was simply doing her diligence.

The sheriff brought him into an interview room—stained

cinder-block walls, a couple of chairs, and a table. Mirrored glass along one wall, scratched all to hell with scrawled names and crude drawings and just plain old war wounds. The room smelled of cleaning products and, underneath, something base and unpleasant.

"You should know that you don't technically have to be here," Hart told Mason, after he'd shooed Derry from the room and offered Mason a chair. "We're not arresting you for anything, not yet, and maybe not ever. If you didn't do anything wrong, I can't see as how you'd need to call a lawyer."

Mason might have laughed; the sheriff's tone was as casual as if he was still jawing about Jess's new house, lulling his suspect into a state of false security. Whether he'd done anything wrong or not, Mason had come to understand that this was the kind of situation where you really could use a lawyer, especially when you found yourself faced off against someone as experienced as the Makah County sheriff.

But Mason didn't know any lawyers. He was still hoping he wouldn't ever have to meet another one.

"This is about Boyd," he told the sheriff. "You got people saw me fight him in front of Tim Turpin's restaurant and now you're thinking I'm the guy put a bullet in his head. You're hoping I'll make your job easy and tell you you're right."

Hart leaned back, the hint of a smile on his face. "And?" he said. "Will you? Tell me I'm right?"

"I'm not a liar, Sheriff. I didn't kill that man."

Hart's smile didn't waver. "But you fought him. You must not have liked him very much."

"I didn't like the way he was talking to my dog," Mason told him. "Not given his history."

"Your dog? I thought he was my deputy's companion animal."

Mason looked at the sheriff. "You bring me in here to question me on custody of Lucy?" he asked. "Because I assure you, me and Jess, we've already hashed that one out."

Hart laughed a little bit, short. Then he leaned forward. "Brock Boyd was murdered the same day as you fought him. I understand that you don't have anyone who can corroborate your whereabouts."

"No, sir, I don't. Jess was at work, and I don't exactly have too many friends."

"You don't like people?" Hart asked.

"I like people fine," Mason said. "They just tend to be suspicious when you're—well, when you have a history like mine."

"Killing people."

Mason knew the sheriff was trying to provoke him. Knowing it didn't make it gnaw at him any less. "I served my time for what I did," he said.

"For what happened in Michigan, sure. What about what you've done since you've been out here?"

Mason stared at him. "You're talking about on the island?"

"You killed a man, didn't you?"

"Self-defense. And you all hired Jess for the same incident, so it can't have been that bad, can it?"

"You're saying I should fire Jess Winslow?"

Mason went stiff. Said, before he could stop himself, "No, god-damn you. You know damn well that's not what I meant."

The sheriff sat back again, and Mason knew he'd let the man beat him. He closed his eyes. Let his breath steady. "I didn't kill Brock Boyd," he said.

The sheriff nodded. "So why don't you tell me what you were doing that night. While you were *not* killing Brock Boyd."

So Mason told him. How he'd been at home—alone—on Joe

Clifford's boat. How he'd had Lucy with him, but he doubted the dog would be willing to vouch for him.

"Fair enough," Hart said. "And what'd you two get up to?"

Lucy slept, Mason told him, recalling how she'd curled up on the settee as usual, snoring most of the time, waking up and groaning and resettling herself whenever the boat shifted on its tie-up lines.

"I made some dinner, read for a little while," Mason told Hart. "Turned in pretty early, as best I recall."

"You do any drinking that night?"

"Not that I remember," Mason said.

The sheriff looked at him.

"I mean, sometimes I'll have a beer with my dinner. It might have been one of those nights."

"Are you a mean drunk, Burke? You get rough when you drink?"

"Not anymore, Sheriff."

"You think Bad Boyd deserved to die?"

Mason studied the sheriff. Hart had asked the question in the same casual, conversational tone as the last three or four before it, but Mason knew this one meant something more.

He let out his breath, long and slow. "'He who follows righteousness and mercy finds life, righteousness, and honor,'" he said.

Hart frowned. "That the Bible, Burke? What's that supposed to mean?"

"It means, Sheriff," Mason said, "that I'm not going to lie to you and tell you I liked the man, or that I cared what he stood for. I won't try to tell you I'm sorry he's gone."

Hart said nothing. Just watched him. Mason wondered who else was watching, behind that scratched-up glass. Wondered if it mattered, what he was saying.

"But as to whether he deserved to die, or didn't," he continued,

77

"I don't reckon that's any of my business. And it sure as hell isn't my place to play judge and executioner, regardless of how I feel."

He pushed himself to his feet; Hart didn't move.

"Now, if you'll excuse me, Sheriff," he said, "I think I've told you all I can."

SIXTEEN

Jess watched from behind the glass as Burke walked past Hart and let himself out of the interview room. She fought the urge to chase him down, catch him in the hall of the Neah Bay detachment, take him in her arms and say — well, what, exactly?

Apologize for how Hart had questioned him?

Tell Burke she didn't believe that he could have killed Boyd, no matter what the sheriff thought? Tell him she loved him and they'd fight this thing together, stand side by side until they found the real killer?

Or — maybe — she'd tell Burke to just clear out and run. Tell him to get the hell out of Makah County while he was still a free man, forget trying to fight. Tell him it wasn't worth the risk that they would lose, not given his history and the way folks in the county still tended to see him.

But Burke wouldn't run, Jess knew. Not if it meant he would have to leave her behind.

She didn't chase Burke down. She didn't even leave the viewing room, and after a short while, Hart stood from the interview table and walked out of the room. A moment later he came into the room where she waited.

"Well," he said. "What do you think?"

She thought that no matter what she believed, the sheriff would need more than just her instincts if he was going to knock Burke off his list of suspects. If she hoped to make him trust her as his deputy, and not just the killer's girlfriend.

Jess looked the sheriff square in the eye and tried to sound confident. "I think we still don't have the murder weapon," she said.

Burke was about a mile out of Neah Bay, walking east on the highway, when she caught up to him in her county cruiser. Rain was pouring now; Burke was soaked, but he walked steadily on the shoulder as if he didn't notice, didn't care.

She put on her flashers and pulled over just ahead of him. Watched him in the rearview as he approached the car. When he'd come up beside her, she lowered her window. "It's twenty miles to Deception, Burke," she said. "Don't tell me you're thinking of walking."

He looked up and down the empty highway. "Don't really like my chances of flagging a ride," he told her. "And it's not like that sheriff of yours offered me a lift."

She looked up at him, his jaw set and stubborn, rain streaming out of his hair and in rivulets down his face. He held her eyes for a moment and then looked away, up and across the top of her cruiser, his expression inscrutable.

"Get in," she said.

He kind of smirked. "You want me in the front seat or the back?"

"Fuck you." She felt anger flare up and glared at him. "Just get in the car, Burke. You want a ride home or not?"

He took the front seat after all, slid in beside her and rubbed his hands together in front of the heater vent as she signaled off the shoulder and pulled back onto the highway. They drove in silence for a while, and then he glanced at her.

"You were watching," he said. "All of that, me and Hart."

She nodded. She didn't say anything.

"I guess he's good at his job," Burke continued. "He knew he'd get me riled up, get me to spill something."

He seemed to be waiting for her to reply, and when she didn't, he looked over at her again, and he sighed.

"I didn't kill Boyd, Jess," he said. "I can't believe it even needs repeating, but I'll say it again. I didn't kill him."

"I know." Her mouth was dry; her voice came out rough, and she coughed it away. "But the whole county's about ready to pin it on you anyway."

Burke frowned. "You mean to tell me you have no other suspects, Jess? A guy like that, in a county like this, and I'm the only one you all can think to pin this on?"

She drove and watched the wipers arc fast across the windshield.

"He was a criminal, same as me," Burke said. "And he was rich, and he was an asshole, and he didn't seem to care if people knew it. But the sheriff and them all think I'm the only one who could have killed him? Over *Lucy*?"

"You love that dog," she said.

"*So do you.*" His voice was sharp, but she could hear the pain behind it.

She closed her eyes, and drove, and took the next bend with her eyes closed and only the sound of the tires on the pavement to guide her.

"We think there was a woman," she said. She opened her eyes, and Burke was watching her. "Or I do, anyway."

She told him about the broken wineglass. The lipstick stain and the partial fingerprint. About how nobody in Deception Cove would admit to seeing Boyd with any woman.

"It's just strange," she said. "Whoever she was, she just

disappeared. And it could be she has nothing to do with the murder at all, but..." She shrugged. "Damn it, we'd still like to talk to her."

She realized she'd probably crossed a line, telling Burke this. But Burke seemed to recognize it was a risk, what she'd done, and he seemed to be grateful for it.

He sat back in his seat. Watched the forest whiz by out his window.

"Thank you," he said. "For telling me."

They sat the rest of the way in silence, and it was a silence that made Jess afraid for what must come next. She wanted to take Burke's hand and feel him close beside her, and she wanted to lie together in bed and laugh at how Lucy chased squirrels in her dreams; she wanted to feel again how Burke's body fit against hers.

She didn't want to lose him, and she wanted to tell him this, but instead, as they came into Deception, she slowed down the cruiser and cleared her throat and asked, "Where do you want me to drop you?"

"Lucy's at the jobsite," he told her. "I figure you'd better take her."

She nodded and drove past the gas station and the motel and the turnoff down Main Street, found her way to her own turn and Timberline Road, a going-nowhere dead end with hardly any neighbors, the property she'd owned with Ty near the end of it. Joe Clifford's truck wasn't parked out front, thank God, but as Jess slowed her cruiser she saw Burke's friend, Rengo, come out from underneath the toolshed with Lucy in tow.

The kid slowed his pace when he saw the cruiser, but Lucy sped up, made a run at the driver's-side door and leaped up for the window before Jess had even stopped the car, the dog's claws undoubtedly scratching that Makah County paint, but neither the dog nor the deputy was particularly inclined to care.

Jess rolled down her window and let Lucy leap up at her, tongue lolling this way and that as, beside her, Burke reached for his door handle.

"Come on over here, girl," he called, and Lucy dropped down from the car and dashed around to his side, leaped up at him and fell short and leaped up again, leaving muddy tracks on his jacket and his jeans.

Burke shepherded Lucy to the open passenger door, where the dog looked in at Jess and then back at Burke and paused, like she could tell, somehow, something was amiss.

"Up you go," Burke was saying. "Get on in there."

He tapped on Lucy's butt and the dog leaped inside, muddy paws on the passenger seat and the center console, her tail wagging as she stretched across the car to assault Jess with her tongue.

Burke closed the passenger door, walked around to the other side of the cruiser, and stood at her window, his hands in his pockets.

"Probably best if I leave you be for a while," he said. "At least while the sheriff still thinks I'm the killer and you're still wearing that badge."

She glanced down at the badge where it was pinned to her chest. Knew Burke was right, but hated it anyway.

Is this what it comes down to? she wondered. *Is this how it's going to be, choosing Burke or the job? The county?*

"We'll catch whoever did this," she said instead, and tried to sound sure. "It'll be over soon, Burke. Just keep your head down until it's done."

Burke nodded, opened his mouth like he wanted to say something else, but he didn't. And there was plenty more *she* wanted to tell him too, but she kept her mouth shut and didn't say any of it, just rolled up her window and put the cruiser in gear, steered away from the shell of her new house, and the man with whom she'd hoped to make it a home.

SEVENTEEN

The man called Logger Fetridge had come by his nickname honestly—or dishonestly, depending on how you wanted to look at it. He traded in timber, mostly, though he'd been known to cook a little bit of glass now and then while Kirby Harwood was alive, and even more so now that Harwood was dead.

The deputy's death had opened up something of a power vacuum in the local drug trade, a free-for-all where once Kirby Harwood had kept some kind of order, using his badge and the threat implied therein as a means of extorting men like Floyd Fetridge, or Ty Winslow, guys who might once have been hauling salmon from the water beyond Deception's harbor, guys who needed some way to put food on the table for their families, and meth just happened to be it.

Fetridge had cooked, sure, while Harwood was still alive. He'd paid his taxes to the deputy too, however grudgingly. But meth hadn't been his main source of income, not until Jess Winslow'd put Harwood in the water. No, for most of his adult life, Floyd Fetridge had made his money in the trees.

The hills and low mountains south of Deception Cove were covered in second-growth timber, on public land and Indian land and straight-up private property, and Logger Fetridge had poached trees from just about every acre. Wasn't much overhead to the business—a chainsaw and a truck and a couple of good men were about all you needed—but the game did require a pair of solid brass balls for when push came to shove in the extralegal timber trade, and in standing up to Kirby Harwood when the situation called for it. And Fetridge knew he'd need them again if he wanted to survive this latest venture, a business proposition he'd supposed would be simple and lucrative, but which was turning out to require a little more concentration than he'd originally planned.

Fetridge sat on a couch in a trailer a few blocks from Deception Cove's Main Street. He was a tall man and imposing, that broad, barrel chest and a healthy tangle of beard only now starting to gray. A lumberjack in the traditional model, a woodsman. An outlaw who held himself to a certain code.

The couch and the trailer belonged to his friend Dax Pruitt, who sat in an easy chair opposite. The television in the corner— a forty-seven-inch RCA with a long crack in the screen—had belonged to a deadbeat no-account named Art Crosby, from whom Pruitt had liberated the set on Fetridge's behalf. The television was tuned in to the Seahawks game, but neither Fetridge nor Pruitt was paying attention.

"It ain't happened yet," Fetridge told Pruitt. "Somebody's got to hang for this murder, before the boss lady gets scared."

She'd called Fetridge again, that afternoon, on the burner. Asking questions he couldn't easily answer, running her mouth, the panic evident in her voice and in the fact she was calling at all.

She'd made Fetridge's head hurt, to be perfectly honest, made him wonder why he'd agreed to this job in the first place, nothing but headaches and fuckups right off the hop.

Fetridge wondered why he even answered the phone anymore when the woman called, and in his darker moments, he wondered if there was something he could do to stop her calling, permanently, just erase that particular line of risk altogether.

But the woman was insulated, holed away somewhere neither Fetridge nor Pruitt could reach her. And Fetridge still held out hope he could somehow solve the problem without jeopardizing the life he'd built for himself in Makah County.

Outside the trailer, an old diesel engine rumbled up the road and eased to a halt outside Pruitt's front door, and Pruitt and Fetridge shared a look and pushed up from the chair and the couch respectively, slipped into their boots and stepped out through the front door to where Chris Jordan's familiar old 2500 sat chugging on the front lawn, Jordan in the driver's seat and Doug Bealing riding shotgun, the same George-and-Lennie act as always.

Jordan was a wiry guy, squinted like a mole, the same chip on his shoulder as nearly every short man Logger Fetridge had ever met. Jordan was a schemer, not a scrapper, though he'd never been particularly smart. As it was, he was mostly just a low-level dealer, ducking the law on account of his being on probation for, of all things, a kiddie porn charge.

Chris Jordan wasn't much, but he was Logger Fetridge's nephew, and blood meaning what it did in Makah, that may have been his only saving grace in the world.

Doug Bealing, on the other hand, was big and clumsy and dumb, and he seemed to have missed the memo that guys like him were supposed to turn out kind of goofy and good-hearted to make up for their intellectual shortcomings. But Bealing wasn't goofy or good-hearted; he was the kind of guy who liked to shoot stray dogs for the fun of it, and then tell the whole crowd at the Cobalt how Fido had bled out all over the damn road.

Logger Fetridge didn't have a dog, but that didn't mean he liked Bealing altogether very much, though at this point the four men were more or less wedded together inextricably.

"Sheriff didn't bite," Fetridge told the men in the truck as Pruitt stood on the front lawn and watched. "Boss lady's getting anxious. I need you to do something to expedite this process."

Jordan and Bealing swapped glances. Jordan frowned out at Fetridge, and his voice when he spoke was the kind of whine that made Fetridge want to slap him.

"Why do we have to do it?" he asked.

Fetridge exhaled, slow, cursing his sister for bringing this waste of space into the world. "Because you're the reason," he replied, "that we're in this fucking mess in the first place."

He'd imagined that even his nephew could dispose of a body. He wouldn't ever make that mistake again.

"What do you want us to do?" Jordan asked. "Just march on into the detachment and tell them a story? We ain't got no proof, Logger. They'll start looking at us."

Behind the men, Pruitt cleared his throat. Fetridge's partner didn't speak much, but when he did, it usually made sense, and all three men turned to listen.

"Sheriff ain't found the murder weapon yet," Pruitt said. "Seems like if he found that gun it'd go a long way toward establishing what happened that night."

For a beat, nobody replied. Then Fetridge turned back to the truck, to his sister's kid and his pylon of a friend. "There," he said. "What do you know? Do you think you dunces can handle that without it all coming back onto us?"

Jordan and Bealing glanced at each other, though if Doug Bealing knew what day of the week it was, even, Fetridge would have been fully impressed.

Then Jordan set his jaw.

"Sure, Logger," he said, puffed up like he was trying for once in his life to sound competent. "We'll get on that right away."

EIGHTEEN

The witness came forward the next morning looking for Sheriff Hart, but she'd turned up at the Deception Cove detachment. Deputy Paul Monk tried to keep her entertained, offered her coffee and a couple of limp comments about how bad it was raining out there, but the witness wanted no part of any of it; she sat on the bench just inside the front door, staring straight ahead at the bulletin board and the Wanted posters, the missing-cat fliers, for the thirty-odd minutes it took Aaron Hart to make it into town.

When the sheriff arrived, he asked to conduct the interview in Kirby Harwood's old office in the back of the building, the room Jess Winslow and Tyner Gillies mostly used for storage now that Harwood was gone. Gillies was on patrol and Winslow had the evening shift, so it fell to Paul Monk to give the sheriff his permission or lack thereof, and Monk didn't quite know the sheriff well enough to withhold permission to anything. He found the spare key on his key ring and unlocked the door and stood aside as Hart ushered the young woman into the space.

"Paul, you'd better come in here too," the sheriff called out to Monk, who'd lingered by the door, unsure of his obligation in a situation like this. "Bring a couple of cups of coffee too."

It took Monk a few minutes to get the coffee put together,

but he made up two mugs and brought in some packets of sugar and some creamers too, not knowing who of the three of them the coffees were for. When he came into the room, Hart was sitting not behind the big beat-up desk that dominated the room but in one of the two chairs in front of it. The witness sat in the other chair.

And that's how Paul Monk found himself in Kirby Harwood's executive-level desk chair in the back end of the Deception Cove detachment, listening to a woman named Charlene Todd explain to the sheriff how she knew it was Mason Burke who'd killed Brock Boyd.

The meeting took over an hour, and by the time it was finished, Tyner Gillies had come in and was standing at the coffee maker, brewing another pot and dripping rainwater all over the linoleum.

Gillies looked up, surprised, when the office door opened and it was Charlene Todd and then Sheriff Hart and then Paul Monk who emerged; the witness ignored him, walked straight to the front doors and out into the rain, and Hart and Monk kind of stood there in the middle of the detachment, watching her go.

"Well, Paul," the sheriff began, when Charlene Todd had disappeared outside, "what did you make of all that?"

Hart had a notebook in his hands where he'd written down everything Charlene Todd had told him, and he'd asked her to tell it a couple of times, run him through every detail until they both were sure she was telling it right. For Monk's part, he'd done nothing but sit there and listen, watched how Hart walked the witness through the interview, watched how the witness worried her hands and kind of looked away, out the window, whenever Hart's eyes were on her.

Now Monk shifted his weight and kind of looked out the window himself. "I mean, I don't know her all too well," he said. "But I don't see as we have any reason to doubt her."

Hart nodded. "No," he said slowly. "I don't think we do."

He looked over at Tyner Gillies for the first time. "Deputy Gillies," he said, "I do believe we need to rustle up a scuba diver."

NINETEEN

Mason supposed he'd been expecting more visitors.

One way or another, he was in the middle of this thing with Brock Boyd. The sheriff sure seemed to consider him a suspect. So whether it was Hart, Tyner Gillies, or some combination thereof, Mason knew the law wouldn't leave him alone for long.

The only person in the county Mason didn't figure would pay him a visit was Jess, and he guessed he couldn't blame her. Objectively speaking, there was plenty on the table to point to him killing Boyd, and she, being a deputy, had to pay attention to all of that. Mason couldn't begrudge her for doing her job.

But hell, it hurt anyway. Truth be told, he relied on Jess plenty, to help him navigate the town and the county beyond, to lend him an air of legitimacy when the rest of the populace seemed to want to see him as a menace. Now he didn't have Jess, and he didn't have Lucy, and Mason already missed them both something terrible.

Either way, he knew Jess and the dog wouldn't be coming back down here, to the boat, in any kind of a hurry. So when he heard boots on the wharf boards outside, the boat swaying a little and the late afternoon light starting to wane, he knew it wasn't a romantic call waiting for him when he stepped out of the wheelhouse.

Sheriff Hart led the parade. He had Jess's fellow deputy with him, Tyner Gillies, and a man Mason had never seen before, who was carrying an oxygen tank and a duffel bag. Hart and Gillies stopped on the wharf beside the boat, and the third man set down his bag and his oxygen tank and peeled off his jacket, and Mason could see he wore a wet suit underneath.

Mason watched the men through the galley window and thought about staying inside, making Hart come to him, but there seemed no point in prolonging the situation, so Mason walked to the wheelhouse door and pulled on a rain slicker and swung the door open.

"Evening, Sheriff," he said, stepping out onto the deck. "Deputy. What can I do for you fellas?"

The question was a formality; Hart had brought a diver, and Mason knew that meant the sheriff thought he'd find something in the water, probably the gun that had killed Brock Boyd. What Mason wasn't sure of, not yet, was whether the gun was down there or not.

"Mason, this is Ed Aymar," Hart said, motioning to the diver. "Ed's just going to check out the bottom of your boat for us. That okay?"

Mason shrugged. Whether it was okay with him or not, Aymar was going in the water, and everyone knew it. Mason pulled the hood over his head and stepped across the deck to the gunwale, watching how Gillies tensed every time he moved, like the deputy was waiting on him to run.

"Go ahead," Mason said, and Hart nodded to Aymar, who checked his mask and his regulator, flipped on a little flashlight, and slipped over the side of the wharf into the oily water beneath, leaving the three other men behind on the surface to watch the water and wait.

The rain had slowed to a drizzle, though the wet still seemed to seep through Mason's jacket all the way to his bones as he stood on the wharf beside Hart and watched the bubbles drift up from where Aymar was diving.

As the late afternoon light continued to fade, the yellow sodium lights on the standards above flickered on, bathing the wharf and the boats and the men in some sickly light, and Mason could see, above and behind Hart, Spinnaker's restaurant was doing good business, the dinner rush already picking up.

"I guess you wouldn't be here if you didn't think you had something," Mason said to Hart after a while.

The sheriff smiled a little bit. "We try not to waste anyone's time."

"That's thoughtful of you."

"Had a witness come in," Hart told him. "Said they heard voices in the harbor—men's voices, fighting—the night Brock Boyd was murdered. Said they heard a gunshot too." He paused. "Then maybe they heard the splash as somebody threw a weapon away."

Mason looked down at the water where Ed Aymar was searching, and he knew that sooner or later the diver was going to come up with the gun the sheriff expected him to find. And he knew, as soon as that happened, he was done for.

Gillies was watching him. The deputy shifted his weight and rested his gun hand on his holster and stood square in the center of the wharf, the only path back to the government dock and dry land.

Mason closed his eyes. "You fellas bring that pistol with you?" he asked Hart, who chuckled and shook his head and didn't bother to answer.

"The way I see it, there's two possibilities," Mason continued. "Either you all are in on this too or you're not."

"Burke," Gillies said.

"I'd like to think the law in this county is a little more honest than when I first arrived," Mason said. "Which means you all aren't the type to chuck a gun in the water just to pin this whole thing on me."

Neither Gillies nor Hart said anything; neither man looked at Mason.

"Which means it was someone else put you up to this," Mason said. "Whoever that witness is, either they chucked that gun away or they know the person who did."

"There's a third possibility, Mason," Hart said.

"I didn't kill Boyd, Sheriff."

Hart wasn't smiling anymore, and he wasn't laughing either, and Mason noticed how he, too, had unsnapped the holster on his belt. For the first time, Mason wondered if he would make it off this wharf alive.

"Let's just wait for the diver," Hart said. "Could be there's no gun down there in the first place."

But there was a gun down there. Mason knew it. He just wasn't sure if Hart knew it too, or if the sheriff was simply playing someone else's hand.

The men waited there. Stood in the drizzle and got steadily colder and wetter as they watched the dark water. And time passed, and Mason couldn't have said how long or how little, except that eventually his jeans and his shoes had soaked through and he was shivering, whether from the cold entirely or from adrenaline too, he didn't know.

Then the diver broke the water. About fifteen feet from the stern of Joe Clifford's little troller, and halfway out into the channel between the two wharf fingers. He spat out his regulator and found Hart on the dock and held up something small and black and shiny in his hand.

"Sheriff," he said, "it's a .38."

TWENTY

There was no point in hanging around to argue.

Hart and Gillies turned to Mason as the diver swam toward them, and Hart's expression seemed to be one of regret or at least sympathy, while Gillies's mouth was tight and he'd drawn himself up fully, blocking the only path off the dock.

"Okay, son," Hart said. "I think you can see how we're going to need you to come back to town with us."

The sheriff advanced on Mason, slow, as if he was a wild animal. Gillies hung back maybe eight or ten paces, keeping a safe distance in case the situation turned ugly. Mason wondered if Jess's buddy would shoot him on this dock, and decided he didn't want to find out. There was no going through these two men, not without someone getting hurt.

But there was no going with them either. He'd never breathe free air again if he did, and even Jess would believe that he'd murdered Brock Boyd.

"Now, just turn around and lie down on that wharf," Hart was saying. "On your front, slow. I'll put the cuffs on you, and we'll get you out of here, easy."

Mason turned around, like the sheriff wanted. Ahead of him, now, the wharf stretched another boat length or so, fifty feet, toward an abrupt end and the water beyond. In the distance, across the harbor, the breakwater and the light and the ocean. To his right, a channel for boats and then a pile of rocks and riprap, and the pilings on which Spinnaker's stood.

"Good," Hart said. "Now, go ahead and lie down, Mason."

There was no hope but to go for it.

Mason made as though he was going to lie down. Bent over a little, anyway. Then he made his move.

He bolted ahead, ran for the water as fast as he could. Heard the sheriff behind him yelling, Gillies too, hoped they were decent enough they wouldn't shoot him in the back in the time it took him to make the end of the wharf.

They didn't, and that was a small mercy, but it wasn't much. Mason made the end of the wharf and dove before he could stop himself, arced out over the water and plunged in, the cold like a thousand knives stealing every last gasp of air from his body, late spring in Deception Cove but the ocean still frigid.

Now they might shoot him. Mason aimed his body deeper into the water, pulling with his arms and kicking with his legs as hard as he could, trying to put distance between himself and the dock. He'd never been much of a swimmer, and the water was cold and soaking into his jeans, his shoes, and his slicker, weighing him down. But he didn't have any choice but to keep pushing forward.

He didn't hear gunshots behind him, and he wasn't sure if that meant the sheriff wasn't shooting at him or if the water around him was muffling the sound. Either way, he couldn't see how it would be a good idea to poke his head up and check, so he kept going, pulling and kicking as his lungs ached for air and his head began to throb.

Finally he could take it no longer, and he kicked for the surface, broke the water with his mouth open, gasping for breath but as quiet as he could, and behind him he could hear the sheriff calling his name, and the sheriff sounded close, but Mason didn't dare look.

He ducked under again and kept swimming, feeling the cold sapping his strength, eating away at the adrenaline that was propelling him forward, and he knew he had to get out of the water quickly, or else he would die.

He angled toward the riprap and the pilings beneath Spinnaker's and came up for air once more, his breath coming in clouds and his teeth chattering; he could feel his mind starting to fog as his body lost heat. The sheriff was still shouting, but he sounded farther away now, and Mason still didn't look back but kept swimming to where the pilings rose out of the water, and underneath them was blackness.

Once under the pilings, he kept his head above water, out of breath and already exhausted. His mind a single track now, desperate for warmth and a dry place to stand or sit or lie down. He paddled between the pilings to where the rocks met the water, and he pulled himself up on barnacled, kelp-covered granite, his lungs burning and his chest heaving.

But there was no rest, not now. The sheriff and Gillies were only two men, but they would call others soon enough, and anyway, between the two of them it wouldn't take long before they figured out where he'd gone. The rocky slope was slippery from high tide and steep, and his hands were numb, but he forced himself to climb anyway, struggling and slipping and gradually gaining ground until he'd reached the underneath side of Spinnaker's, and then he followed the rocks to the north end of the restaurant.

The air seemed to have dropped ten degrees since he'd stood on the dock with Hart and Gillies. Mason was cold, and he knew he would succumb to hypothermia if he didn't find some warmth and a change of clothes soon. Around the far side of the restaurant was the parking area, and beyond that he could hear the siren from Hart's or Gillies's vehicle. There was no time to waste thinking about a plan. Mason stayed low on the rocks and crept clumsily away from the restaurant and the town, kept going until he reached the rusted chain-link fence that marked the edge of the restaurant's property and the start of Brad Anderson's marine ways and boatyard.

Anderson was the lead volunteer for the Deception Cove Fire Department, and he'd struck Mason as a stand-up guy the odd time they'd crossed paths. The light was on in Anderson's workshop, and at any other time, Mason wouldn't have hesitated to ask the man for help, but tonight's problem wasn't something a stand-up guy like Brad Anderson was equipped to deal with. He'd likely take the sheriff's side, and Mason knew he couldn't blame him. He crept along the fence line to where it opened at Anderson's driveway, and then he followed the road away from it into the forest.

He was still cold. He was very cold and wet, and his clothes were heavy and his limbs were heavy too, and the cold was still slowing his thoughts to a crawl, and there was only one place he could think of to go.

He walked deeper into the forest, away from the water and toward the lights of the town. Kept himself hidden as best he could in the shadows, and willed his body to keep upright just a little longer, just as long as it took.

TWENTY-ONE

The way Lucy's tail thumped on the bed, Jess knew it had to be Burke outside.

The dog had a sixth sense for when Burke was around, some kind of bond forged before she knew Jess. Before Burke had trained her, when she'd been so traumatized from the dogfighting that she'd peed all over Burke's lap practically the moment they'd been introduced to each other.

She was a different dog when Jess met her. There'd been no sign of that terrified creature then, when they created their own bond together on a ranch a couple hundred miles inland, a bunch of fucked-in-the-head veterans like Jess and a pack of dogs the military promised would help them. It wasn't until Jess had known Burke a while that he'd told her how Lucy was when he met her, how far she'd come.

"Runt of the pack, she was," he'd said, and he'd smiled affection-ately at Lucy as he talked, scratched between her ears, the dog grumbling with a grudging kind of approval. "I caught all kinds of hell from the other guys about her—and honestly, Jess, I was pretty pissed off myself, at first."

The other inmates had been given golden retrievers, German shepherds—happy, playful dogs without any issues. He'd resented the agency lady for sticking him with Lucy, but he'd gradually come to see how desperately the dog needed him, needed someone to treat her with love.

He'd told her how Lucy had stuck up for him toward the end of the program, an almost-fight between Burke and a couple of gangbangers. She'd had his back the same way she had Jess's, like she knew they were family and she was going to stay loyal.

"That's why I wound up coming out here, I guess," Burke had said. "She was the only one had my back when I needed it. I couldn't let her down when she needed me."

They hadn't really talked about whose dog Lucy was, after Burke had come to Deception Cove and Jess had asked him to stay. Burke had assured her he wasn't there to take Lucy from her, just to make sure Kirby Harwood and his gang didn't kill her. But the bond was there, and it was obvious, and it had made Jess feel jealous at first, *her* dog liking this ex-con so much.

Later, she'd come to see it as a point in Burke's favor. All the more so since he seemed happy to let Jess's relationship with Lucy come first.

But there was a bond, and it was evident now as Lucy's ears perked up on the motel-room bed, tail beating the blanket like she was dusting a rug.

And sure enough, a moment later someone tapped on the door, and Jess went to the peephole and looked out, and it was Burke. Lucy stood, stretching, jumped down from the bed and padded across the room to join Jess at the door, and Jess hesitated just a beat before she unlatched the chain and unlocked the door and swung it open.

She'd been in the middle of getting dressed for the night shift, her hair up in a ponytail and her uniform shirt unbuttoned, had only another twenty-five minutes before she was supposed to be at the detachment, and she'd yet to eat her dinner, besides.

One good look at Burke, though, and Jess forgot about the night shift. The man was soaking wet, shivering, his skin pale and his lips tinged blue. He hugged a rain slicker around himself, though it didn't seem to be doing him any good; his clothes were as wet as the rest of him, and he smelled faintly of salt water and diesel.

"God's sake, Burke," she said, staring at him. "What in the hell happened to you?"

He shrugged out of the slicker and dropped it to the pavement outside her door, and she could see how his shirt underneath was drenched too; he was soaked to the bone. He looked up and down the line of doors and out into the parking lot.

"Can I come in?" he asked. "Just for a second?"

Wordless, she stepped aside, and his boots made wet, sloppy sounds on the floor as he walked past her into the room, Lucy circling around his legs now, kind of whimpering and nuzzling up to his hands. He was shaking, and his eyes were dull. There was no point in asking any more questions, not yet.

Jess closed the door, locked it. Shooed Lucy away and went to Burke, took hold of his hands where they were struggling with the buttons on his shirt. His hands were as cold as ice, and he couldn't seem to get his fingers to work right; she set his arms at his sides and began to unbutton his shirt herself, feeling the cold radiate off his body, the smell of diesel stronger now, almost overpowering.

"Did you fall in the chuck, Burke?" she asked. "Is that what you did?"

She'd never known him to drink to excess, but maybe he'd been drinking; it had happened to her husband, and he'd died for it. But Burke shook his head, tried to form words and couldn't.

She got the shirt off of him and tore the blanket from the bed, wrapped his shoulders inside it as she started on his pants. "Hush," she said.

———

By the time Jess had Burke naked, he seemed to have warmed up some, and she wrapped the blanket tighter around him and went away into the bathroom to run a shower, scalding hot. But when she came back, she found the blanket on the bed and Burke in fresh skivvies, rooting around in the dresser drawer where he kept his spare clothing for the nights he slept over.

"The hell are you doing?" she asked him. "You're a block of ice, Burke. You gotta warm up some more before you——"

"No time," he told her, and there was at least some semblance of strength in his voice. "They'll come looking for me; here's the first place they'll check."

Her stomach fell. She watched him pull out fresh jeans, a sweater, and she wondered why she'd opened the door for him at all.

"What are you——"

"They're setting me up." He stepped into the jeans and pulled them up his legs. Looked over at her, and his eyes were dark and serious. "Someone told Hart to send a diver to the harbor. They found a gun in the water underneath my boat."

Jess stared at him. Her mind struggled to catch up. Somewhere in the room were her belt and her service pistol. Her handcuffs, her radio.

Burke watched her eyes, and his shoulders slumped. "Look," he said. "You can call Hart if you want; I won't fight you. If you truly believe I'd do something like this . . ."

He trailed off. She didn't move, felt her heart pounding. Even Lucy was still, like she was waiting to see what would happen next.

"You know me, Jess," Burke continued. "And I've never lied to you. I didn't kill Brock Boyd, but somebody in this county sure wants it to look like I did."

There was resignation in his voice. Like he suspected already that she wouldn't believe him, she'd already sold him out in her mind. Like there was no point in running if he couldn't even keep her on his side.

Your career, or the man you love.

"What do you need?" she asked him, her voice rough. "What is it you expect me to do for you, Burke? You said it yourself: here's the first place they'll look."

He blinked. Studied her a beat, and then he shook his head and pulled the sweater down. "No," he said. "Don't risk your job for me. Just don't—don't turn me in to the law just yet, if you can."

"You could run." She crossed to where her purse sat on the room's little dining table. "I have some cash and you could take the Blazer; I won't tell Hart. Just get the hell out of Makah, Burke, and don't look back. You—"

"I didn't kill anyone." Frustrated, an edge to his words. "I'm not running."

She didn't say anything. Watched him finish dressing, and Lucy did too, her head between her paws as she stretched out on the bed. The dog's eyes were sad, as always, and maybe a little sadder; surely she could tell that something in her world had gone drastically wrong.

Burke slipped back into his soaking-wet shoes. Made a face, but bent down to tie up his laces. Jess found the spare key to the Blazer, held it out to him. But he waved it off as he stood. They were close now; he seemed to tower over her.

"I don't need anything from you, Jess," he said. "You don't even have to cover for me if you don't think it's right."

"What are you going to do?" she asked, but he was already turning away, and she watched as he swung open the front door and peered out into the parking lot, surveyed the lot quickly and stepped out into the night. She made no move to stop him, and then he was gone, and the door swung closed behind him and she was left there in that little room with the scent of him lingering beside the smell of diesel fuel and the ocean, the memory of the hurt she could see in his eyes, and the dog watching her from the bed as if she had any answers.

TWENTY-TWO

Jess stood in that room for a long time, not moving. Lucy lay on the bed and watched her, and it was like time seemed to stall for both of them. Outside, the rain fell on the roof of the motel. Burke was out there somewhere, and she didn't know where or what he planned to do, but she was afraid for him and wished he hadn't gone.

She couldn't make herself think straight. Before he'd come in, she'd believed he was innocent, and she still didn't see how he could have murdered Brock Boyd. There was a part of her now, though, that wondered if she could be wrong. If she was blind. She'd fallen in love with men before, after all, and believed they were good. And some had been anything but, in the end.

They found a gun in the water underneath my boat.

I've never lied to you.

Jess didn't know what to think, not now that Burke was gone again. But she was afraid for him anyway, and she hoped he was running.

Then came another knock at the door.

Jess thought it was Burke, at first, and her heart leaped and she reached for the handle and thought to swing it open and take him inside and tell him to just hide out for a spell while she thought of a way to solve this, but somehow she thought better of it, caught herself, and when she checked the peephole, it wasn't Burke but Sheriff Hart, and Jess was damn glad she hadn't opened the door.

The room was a mess. The blanket lay in a heap at the foot of the bed, Lucy half on it and half off, and it was damp from Burke and probably smelled like him too. Burke's wet clothes were on the floor, and there were footprints where he'd walked in his soaking shoes. Anyone could see that he'd been here.

Hart knocked again. "Jess?"

It snapped her to life. Quickly, she gathered Burke's clothes and took them into the bathroom, dumped them into the tub. She brought a towel out with her, mopped up the puddle by the door and tried to wipe away the footprints. Then, as quiet as she could, she shooed Lucy from the bed and relaid the blanket, smoothing it over the mattress and hoping the damp spots didn't show. It was the best she could do; any longer and Hart would get suspicious, if he wasn't already.

There was nothing she could do about the lingering smell; Jess could only hope the sheriff had a cold.

She herded Lucy toward the door, praying the dog would be a distraction. Kept her uniform shirt unbuttoned for more or less the same reason, and she turned the knob and pulled the door open and reached down to catch Lucy with her free hand.

"Sheriff," she said, making her voice breathless. "Running a bit late—sorry. Come on in."

She pulled Lucy back so that Hart could enter, the dog looking askance at her, like *What exactly do you want from me?* as Hart took a step inside, surveyed the room.

"The place is a mess," Jess said. "I'm sorry. Really looking forward to when my house is finally finished."

Hart nodded but said nothing, his face revealing nothing either. She wondered if the sheriff already knew Burke had been here. If he did, he wasn't letting on.

"You, ah, heard from Burke tonight?" he asked her. She saw

fatigue in his eyes, concern, but nothing more. No guile, though she knew better than to assume that meant it wasn't there.

"No, sir," she replied, buttoning her shirt. "We haven't talked since yesterday, and I don't expect to see him again any time soon either, not with this whole Boyd thing still up in the air."

She was lying to the sheriff. She supposed that made her complicit, and she knew Hart would take her badge if he ever found out.

Your career, or the man you love.

Hart asked her, "Was that your decision?"

"Mutual, Sheriff," Jess said. "We both figured it wouldn't look all that good on me or the detachment, not while Burke's still a person of interest."

Run, Burke. Run.

Hart nodded. Took a couple of steps over toward the bed, held his hand out and let Lucy sniff at it. She'd taken up her spot on the blanket again, and if Hart looked past her and up toward the pillows, he might see the damp spot. Jess waited, hardly daring to breathe.

Then Hart turned away from the dog, squared his shoulders.

"We had a witness come in, said she heard men fighting down in the boat basin the night of the murder," he said. "Said she heard a gunshot too. Then maybe a sound like somebody was throwing a gun in the water."

Jess waited. Thinking if she did speak, interrupt him, she might give the game away.

"We brought a diver down," Hart continued. "Me and Tyner. The diver found a .38 just off the stern of Burke's boat."

Jess tried to make herself look surprised. "Did you—is he—"

"Made a run for it," Hart said. "Or rather, he swam. Jumped into the water off the end of the wharf and we haven't seen him since.

Might be he drowned out there or might be he slipped away. It was only me and Gillies out there, after all."

He looked at her, made a face.

"Best as we can figure, there must have been an altercation," he said. "Maybe Boyd came back for another round, found Burke on the docks."

Jess remembered how Burke told her Boyd had found him on the *Nootka* a few days before the fight. Boyd knew where Burke was staying, that much was certain.

"You never saw Burke with a .38, did you?" Hart asked.

Jess shook her head. "No, sir."

The sheriff shrugged. "Well," he said. "Not too hard to find a weapon in this part of the world." He paused, looked around the room again. "Boyd's body was too far gone to tell if there'd been any violence before the gunshot. But Burke must have put the bullet in his head, fired up that old boat and driven out into the strait, dumped the body. Just his bad luck Boyd washed up how he did."

Jess tried to picture Burke piloting that old *Nootka,* couldn't see it happening. The ex-con was from Michigan, wasn't much of a mariner. But then she still couldn't fathom him killing Brock Boyd in the first place.

"What do we do about this, Sheriff?" she asked. "I can keep my eye out for him on patrol, but we're kind of lacking bodies for a manhunt, aren't we?"

Hart rubbed his face. "Not for long, we aren't," he said. "A murder racket like Burke's, a killer on the loose? We can't afford to waste any time."

Jess said. "So—"

"I called the state police, Jess," Hart said. "They're en route from Port Angeles. This county's on full-on lockdown, starting now."

TWENTY-THREE

Chris Jordan hesitated, but not long, before he knocked on the door. The woman opened up quickly, like she'd been waiting for him. Looked out with wide eyes and dark circles beneath, scanned behind and beside him like she was afraid who else might see.

Jordan studied her face in the doorway for a time. When was it that she'd gotten so old? The lines on her face were etched deep like canyons, a topographical map of anxiety and addiction.

She'd been pretty, in high school, and he'd lusted after her and loved her and never quite found the courage to ask her on a date or even say more than a couple of words to her at a time. She'd chosen another, married him quick, and it wasn't until her old man went and got himself drowned in a fishing-boat accident, out in the strait, that Jordan had seen her again.

She'd been living off the settlement checks, she'd told him, waiting to figure out her next move. By that point, he was running glass for his uncle and Dax Pruitt, and little by little, she'd become his best customer.

Occasionally she'd become something more, though there wasn't any romance to it, nothing like those schoolboy fantasies he'd harbored back when, before she'd even known he existed.

Jordan had asked her, once, what she thought her next move

would be, and she'd kind of looked off and muttered something about maybe being an artist or maybe going back to school, and then she'd taken the glass from him and handed over the money, and the conversation had more or less fizzled out from there.

She hadn't gone back to school, and she didn't make art. She'd stuck around in Makah as the settlement checks dwindled. And here she was, still, just another sad story.

"I did what you said," she told Jordan. "Everything you told me, I told them just how you said to. About the gun and what I heard and — and everything."

Jordan hoped his uncle would be impressed, what he was doing here. Tying up loose ends, keeping the story straight. Mitigating the risk, to Fetridge and Pruitt and the boss lady, whoever she was, up above them.

"You want to invite me in?" he asked the woman.

She hesitated. "You said," she began. "You said if I did it, you'd . . . you said there'd be something in it for me."

Jordan dug into his coat pocket, pulled out a baggie, Fetridge's best glass and a fair couple grams of it.

The woman's eyes widened and she stepped back, let Jordan walk across the threshold and into the room beyond. He nudged the door closed behind him, locked it. When he turned back, she was standing there, eyeing the baggie.

"You said," she said, and she was nothing like the girl he'd wanted in high school, tall and striking and confident and proud. She held out her hand and stared at him, beseeching, and he couldn't even see the resemblance anymore, couldn't see how he'd ever pined over her in the first place.

He hoped his uncle would appreciate what he was doing. His initiative, for the family. Maybe Fetridge would promote him, move him up from just straight selling glass all the time. Maybe Fetridge might finally respect him.

In the pocket of his jeans, Jordan carried a knife. He slipped it out and watched how the woman shrank back as she saw it.

"You said," she said weakly. Resignation in her voice. "But I did everything like you said."

TWENTY-FOUR

"Charlene Todd," **Rengo** told Mason. "That's the woman who ratted you out."

It was the next afternoon. Still pissing rain. Mason had been inside all day, warm, and he still couldn't chase that cold, that permeating damp. Still couldn't scrub the taste of diesel from his mouth.

He'd taken most of last night to find his way up here, to Rengo's ramshackle collection of broken-down trailers and detritus in the woods. The compound sat at the ass end of an old logging spur, had belonged to Ty Winslow once upon a time, back when he used to cook meth with Rengo.

Ty had died, and Rengo had moved in, and though Mason had seen to it that the kid stopped trying to cook, he'd yet to convince him to move out of the rainforest and down into town.

For once, he was grateful that Rengo was stubborn.

The compound was a long climb through the forest from town, plenty tough on a four-wheel-drive vehicle and about fifty times tougher on foot, in the dark, in the rain. Mason had been up here only a handful of times, but he'd found the place fine, after three or four hours. Showed up at Rengo's door and knocked and prayed the kid wouldn't shoot his head off, and Rengo had opened up sleepy-eyed in a pair of stained-yellow tighty-whities, scratching his head and staring out at Mason like he'd sooner have expected a ghost.

But he'd let Mason into his trailer anyway, welcomed him to the taped-up couch in the corner and a moth-eaten old blanket, told Mason to get some shut-eye and they'd discuss it in the morning. The kid carried himself different when he thought he was in charge; something changed in his voice and the way he used it, like he was trying to live up to this new responsibility, prove to the world he deserved it.

Mason hoped the kid did.

Next morning, Mason had explained the whole thing, the gun in the water and the witness and everything. Rengo wasn't surprised.

"Sure, it only makes sense," he told Mason. "You probably got a few more enemies than you realize. Whoever kilt Bad Boyd for real probably sees you as—"

He stopped. Cocked his head.

"Just so's we're clear, you *didn't* kill him, right?"

Mason looked at him. Said nothing.

"I mean," Rengo said. "It wouldn't be much matter if you did, but you can tell me the truth, right? I mean, you got at least one friend in this town."

Mason sighed. "I didn't kill Boyd," he said. "But someone surely wants the law to think I did. They sent a witness to see Hart, planted the gun."

Rengo had sparked up a joint, sat back and inhaled, deep. Held the smoke in his lungs for a long beat and then exhaled.

"It's a solid frame job," he said. "What are you thinking to do?"

Mason had thought about this the whole climb up the hill, slogging through mud and wiping rain from his eyes, tripping over deadfall whenever he veered from the road.

"I guess I ought to find that witness," he said. "See if I can't talk to her, whoever she is."

So Rengo went into town the next morning, worked a full day with Joe Clifford, building more of Jess's new house. That was Mason's idea; the kid wanted to stay home, gather his weapons, and hunker down, make a plan, but Mason figured the sheriff would have a pretty good search going by this point, and someone was sure to tell him how Chris Rengo was about the ex-con's only friend.

In the meanwhile, Mason rested and looked for something to eat among Rengo's assortment of candy bars, pork rinds, and sugary breakfast cereals. He understood now why the kid stayed so scrawny no matter how hard he worked on the jobsite.

Mason walked the perimeter of Rengo's compound in the rain, wondering at who might find the place and where they would come from, and when he started to shiver again, he went back inside and sat on the couch and wrapped the blanket around his shoulders and tried to think things through.

He hadn't made much progress by the time Rengo returned, about an hour before dusk and the rain still coming. Rengo had the name—and he had news too, and it wasn't good.

"State patrol's all over the damn town," he told Mason, handing him a takeout carton from Rosemary's diner. "Got boats and men searching the harbor too. Guess they think you might have drowned?"

State patrol. Mason opened the carton and took out a long-gone-cold hamburger, chewed it and wondered if he should have just taken Jess's advice, got to running and hoping he made it out of Makah, off the Olympic Peninsula, maybe up to Canada. Hell, maybe even try for Mexico, hope he got lucky.

But it wasn't a future Mason wanted for himself. He didn't want to run. He'd made a commitment to Jess, to Lucy. To himself. He wanted to stay here and see this thing through.

And, damn it, he wanted to prove the town wrong. Clear his name and make something of himself, show the people of Deception he was more than just a killer. He'd had fifteen years to prepare for this second chance; he'd be damned if he was going to cave so quickly.

Charlene Todd. That was the name of the witness.

"Rents a room above the Cobalt," Rengo told Mason. "In case you needed any indication of where *her* life's at."

The Cobalt sat downtown, right square on Main Street. Down the block from the sheriff's detachment, where Jess would be working, maybe even helping the sheriff plot a way to bring him in.

Mason wished Charlene Todd lived in a nice house somewhere, out in the boonies, but he supposed he must have known that it wouldn't be easy.

Outside Rengo's trailer, the forest was dark now. The rain was still falling, and Mason still felt cold.

He pushed himself off the couch. There was no point in waiting.

"Charlene Todd," he told Rengo. "Guess I'll go find her."

TWENTY-FIVE

The state police officers whom Sheriff Hart had called were all tall and broad-shouldered young men, brawny and self-serious and competent and, it seemed to Jess, completely incapable of smiling. She supposed she'd been like them, once upon a time, when she'd arrived at Parris Island for boot camp scared out of her mind and determined to focus only on doing what it took to succeed as a young Marine. She *had* succeeded, so it must have worked, though she hadn't made many friends or laughed much over those grueling thirteen weeks.

Later, in the field, she'd learned to laugh. Learned that laser focus only took you so far if you weren't mentally prepared to stand in a hailstorm of shit, all the horrors of war, and deflect it and retain some humanity. The Marines who couldn't joke, never smiled—they were the ones who cracked first.

Jess watched the state police taking over her detachment and she didn't see any jokers among them. Wondered if they ever cracked, and how bad things had to get before they did.

The lead guy was a cop named Shipps, probably a shade over six feet, a firm handshake and an unwavering stare. He'd shown up about an hour after Jess arrived at the detachment last night, said he'd picked up from Port Angeles and driven out as soon as he'd heard.

"A killer on the loose," he told Jess and Hart. "It's not a time to sit around with our thumbs up our asses."

He didn't excuse himself for the language, not to Jess or anyone else, and Jess was grateful for that at least. But Shipps scared her; he carried himself like he knew what he was doing, like he fully expected to catch up to Mason Burke before dawn. Like he might even relish the opportunity to put Burke in the ground.

But Shipps hadn't caught Burke by dawn, or even through the next day, though more of his colleagues had arrived in Deception and the surrounding county, prowling down back roads and peering into windows. It was only a matter of time, Jess knew. She hoped Burke had had the good sense to run, or that he'd at the very least go quietly when Shipps and his men came for him.

But she had to be hopeful in secret. Right now she stood in the detachment with Sheriff Hart and Paul Monk and Tyner Gillies, the entire Deception Cove deputy complement, a couple more from Neah Bay, and Shipps and a few of his men besides. Everyone but the state guys looked sleep-deprived and anxious; they'd over-whelmed the coffee maker four hours ago and were sending out for Rosemary's house blend at a rate of one trip across the street every hour or so. The purpose of this tête-à-tête was to try to, as Shipps put it, *think like this guy Burke does.*

"We're trying to get inside his head," Shipps told the assembled. "But any information at all is going to help us. Is he a runner? Is he hiding? Who are his friends? Where's he likely to turn?"

Every eye on the Makah County side of the room turned to look at Jess. Shipps didn't miss it; he turned his gaze on her too.

Jess met it, head-on. Figured that was the only way she'd keep her seat at the table. "Burke's not from around here," she said. "He doesn't have many friends. The way this town sees him, he's not likely to have many hiding places."

Shipps studied her a long beat. "You're Winslow," he said. "The Marine. You and Burke have history together."

"Yes, sir," Jess said.

Shipps turned to Hart. "You think it's wise, Sheriff, to keep her on this case? Everything she and Mason Burke have been through?"

"Everyone in this room has connections to this county's criminal element, Sergeant," Hart replied. "What matters is whether they can put the badge first in a situation like this. I trust that Deputy Winslow can."

Shipps turned and looked at Jess again. A long time. She felt the rest of the room watching her too.

"Friends," Shipps said finally. "Lovers. Acquaintances. Where's he working? Who're his contacts in the community, aside from —" He lifted a hand in Jess's direction.

Once more, the room waited on Jess. She cleared her throat.

Run, Burke. Run.

"I'm his primary contact in the community, Sergeant," she said. "Aside from me, there's his employer, Joe Clifford, and one known associate, a man named Christopher Rengo."

"We've checked in with Clifford," Hart said. "He's a family man, respected in Deception. Agreed to let us know if Burke shows up at his door."

"And this other person," Shipps said. "Ringo?"

"Rengo," Hart said. "Young kid, bit of a troublemaker. Or he was, until Burke came along. Right now he's of no fixed address; we're having trouble pinning him down."

Shipps snapped his fingers. "Find this guy. Maybe he knows something. We're watching the highways, buses, Amtrak in Seattle, and every road in and out of Makah County, got Burke's face on the news and in the newspapers. It's a matter of time before Burke trips a wire somewhere, but maybe we can force it in the meantime. Sounds like this guy Ringo might be our best bet."

"It's Rengo," Jess said, but Shipps was no longer listening.

The way Shipps had looked at her, Jess knew it was coming eventually. She sat alone at her desk and tried not to notice how the rest of the room watched her, how voices hushed whenever she walked within earshot. How Shipps beckoned the sheriff over and the two men conversed in quiet, every so often glancing in her direction.

She was as good as done. Jess knew it.

She pretended not to see as Hart broke off from Shipps. Crossed the room toward her and sidled up to her chair.

"Hey, boss," she said, looking up. "Thanks for sticking up for me."

Hart couldn't meet her eyes. "You haven't heard from him, have you?" he asked softly. "Not that I don't believe you'd tell me if you did, but these guys—" He gestured toward the state contingent. "I can understand if you'd feel a bit shy bringing it up to them."

Jess shook her head. "Nothing," she said. "I really think he might have run, Sheriff. Or . . ."

"Or?" Hart said.

"Look," Jess said, not knowing where she was going, and scared like shit she would crash. "He swore he was innocent, last time we talked and every time before that too."

"We found the gun, Jess."

"Given to you by some miraculous witness who says she heard everything." Heads were starting to turn now; people were listening. "One word from this woman and—bam—the smoking gun is right where we need it. You don't think that's odd?"

Hart took her by the shoulders, not rough but plenty firm.

Pulled her away from Shipps and the rest, took her around the corner to where the holding cell was.

"You need to watch how you're talking around those guys out here," he said, and his tone wasn't angry, exactly, but it was urgent. "They hear you spouting this shit, Jess, they'll come for your badge."

"What if it's not *shit* I'm spouting?" Jess asked him. "I don't make Burke for Boyd's killer, Sheriff; I'll be honest. And I respect how you might not put much stock in my opinion, but you've still got to admit that it's pretty damn convenient the way this is all wrapping up. You don't think we ought to at least consider—"

"Deputy." Hart held up his hand. Then he sighed. "Jess. You haven't worked a case this big before; I understand that. You've got a lot to learn, and sometimes I forget, but—"

"Sheriff—"

"But you're going to find," Hart continued, talking over her interruption, "that cases like these, they're not generally head-scratchers. Most of the murders you'll see, they'll wrap up just about the way you expect them to. People get angry, they do something stupid. They, by and large, lack the capacity to cover it up."

Jess made to speak again, but Hart wasn't having it. He held his hand up again, palm out toward her.

"I've got to take you off this case," he said. "Shipps is forcing my hand here, and I can't say that I blame him. He doesn't know you, Jess, but he knows about you and Burke. And the optics..."

He trailed off. Watching her, and it wasn't like Shipps; there was no judgment, no suspicion. She could tell Hart cared about her, knew this must be tough on him.

"It's nothing to be ashamed about," he said. "There's plenty more police work to be done in this county while the state patrol's looking for Burke. Hell, it's not like the rest of the criminals in this county just all up and went on vacation."

Jess studied his face. Wondered if she'd just torpedoed her career, speaking up on Burke's side. It didn't matter now. She couldn't blame Hart, and there was no point in fighting it.

She looked Hart in the eyes. "Fine, Sheriff," she told him. "I guess I'll get out of your hair." And she excused herself then, slipped past him, and walked out into the main room of the detachment, past Shipps and his troopers and Tyner Gillies and Paul Monk and the rest, and she felt their eyes on her and knew what they must be thinking, and she tried not to care, about the men and about what they'd surely do to Burke when they found him.

TWENTY-SIX

The Cobalt occupied the first floor of a dirty brick building on a corner lot on Main Street, just up the hill from the government wharf and the boat basin, and just north of where the road up to the highway really got steep. It was the kind of bar that looked abandoned in daylight and worse after night fell, windows boarded and graffitied over, the only entrance a plain steel door painted flat black.

Above the first floor, the building rose from the pavement another two stories, four windows per level facing out onto the street, bedsheets or Seattle Seahawks flags for curtains, greasy anemic light emanating from behind. Apartments, or rooms at least: Deception Cove downtown living at its finest.

Doubtless there was a front door to the residential component of the building, but Mason didn't figure he could risk a look. Anyway, there was a fire-escape structure tacked onto the rear, flimsy wooden stairs backing onto the alley, and those ought to do well enough.

Rengo had driven him as far as the top of the hill, in a beat-up old Toyota pickup with a rusted-through body but a motor the kid swore still purred. He'd dropped Mason off and turned around and driven off to hide again, Mason finally establishing in the kid's mind that the state cops were likely to come looking after him too, sooner or later. Mason had watched Rengo go, his taillights red smears in the rain, and then he'd turned and found a side road a ways down from Main Street, hiked down the hill, and hoped nobody saw him.

Nobody did.

Now he stood at the rear of the Cobalt, listening to the throb of rock music from the first-story bar, uneven drums and an angry guitar. Down the block was the sheriff's detachment and Jess probably in there, and Mason missed her like anything and wished she were with him. Wished he'd taken her away from Deception Cove after the Harwood thing, convinced her to make a life somewhere else, somewhere new.

But Jess would never leave Makah County again; Mason knew it. What he really should have done was walk away from Brock Boyd outside Spinnaker's restaurant.

Do not resist an evil person. If anyone slaps you on the right cheek, turn to them the other cheek also.

If he'd let Brock Boyd claim his victory, just taken Lucy and walked, nobody would have seen him hit the dogfighter. Nobody would have any reason to believe he held a grudge.

Mason knew he'd been stupid, and he was paying for it now.

According to Rengo, Charlene Todd lived on the top floor of the Cobalt, the farthest unit from the harbor. Mason found his way to the fire escape and started climbing, hoping the "witness" would be home.

The fire escape was flimsy, waterlogged wood. It swayed and creaked as Mason climbed, and he feared for some time that the whole thing would collapse underneath him. He hurried, trying to keep quiet, hoping the noise from the bar below was drowning out his boot steps.

There was a wooden door at the second-floor landing; Mason tried the handle and it swung open. He closed it again, climbed to the top floor of the building and found another door there, and it, too, was unlocked. He pushed it open and walked inside.

A narrow hallway. Dirty light bulbs spaced far apart, carpet tracked with mud and wet and who knows what else. A communal bathroom off to one side, the toilet seat up, the mirror a mess of more graffiti. A stink wafting out through the open doorway — weeks or months of uncleanliness. Opposite the bathroom door was Charlene Todd's known address.

Mason knocked on the door. There was no answer, no sound of movement from within. He waited in the hall and listened to the buzzing of the light bulb overhead, felt the throb of the bass from two floors below, resonating through the whole building and inescapable.

This was not a happy place. It looked nothing like the Chippewa pen, but it reminded Mason of prison all the same — an undercurrent of desperation, thinly masked volatility. A violence coiled up and hidden and waiting to strike.

He knocked on the door again and there was again no answer. He could have turned around and left and come back another time, and he probably should have, but instead Mason tried the door handle and it was unlocked and he'd pushed the door open before he could stop himself.

Charlene Todd's home was a single room with a window that looked out to Main Street. On a nice day, you'd have been able to see the water, if you craned your neck some. Square, more or less, enough space for a small bed and a table and chair; no cooking facilities to speak of, but a hot plate on a shelf by the door. Sketches taped to the walls, ballpoint pen on printer paper, landscapes of the harbor and the town and some profiles of animals — a bald eagle, a killer whale. A raven.

Charlene Todd lay on the bed, beneath the window, and Mason knew she was dead before he'd even crossed the threshold.

She lay on her back on the bed, her feet toward Mason at the door and her head resting on the pillow.

Her throat had been slashed. She'd bled out onto the bed, and the blanket and pillow beneath her were stained dark and damp. It was impossible to say how long she'd been dead, but she was dead and there was nothing Mason could do for her. She'd been about Jess's age, he suspected, in her midtwenties, though it was hard to know for certain in the darkness of the room. He realized he should have expected this, that whoever had convinced Charlene to lie to the sheriff would likely want to keep her quiet now, now that she'd done the job for them.

Mason stepped fully into the room. Closed the door behind him. He looked at Charlene Todd and felt guilty and empty and sick, that this woman had died to serve some machine with him at its center, that he'd fought with Brock Boyd and now another person was dead.

He stood in the room with Charlene Todd's body for some time, and he didn't know how long. The music played far below and cars passed on the street outside, and rain fell against the window and Charlene lay on her back on her bloody bed and couldn't provide Mason with any answers.

Mason turned back to the door and pulled it open, and then he wrapped his hand in his jacket sleeve and wiped the door handle down as best he could, on both sides. He stepped out into the hall again and pulled the door closed with his hand wrapped in his jacket, and he went down the hall to the fire escape and prepared to let himself out.

But the bathroom door was closed. Mason should have noticed

but he didn't, and then he heard the toilet flush and the door swung open. A man stepped into the hall, buttoning his pants, and if he'd just turned the other way, he might have walked back to his room without noticing Mason.

But the man stood there in front of the bathroom for a beat; he was an older man, with a lined face and a stooped-over posture, stained Carhartts and a flannel shirt. Mason waited, frozen, the music pounding up from beneath, and maybe it wasn't the bass resonating now but his heart, and then, slowly, the man turned and saw him.

"Another friend of Charlene's," he said, his voice betraying no surprise. He hadn't asked a question, but he looked at Mason through bleary eyes as though expecting an answer.

He might have been drunk or it might have been drugs, or it might have been something else entirely. Mason wondered if there was a chance the man might forget about him after he'd found his way back to his own room.

But then the man blinked, and his eyes cleared and he frowned. "You're the one they're looking for," he said. "The one killed Bad Boyd."

There was no hope then but to leave and leave quickly, and that was all Mason could figure to do.

He met the man's gaze, and the man didn't look afraid but rather curious, as though he was wondering what the man who'd killed Bad Boyd was doing here, in his hallway.

"Call the sheriff," Mason told him. "There's been another murder." Then he turned and reached for the fire door. Let himself out and into the rain again.

TWENTY-SEVEN

It was the last thing Aaron Hart needed, another body on his hands. For all of the spiel the sheriff had spun to his favorite deputy about crime in Makah County being more or less simple, he couldn't quite convince himself the Charlene Todd murder wrapped up as nicely as it should have.

The call had come in about an hour previous, closer to nine in the evening than eight, breaking up the meeting of the minds with Sergeant Shipps and the state patrol. Ernie Saint Louis at the Cobalt had a murder to report, and he was saying it was the man who'd killed Bad Boyd who'd done it.

Ernie was in his cups, and deep, by the time Hart had trekked across the street to the Cobalt Hotel, a forensics team on its way from Port Angeles to meet him. No elevator in the Cobalt, of course, and Hart was near out of breath by the time he'd reached the third floor, found Ernie in his room with an open bottle and a couple more of them empty, asked him to explain the whole thing over again.

Ernie swore it was Mason Burke who'd met him in the hall, had come out of Charlene Todd's room and told Ernie there'd been a murder. And Charlene Todd was dead and murdered; there was no doubt about that. Her throat had been cut, and she'd died in her bed, not even forty-eight hours since she'd walked into the detachment and pointed Hart to the murder weapon at the bottom of the Deception Cove boat basin.

From any logical point of view, Mason Burke was the prime and only suspect. And Hart figured that was probably the way it would all shake out in the end. But in the meantime, there was plenty that niggled at him. The first thing was how Burke had figured out so quick it was Charlene Todd who'd snitched on him. The second was, why'd he go and tell old Ernie to call the law and there'd been a murder, when he could have said nothing and bought himself time to keep running? But the most troubling thing about this whole development, from Hart's eyes, was why Burke would bother to kill Charlene Todd at all.

Hart didn't know Mason Burke very well. He knew the man's history, and they'd shaken hands once or twice. But he knew Jess Winslow, better than a little bit. He figured he knew her well enough to trust she was an all-right judge of character.

Hart could believe that Mason Burke had killed Brock Boyd. The men didn't like each other, and from the sound of it, both of them had had something to prove. Burke had a killer's pedigree to start with, and he'd likely seen Boyd as pretty close to fair game, Boyd being a criminal himself, and a dogfighter at that.

The way Hart saw it, if Burke *had* killed Boyd, he probably slept just fine at night afterward. Just as he'd likely not lost any sleep after what had happened with Jess and Kirby Harwood on Dixie Island. But Jess swore the first murder—the one down in Michigan that had sent Burke down this path—had been a long-ago mistake, something that had changed Burke almost as much as it had changed the unlucky bastard on the other side of the equation.

As Hart surveyed Charlene Todd's little room, and Charlene lying dead in the middle of it, he didn't see fair game, and he didn't see how Burke could have either. Charlene was destitute, and she was by and large harmless. She'd done nothing wrong but tell the law what she'd seen.

Why would Mason Burke risk capture just to punish her? It was a hell of a chance to take when Charlene had already told her story. And Burke, to Hart's mind, seemed smarter than to do it—or at least the sheriff hoped his favorite deputy wasn't shacking up with a guy that dumb.

But if Burke hadn't come to kill Charlene Todd, then why had he come here? And if not Burke, then who had killed her?

Hart knew he was playing the same game Jess Winslow had been playing, letting his mind spool out with conspiracy theories and hunches, not seeing the facts laid out before him. Charlene Todd was dead, and Mason Burke had been in the room with her. Smart money said Burke had killed her, and Hart might never know exactly why.

All the same, the questions bothered him. And when Doc Trimble showed up from the coroner's office, and the forensics technicians arrived on loan from Clallam County, Hart decided he'd put them to work.

"I need it all, Shay," he told Trimble as they stood in the doorway and looked in at Charlene's body. "Full workup on the deceased. Everything you can tell me."

Trimble nodded, but she looked skeptical. "You're the boss, Sheriff," she said, "but I can tell you right now, it looks like she died from a knife."

The doc was wearing more makeup than usual, a nice crimson dress underneath her lab coat. Hart surmised he'd interrupted some kind of evening.

"Yeah, I get that," he told her. "Time of death, though—that's what I'm after. As close to the minute as you can peg it."

Mason Burke had been in with Charlene around quarter past eight, Hart figured. If the coroner could pin down a time of death within a reasonable proximity, the sheriff knew it would go a long way toward erasing the nagging doubts in his head.

But in the meantime . . .

"Dust the room; all of it," he told the forensics team, Bobby Yee and Ray Franklin, with whom he'd worked more than a few cases in Clallam County. "You might probably get the phone book, but I want every fingerprint accounted for. Anything unusual in this room, document it."

He stepped back and watched the team get to business. Figured to work this case harder than any open-and-shut case had ever been worked in Makah County, get ahead of this homicide spree before it claimed any more victims. Probably it was Mason Burke who'd killed Charlene Todd. Undoubtedly he'd killed Brock Boyd.

But just in case it wasn't Burke who was doing this, Aaron Hart figured he'd need every scrap of a clue he could get his hands on.

TWENTY-EIGHT

She'd been bumped off the Boyd case, but Sheriff Hart had let Jess keep her badge, and that's how she found herself parked with Lucy in a county cruiser a day or so later and a couple of miles west of Deception, aiming a radar gun at eastbound traffic coming out of Finlayson's Bend.

She had the dog in the back seat and Gillies riding shotgun. Gillies, who ought to have been working the night shift that evening and instead had been downgraded to babysitting duty, working tandem with Jess while Mitch Derry out of Neah Bay caught the overtime and the state patrol handled the manhunt.

It was embarrassing, Jess thought, for her and Gillies both. Sheriff Hart obviously felt like she needed caretaking, someone to keep an eye on her while Shipps and his men left no stone in the county unturned in their search for Burke. Jess might have been insulted if she'd believed Hart meant it personally. But she figured he was trying to look out for her, keep her busy without jeopardizing the case, and she supposed she'd have done the same thing if the roles had been reversed.

Gillies, for his part, had just about bent over backward trying to convince Jess that he didn't blame her for their newfound partnership.

"I don't care what Burke did or didn't do," he told her, studiously avoiding eye contact. "You're still a hell of a deputy, and I can't see how this case changes any of it."

His disappointment was obvious, though he tried to put a brave face to it. "Hell, those state police assholes are more or less crowding us out anyway," he said. "Wouldn't be much to do even if they did let us help investigate."

That was a lie, and they both knew it. Shipps and his men may have been handling the hunt for Mason Burke, but Hart still had to work the Boyd murder case—and the new one, Charlene Todd, with Burke pinned for that too.

That one was a head-scratcher, and even Hart knew it. And Jess hoped the sheriff would see soon enough that there was no way Burke could have done it, or *would* have done it. Though Charlene Todd had more or less damned Burke with her testimony, Jess knew he wasn't the kind of man who'd ever seek vengeance. Especially now, with the whole county knowing his face and looking hard for it.

Burke hadn't killed Charlene Todd. Jess was certain. But nobody else in the county seemed ready to listen to her, and it drove her crazy to be sitting here with Gillies playing speed trap instead of actually hunting for the real killer.

The lipstick on the broken wineglass in Boyd's garbage—as far as Jess knew, neither Sheriff Hart nor the state police had come up with an explanation yet. Nor did it seem to Jess that anyone cared to look for any motive Charlene might have had to point the finger at Burke for Boyd's murder. Hart wouldn't know that Charlene had been lying, but Jess did. What she didn't know yet was *why*.

A mustard-yellow Chevette, a hatchback about three decades old sagging low on overloaded springs, came racing out from around Finlayson's Bend and tripped the radar gun first at fifty-three per.

Thirty-five miles an hour was the speed limit here, down from fifty on the other side of the bend, more than a few wrecks in the trees and crosses by the roadside, thanks to drivers who'd ignored the slowdown and skidded, especially in the dark and the wet.

Jess hit the lights and pulled out after the hatchback, the little car chugging along steady at a speed that defied explanation once you caught a look at the smoke churning out of its exhaust pipe. In the back of the cruiser, Lucy settled in for the chase, though it wasn't much of a pursuit; Jess and Gillies were coughing as they pulled up behind the Chevette, the driver glancing through the acrid fog in his rearview and his shoulders slumping, the car slowing and pulling over to the side of the road.

Jess and Gillies swapped glances, reaching for their seat belts. "Here we go," Gillies said, and he tried to sound excited, but Jess could tell he wasn't exactly turned on.

The driver was a man named Douglas Bealing, address out in Neah Bay. He was four years older than Jess, according to his license, and she didn't recognize him. He sat behind the wheel with his hands at ten and two, stared straight ahead with a look of confusion that might well have been permanent. Jess leaned in through the open driver's-side window to chat with him; Gillies stuck to the passenger-side, his hand on his holster.

"You know why we pulled you over?" Jess asked Bealing.

Bealing didn't respond. He was shaking, she saw, his hands gripping the wheel tight.

"Douglas," Jess said. "Are you hearing me?"

Still no answer, and Jess straightened, caught Gillies's eye over top of the hatchback. Figured they'd have to haul Bealing out of the car, administer a sobriety test, no telling what kind of junk he was on.

Then Bealing spoke. Clumsy and abrupt. "I got nothing to say to you," he said. "I don't know nothing about what he done."

Jess leaned down again. "What *who* done, Douglas?" she asked. "What are you talking about?"

But Bealing just stared straight ahead. "I don't know anything," he said again. "Honest, he didn't tell me he was going to do it, not *that*."

At the far side of the car, Gillies shifted his weight. Straining to hear. Jess kept focused on Bealing, her spidey sense going haywire.

"Who're you talking about, Douglas?" she asked. "What's going on here? You want to step out of the car so we can talk about it?"

"*No.*" Bealing was still shaking. "He doesn't tell me anything," he said. "Not until it's done."

This was something. This was something, and Jess knew it, but she didn't know what. And she didn't know how to get Bealing to tell her.

"Douglas," she said. Kept her voice calm. "Why don't you step out of that car so we can talk this thing through, huh? Get to the bottom of it."

She wasn't aware of the pickup truck until it had pulled up beside her, in the eastbound lane, sandwiching her a little too close for comfort between the Chevette and its passenger door.

"Problem, Deputies?"

Jess straightened and turned, found the passenger-side window open on a Chevy Silverado, the face of Dax Pruitt leaning across and looking out at her, polite and nonthreatening, everything normal.

Jess knew Pruitt, by sight and reputation. Older than Burke, pushing middle age, he might have been handsome, if he'd just cut his hair, shave away that awful goatee, put on a clean shirt every once in a while. Simple stuff, cosmetic changes.

But there was nothing cosmetic that could chase the hunger from his eyes. The seedy look of desperation that spoke to how he'd mortgaged his principles, a long time running, how there wasn't much anymore he wouldn't do for a dollar. Nothing you could buy in a store would hide that.

Pruitt wasn't a bad man, not as Jess had heard it. But he wasn't a particularly *good* man either.

"Just a routine traffic stop, Dax," she told him. "Nothing to concern yourself about."

Pruitt leaned farther, looked past her to the mustard Chevette. "That Dougie Bealing over there?" he called. "How're you doing, Dougie? These deputies treating you okay?"

Bealing didn't turn to Pruitt. He continued to stare straight ahead and muttered something that might have been a yes or it might not.

"You're obstructing traffic, Dax," Jess told Pruitt. "We've got this under control. Move along."

But Pruitt didn't move. "You know Dougie, don't you, Deputy?" he asked Jess. "Little slow, if you know what I mean. I'll just hang around with you, make sure he's all right. Sometimes it helps if he knows he's got a friend waiting on him."

"That's really not necessary—" Jess began, but Pruitt looked past her again and called out to Bealing.

"I'm right here, Dougie," he said. "Everything's fine. I'm not leaving until these deputies are gone."

He shifted the Silverado into gear. Hit his blinkers and rolled forward, pulled onto the shoulder in front of the Chevette.

Jess watched him park. Looked over at Gillies again, who shrugged.

"Shit," Jess said. She leaned down to peer through the Chevette's window again. Dougie Bealing was watching the Silverado. She said, "Dougie," and he flinched.

"Just give me my ticket," he whispered. "I got nothing to say to you."

This was a lie. Jess knew it, and Gillies knew it, and even Dax Pruitt would have known it had he heard Bealing say it. But Jess knew there was no way she'd get Bealing to reverse his course, not with Pruitt in that Silverado filling up Dougie Bealing's windshield.

She wrote her phone number in her notepad. Reached inside the Chevette and laid it on Bealing's dash.

"I'm going to let you off with a warning," she told him. "You want to talk, now you know where to find me."

Bealing didn't answer. Didn't even look at the paper. Jess waited there another beat or two, trying to compute in her head whether anything Dougie Bealing had told her gave them cause to hold him, bring him in, search the car, anything. But she couldn't see a way in, not that would hold up in court. And she could tell that whatever she tried, Dax Pruitt would be ready to fight her the whole way.

Reluctantly, she straightened. Tapped the hood of the Chevette and glanced once more to the Silverado parked ahead, Pruitt watching her in his side-view mirror, their eyes meeting just once, for an instant.

"Okay, Dougie," Jess said, motioning Gillies back toward the cruiser. "I guess we'll be seeing you."

TWENTY-NINE

"The way I see it, we've got a few possibilities," Mason told Rengo.

They'd holed up back at Rengo's compound, though for how much longer, Mason couldn't be sure. He'd seen the state police contingent on his venture into town to find Charlene Todd, and now that Charlene was dead, Mason couldn't imagine there were many folks left in Makah or the neighboring counties who weren't aware of what was happening—or, for that matter, of his association with one Christopher Rengo.

Mason knew the state police, sooner or later, were going to find their way up the spur line that led into the compound. And if Mason was here when they did, there was no way either man was leaving in anything other than handcuffs or body bags.

It didn't sit right with Mason, not at all, being in opposition to the law once again. He'd imagined those days had passed along with his prison term, that he would live out his life as a model kind of citizen, a man who played by the rules and stayed within the lines.

Even when he'd fought against Kirby Harwood, he'd done it because the lawman was corrupt and he'd known he and Jess were right.

Now, though, Mason knew that the men who searched for him believed they were doing good, believed he'd killed Brock Boyd and it was their duty to catch him. He had no issue with these men beyond that they aimed to imprison him, and he wished, fervently, to avoid confrontation.

He'd wondered, again, if he might not be better off turning himself in, putting his faith in the law and avoiding the possibility of further violence. But Mason knew he couldn't do it.

If he wanted his name cleared, he would have to do it himself. And he would have to do it in a way that ensured no more innocent people were hurt.

Rengo drank from a fifth of Wild Turkey. He was trying not to look scared, Mason could tell, but the kid was all of twenty, twenty-two, and if he didn't show his face soon, he'd be a wanted man, the same as Mason was.

"So out with it," Rengo said. "What are we looking at here?"

Mason replied, "First thing, you go on down the hill and turn yourself in to the state troopers. Tell them you haven't seen me, and you don't know where I'd run to."

"And what are you doing while I'm giving myself up?" Rengo asked.

"Charlene Todd," he told Rengo. "That's the first thread I could pull. She lied to that sheriff, and someone put her up to it."

"And then someone killed her for doing it," Rengo said.

"It sure seems that way. I chase down who was leaning on Charlene, I maybe find my way to whoever's trying to frame me."

"And then we'd likely know who killed Boyd. What's the other option?"

"The other option is Boyd himself," Mason said. "Start at the beginning. Jess said there a woman he was with, sometime before he died. So far, they haven't been able to find her."

"And you think we can? If the law—"

"The law's thinking I did it," Mason said. "They're not looking too hard at the alternate possibilities."

Rengo drank again from his bottle, and was silent, and Mason knew the kid wasn't fully on board with the idea.

Hasn't exactly worked out so far, he thought, *you tracking down witnesses and trying to find answers.*

"Look," Mason said. "Someone killed Brock Boyd, and they had a reason for doing so. I'm not saying I need to find this woman, necessarily. But I would like to know a little more about Boyd, preferably a good reason or two why somebody would kill him. That's all I'm saying."

Rengo set down his bottle. Stood, and on unsteady legs he walked to the door of his trailer and looked out across the litter-strewn compound to the forest beyond. "You keep saying 'I,'" he said. "Like I don't have a part in this too."

"We talked about your part," Mason told him. "You go on down to Deception and disavow all knowledge of my whereabouts to the sheriff. Find somewhere else to sleep for a while."

Rengo looked out the door and didn't respond. Mason could see how he gripped the frame of the door, gripped it tight, like he was trying to pull it free from the trailer. "It don't work," the kid said finally.

"What's that?"

"What you're saying. The plan. Me turning myself in." Rengo turned back to Mason, impatient. "It just don't work."

Mason frowned. "Why not?"

"Because, Burke, you're a wanted man, and everyone knows it. And you ain't been in Makah long enough to know your way around here without getting caught. You think you can track down Charlene Todd's people without the whole damn county getting wise?"

Mason said nothing.

"Secondly, you know jack shit about Bad Boyd," Rengo said. "What, you're going to march into the library and look him up on Wikipedia? *You ain't from around here,* Burke. You want to stay here and solve this, you're going to need someone who knows Deception."

Mason stared at Rengo for a beat, and Rengo stared back, holding his gaze, courage drawn from the bottle or maybe something more fundamental.

"I'm not dragging you into this with me," Mason said. "People are dying, and it isn't your fight."

Rengo didn't reply right away. When he did, his voice was lower, and his eyes weren't meeting Burke's anymore. "You stuck up for me," he said. "This construction thing? You could have left me alone up here in the woods."

He paused.

"I don't have any friends either, Burke," he said. "You're it. And how I was raised, you don't let your friends handle the tough shit alone."

Mason said nothing. Neither did Rengo. The wind rustled the trees outside the trailer and blew the clouds past overhead.

"Goddamn it," Mason said finally. "Just don't get yourself killed on my account, understand?"

THIRTY

The plan was collapsing, and Dax Pruitt could see it happening.

It was Pruitt who told Logger Fetridge how he'd run across Dougie Bealing on the highway into Deception, parked on the shoulder in that shitbox Chevette with the new deputy, Winslow, leaning in through the driver's-side window.

Bealing, who couldn't be counted on to right weigh down a body. Who sure as hell couldn't be trusted to keep a secret. Pruitt had taken one look at the man through the passenger window of his own Silverado, seen how Jess Winslow and her partner, Gillies, were perked up and on the hunt, and he'd known he and Fetridge were just about hooped. It had taken all he could muster to get Bealing out of the traffic stop without giving the game away then and there.

Of course that wasn't where the trouble had started. The trouble had started, Pruitt and Fetridge both knew, when they'd taken the job from the boss lady, and it had snowballed into something else when Jordan and Bealing couldn't see to it that Bad Boyd's body disappeared and never turned up again.

At least then they'd had Burke, though, to take the fall for the crime.

No, Dax Pruitt knew that the situation had really, *really* fucked up at the moment when Chris Jordan had the bright idea to murder Charlene Todd. He'd killed her and told Fetridge proudly what he'd done, as if another murder in Makah County was going to make anyone *calmer*.

"Had to do it," Jordan'd said, protesting when his uncle and Pruitt'd told him what a stupid piece of dead weight he was. "What if she talked, went back on her story?"

"You slit her fucking throat, Nephew," Fetridge had replied. "You wanted to kill her, you couldn't slip her a dose?"

Jordan'd had no answer to that, couldn't meet anyone's eyes, and Pruitt had the sneaking suspicion the younger man had used his knife because he'd wanted to, because in some sick way he'd enjoyed it. It turned Pruitt's stomach, but it didn't surprise him. Chris Jordan was a damaged man, and if his mother hadn't been Floyd Fetridge's sister, someone might ought to have killed him by now, spared Makah County further pain and embarrassment.

As it was, Jordan was untouchable, and woe betide anyone who tried to teach him right from wrong. Anyway, Fetridge needed him to keep Dougie Bealing under wraps, being as how the big man hadn't ever seemed willing to listen to anyone else.

"Hide him," the poacher'd told his nephew. "Don't let him see daylight until the law catches up to Mason Burke."

As far as Pruitt was concerned, it was only Jordan's dumb luck that Mason Burke had stumbled onto Charlene Todd's body, and that Ernie Saint Louis had then stumbled on to Mason Burke. It meant the law was still focused on the ex-convict from Michigan and wouldn't be looking too deep into the Charlene Todd situation.

It meant there was still a way out of this mess, for Fetridge and Pruitt and even Jordan and Bealing. If they all kept their heads down and their mouths shut, and the next few days broke right. It meant they maybe weren't as fucked as Dax Pruitt had thought.

Still, Pruitt wasn't quite ready to breathe easy just yet. Not when he knew what he'd done, and what Logger Fetridge had done, and what had been done in their names. Pruitt knew that kind of violence tended to seek an answer. He couldn't quite shake the feeling there was a reckoning to come.

THIRTY-ONE

She missed him. She missed him more than she'd imagined she could, more than made sense when you considered how little, still, they knew of each other. She missed him regardless, and it ached like a hole in her chest.

Mason Burke wasn't a killer anymore. Jess simply couldn't see how he'd do it, not to Charlene Todd. And she believed he hadn't killed Brock Boyd either, though in truth, on that count, she couldn't be as sure.

He killed before, didn't he? And didn't you already prove you're a piss-poor judge of a man's character? Wasn't your husband already the plain proof of that fact?

You need proof, she thought. *Something concrete.*

She missed Burke, anyway. And she wished for the time they'd had before, between Kirby Harwood and Brock Boyd, when she'd imagined, and Burke probably had too, that they could build a life together, peaceful and ordinary.

She missed that time, and she knew it was gone, maybe forever. And so she searched for distraction and threw herself into her work.

The home at the address on Dougie Bealing's driver's license belonged to his mother, Martha, who swore she hadn't seen her son in weeks. She told Jess and Gillies he'd been living with a woman on Indian land. But when Jess and Gillies and a tribal officer drove out to the home in question, the woman—her name was Denise—more or less convinced them pretty quick that Dougie Bealing wouldn't be coming around her place any longer.

"You see that bastard, you go ahead and shoot him," she told Jess. "Stole my TV and half my goddamn silverware. Plus I think he was putting his cigarettes out on my cat." She glared at Jess. "On my fucking *cat*."

"You have any idea where he might be now?" Jess asked, already dreading the response.

Denise shook her head. "None whatsoever," she said. "But you all had better hope you find him before I do. Otherwise you'll be digging him out of the ground."

Jess knew Tyner Gillies wasn't especially on board with the goose chase she was leading them on, hunting down Dougie Bealing in hopes he'd have something to tell them that he wasn't able or willing to say in Dax Pruitt's presence. But Gillies stayed quiet and played along; if he had any reservations, he was keeping them to himself. And Jess, after that traffic stop, found she was pretty damn curious to hear what Bealing was talking about.

But Bealing's record gave no indication of where he might be hiding. The man had served time for a variety of offenses, ranging from assault to animal cruelty to possession with intent, but he'd never stayed in lockup more than a couple of years at a stretch— and he hadn't been arrested, Jess read in his file, since his last release three years ago.

Those three years coincided, of course, with the Kirby Harwood era, and though Jess wanted to believe that Bealing had cleaned up his act after his last stint in prison, she figured it was more likely he'd benefited from Harwood's particular brand of lawlessness.

She'd returned to her desk at the Deception Cove detachment, was procrastinating by running Bealing's file on the National Crime Information Center database, when Mitch Derry wandered over to her desk, bent down to where Lucy lay on the floor, and gave her a good belly rub.

"That's a good girl," he told Lucy, the dog rolling onto her side to give Derry better access. Then, to Jess, Derry said, "Boy, it's hard not to be jealous, huh? Dog gets to pretty well sleep all day while we're out here busting our humps."

Jess smiled. She liked Derry, what she'd seen of him. And if Lucy liked him, that was enough of a seal of approval. "You ask Lucy, she'd say this is work," she told the Neah Bay deputy. "I guess she'd much rather be out chasing squirrels somewhere."

"Wouldn't we all?" Derry said. He pushed himself to his feet and happened to glance at her computer screen. He chuckled. "Dougie Bealing," he said. "That boy's mighty popular these days. What's your business with him?"

Jess ran it down for him, the mustard hatchback and Dax Pruitt. How she'd hoped to get Bealing alone, maybe hear more of his story.

Derry listened and nodded. "Well, Dougie's hardly ever alone," he said. "If it's anything like he was in high school, he's more or less inseparable from a guy named Chris Jordan."

"Chris Jordan." Jess made to type the name into a search window. Derry stopped her.

"Hell, let me save you the trouble," he said. "Jordan and Bealing are holed up on some derelict freighter. Shipps and the state patrol were down those parts looking for Burke last night."

"Chris Jordan," Rengo said. "What I heard, Charlene Todd used to run with him for a while before she got too strung out on the glass."

Dusk in the compound now. Mason restless, having squandered another day on Rengo's busted couch, waiting for the kid to come up with a story from town, some direction that would lead them to whoever'd killed Brock Boyd. He'd paced, tense, in the trailer until he grew so bored he felt physically sick, and then he'd gone out into the compound and tried to put a workout together, push-ups and sit-ups until his muscles ached.

It didn't help. Time was wasting, and sooner or later the law would be up here. And the trail from Charlene Todd to her killer would grow cold.

"Chris Jordan," Mason said. "Who the hell's he?"

"Chris Jordan's a lowlife," Rengo replied. "He's a scumbag. Likes his women young—real young—and spent some time in lockup on account of it. Nowadays he mostly moves glass for his uncle."

Fetridge. That was the uncle's name, Rengo said. Logger Fetridge, a tree poacher and all-around ne'er-do-well who Rengo couldn't remember ever making any connection whatsoever with Brock Boyd. But that didn't mean his nephew mightn't have made his own history.

"There's one other thing," Rengo told Mason. "Folks are getting wise to me asking so many questions. I could see it, Burke. With the state troopers so heavy down there, someone's going to tell them how I've been around."

Whether they talked or they didn't talk, Mason knew time in this compound was running extremely short.

"So let's find Chris Jordan," he told the kid. "And maybe he gives us some answers."

THIRTY-TWO

Jess knew the ship. Burke had told her about it, an abandoned old freighter tied to a rickety dock, a patch of cleared land at the end of a dead-end gravel road, enough PRIVATE PROPERTY signs and razor wire to keep the curious at bay. It had been a cook spot, once, to hear Burke tell it, though by the time Sheriff Hart had seen fit to investigate, the ship was half sunk and nobody was aboard, no signs but trash and that acrid chemical smell to betray the hulk's history.

Amy Usen, the ship was called. Burke said he'd been here, once, when he was looking for Kirby Harwood. Said a man named Yancy had pulled a gun on him, suspicious.

Burke said after he'd calmed Yancy down he'd bought a motorbike from him, of all things. Owned it half an hour before the damn thing was destroyed.

None of that meant anything now.

Jess brought Gillies down to the water with her and Lucy, in a Makah County cruiser this time. They parked at the tree line, just beyond the fence and a midden of rusted-out cars and fishing tackle and detritus, out of viewing range from the hulk. Mitch Derry had said the state patrol'd found Bealing and Jordan on the ship, their purpose for being there unclear, but it looked like they were camped out in a couple of the old staterooms. Said Sergeant Shipps had asked them if they'd seen Mason Burke and been answered in a resounding negative.

"If we had any time, I'd go down there," Derry had told Jess. "Clean out those boys and call the Coast Guard to haul that ship out and sink it. It's a danger, what it is, and an eyesore. But I guess we've got bigger problems at the moment."

Derry might have had bigger problems. But Jess had figured she and Gillies might as well head down on behalf of the county.

They left Lucy in the cruiser and crept toward the spindly dock, lit up here and there with camp lanterns, the hum of a generator from somewhere belowdecks. Amid the piles of scrap and rust near the dock were a couple of vehicles that appeared to be in working order, a big old Dodge pickup and Dougie Bealing's mustard hatchback.

Faint music carried from within the ship's hull. It wasn't a large freighter, a couple hundred feet, tops, a red hull and rusted, a white superstructure toward the stern. No rain tonight, but a soft wind overhead, rustling through the branches and blowing clouds around, obscuring the moon and rocking the ship on its tie-up lines.

They'd driven out from the detachment and it had taken all of ten minutes, but Jess felt as though they'd landed on the other side of the world.

She made it to the edge of the dock and paused for a moment to survey the ship again. No movement on deck or within the lit windows, and she wondered where Dougie Bealing and his friend Jordan were. Wondered what kind of a reception they might receive.

"If it gets hairy for any reason, you walk away," Sheriff Hart had told her when she'd called him up to okay the excursion. "Step back and let it rest for the evening. We'll bring a whole crew out in the morning."

But Jess knew Hart didn't *have* a whole crew, even if he could spare any from the manhunt.

Jess squared her shoulders. Walked up the dock and braced herself as it wobbled beneath her feet. Reached the ladder that climbed the hull of the freighter to the main deck, and cupped her hands around her mouth and prayed she wouldn't actually have to climb aboard.

"Dougie Bealing, Chris Jordan," she called. *"Sheriff's Department. Anyone on this boat?"*

———————

Mason heard Lucy whining before he saw her.

He'd had Rengo drop him off at the highway. The kid had protested, but Mason had a decent reason aside from not wanting to drag him any further into what could turn into a fairly ugly night.

"Watch the logging main line," he told Rengo. "Sooner or later, those state troopers are going to find their way to the turnoff, and I'd rather know before we get back to the compound whether they're waiting for us up there or not."

Rengo had protested and tried to hand Mason a pistol before he beat his retreat.

"No guns," Mason told him. "I didn't kill Boyd and I didn't kill Charlene Todd. I don't intend to kill this Jordan fellow either."

Rengo stared at him. Shook his head and tucked the pistol away. "I'm thinking old Jordan might not be playing by the same rules, Burke," he said. "But you suit yourself."

Mason hurried away from Rengo's little Toyota, headed for the gravel turnoff he remembered marked the road down to the derelict freighter where Chris Jordan, apparently, made a squatter's home. He came down the hill toward the shore and saw a vehicle in the shadows ahead of him, a car parked on the shoulder, and as he came closer he could make out the light bar on the roof and knew it must be a county cruiser, and he thought about turning around or at least hiding out somewhere, waiting for the law to finish *their* business with Chris Jordan.

But then he heard Lucy whining.

She was sitting upright in the driver's seat of the cruiser, posed like the getaway driver waiting on Jess to come running out with the score. The way Lucy wagged her tail and pawed at the door, Mason could tell she'd heard him coming, sniffed him out and was waiting for him, and as he came closer and a stray lick of moonlight cast over the cruiser, he caught sight of the dog's face and that big lolling tongue, and he felt the dog's absence like a knife to his chest.

He'd missed the dog, and the dog had missed him, and Mason realized he hadn't been sure he'd ever see her again. And now that he'd seen her, he couldn't resist.

The door to Jess's cruiser was unlocked, and Mason opened it partway and pressed his body into the gap, blocking Lucy from leaping out at him, her tail whipping violently and her whole body wriggling with excitement.

"Okay," he told her as he nudged her back and slipped into the driver's seat, reaching up to flick off the dome light. "Okay, girl, I missed you too."

Lucy licked his face nonstop, crowding him, pushing against him as though she, too, had worried he was gone forever. Mason petted her and scratched her and withstood the onslaught and tried to let himself just enjoy the dog's company for a moment. But if Lucy was here, it meant Jess was paying Chris Jordan a visit herself. Mason didn't know what Jess was looking for in Jordan, what she hoped the glass dealer would tell her, but he did know he didn't like the thought of her out here without him. And he knew he wouldn't be hiding in the woods until she was done.

He pulled Lucy closer to him, touched his forehead to hers. Gave her neck a good scratch and then released her, held her back as he pushed the door open again and stepped out onto the soft muddy shoulder. Lucy watched him, watched the gap in the door, her ears perked and her eyes beseeching, like she was asking Mason to take her with him.

"Don't you worry about Jess, girl," Mason told her. "I'll make sure she's all right."

Then he closed the door just firm enough that it caught, and ventured out past the cruiser toward the clearing beyond.

THIRTY-THREE

Chris Jordan was a short man, and ugly, that ugliness made all the more so by the sneer that marked his face and the condescension in his tone.

"Evening, Deputy," he said to Jess, peering down at the dock from the main deck of the freighter, his eyes roving down her body and then up again. "What brings you out here tonight?"

Jess looked past him and up toward the hulk's rusting superstructure. Smelled low tide and diesel and heard music still playing from somewhere inside the ship. No sign of Dougie Bealing.

She'd debated how to play this. By rights, she and Gillies could evict Jordan and Bealing from their squat on this freighter, cite them for trespassing and probably a hundred other things besides. Jess was certain that if she searched Jordan, she would find something illegal, some reason to violate his probation, knew she could drag him down to the Deception Cove detachment, and Bealing too, wherever he was, lean on them for answers the old-school way, sweat Bealing's story out of him over the course of a few long, uncomfortable hours.

She supposed it might yet come to that, but she hoped it wouldn't have to. Knew if she and Gillies came at the squatters strong, there was a possibility that violence might result.

She was hoping to get answers without anyone getting hurt. Later, she'd wonder at how naive she'd been.

* * *

"I'm looking for a friend of yours," she told Jordan. "Dougie Bealing. He around?"

Jordan's expression didn't waver. "Not here."

"That's his car parked back there in the clearing, isn't it?"

Jordan craned his neck out from the deck, scanned back over the dock to the rusted black pickup and Bealing's Chevette just behind it. Jess could smell something on Jordan now, overpowering the scent of the water and the ship: alcohol and stale tobacco and something else, something chemical. Jordan's eyes seemed calm; she couldn't tell if he'd been using, but she was thankful for her sidearm anyway, and for Gillies behind her with his own.

"So it is," Jordan said, rocking back on his heels and smirking down at her. "So?"

Jess glanced back at Gillies. The deputy stood ready, a wide stance and his hand on his holster. He watched her, waiting on a cue.

"Look, we could book you right now," Jess told Jordan. "You're trespassing on this vessel, and I'm sure you've got some things in there you'd prefer the law wasn't aware of. All I'm asking is you let me talk to Dougie, then maybe my partner and I walk away and let you move off this wreck on your own time."

Jordan didn't say anything. He just grinned his unpleasant grin and let his eyes wander down to her boots and back up.

"You could almost pass for real law," he said finally. "Dressed all up in your little uniform, asking your questions. Hell, it's almost like you're an actual deputy."

"I'm real, Jordan," Jess replied, "and so's Deputy Gillies behind me. This isn't a game."

"What I don't understand is how they let you walk around with that badge," Jordan said. "Your boyfriend's a fucking murderer, and you—ain't you supposed to be fucked in the head?"

Jess didn't say anything.

"Got that dog, don't you? Supposed to keep you from, what, blowing your brains out? Hallucinating, seeing ghosts? How do you know I'm not a goddamn hallucination right now?"

Jess kept her mouth shut. Could feel a hot kind of anger simmering up inside her, was afraid of where it might lead her.

Then Gillies spoke up, before she could find out. "Forget this," he said, stepping forward to the ladder. "Mr. Jordan, you have five minutes to get your ass off of this ship. Otherwise we're coming up there and dragging you off ourselves."

"No, the fuck you will not," Jordan said, and something changed in his voice, a menace barely restrained. And then Jess saw the gun.

He'd had a pistol stashed somewhere, Jess didn't know where, but she imagined it must have been tucked into his waistband, the small of his back, and it didn't matter anyway where it came from. Jordan had a pistol, and that was a clear violation of his probation, and now, Jess realized, they had to take him in.

But something in Jordan had been triggered.

"You stay the fuck back," he told the deputies as Jess pulled her own weapon and Gillies beside her hollered at Jordan to put the gun down.

"*Chris,*" Jess said, fighting to be heard. Fighting to break through the fog and malevolence in his eyes. "Now, just wait a second, all right? Let's just talk this out."

She could see in Jordan's expression, though, that there wouldn't be any talking, knew it even before the dealer raised the pistol he was holding and aimed it down in their direction. Jess saw it in slow motion, knew what must come next. But before she could call out or do anything, Gillies's pistol was firing beside her, and then there was a hole in Chris Jordan, and the dealer was staggering backward and down to the deck.

And then the porthole beside Gillies blew out with a sound like artillery fire. Gillies stumbled back a few steps, eyes wide, and collapsed on the dock, and Jess knew that somewhere behind that porthole was Dougie Bealing with a shotgun.

She hit the dock and rolled, landed in the water and felt the shock of cold and rocks in her back, and she scrambled to stay afloat and wade her way back to shore, suddenly aware of just how perfectly the whole night had turned to shit.

———

Mason heard the gunfire, small arms and then the shotgun, and it was everything he'd worried he would hear. Two shots and then silence, and he ran into the clearing and the piles of junk that bordered the water, thinking he was bound to come across Jess filled with buckshot somewhere near the shore.

He heard a man cry out like he was in pain.

The wreck stood ahead, with enough light from the camp lanterns and Christmas lights on the ship to see the dock and the water and the body.

The shotgun blasted again from somewhere inside the ship, and the man on the dock tried to pull himself to some kind of cover, and he couldn't—rendered immobile by the way he'd been shot.

The night flared as shots rang out beside Mason, and he looked over and saw Jess at the shore by the foot of the dock, opening up with her service pistol at the hull of the freighter. She was alive, and the power of his relief nearly stopped him where he stood, but he forced himself to stay focused.

"Jess," he called out, during a break in the gunfire. She swung over with her pistol and damn near shot him, and in the light from the freighter and the moon overhead he could see her surprise and confusion.

"We got to get that man off the dock," he told her. *"Cover me."*

She stared at him a moment, blinked, like her thoughts were still trying to process just how and why he'd showed up here. But then Gillies screamed, and Jess seemed to get it; she nodded at Mason and took aim at the freighter again. He hurried to the edge of the dock, feeling naked and exposed and well clear of any usable cover, the dock stretching out long and open in front of him, and the man who'd been shot waiting at the end of it. Mason tensed his body to run and waited for Jess to start shooting again.

THIRTY-FOUR

She could have shot him. Accidentally, the first time, when he'd appeared from somewhere in the junk pile, calling her name, and then on purpose the next time, when her brain had processed the whole freaking fiasco and decided that, *yes,* not only had Burke showed up at her shoot-out, but he was proposing to go running into shotgun fire to drag Gillies off that dock.

Jess could have shot him herself, to save the heartbreak later.

But she didn't shoot Burke. She kept her pistol trained on the wreck as he inched up toward the dock, and when he glanced over to where she crouched, half covered behind an old fishing tote, she waited until she saw him nod to her. Then she stood and opened fire on the ship at where she'd last seen the shotgun, and she fired and kept firing and could hardly bear to watch as Burke dashed down the length of the dock to where Gillies lay perforated and probably dying.

Burke made it to Gillies at about the same time as Jess emptied her magazine. She glanced across the dock and saw Burke bend over in front of Gillies and grab him under the shoulders and start dragging him back down the dock.

She slammed another magazine into her pistol and swung around toward the ship again, and as she did she saw Dougie Bealing rise up with the shotgun from the main deck now, swinging that boomstick he was carrying down toward Burke. There was no time to think; Jess squeezed off as many shots as it took to knock Bealing backward, and as Bealing fell, that big shotgun fired off, and on the dock Burke flinched, and Jess thought, for a heart-stopping moment, he'd been shot.

But Burke hadn't been shot. He kept going. Dragged Gillies backward as the last echoes from Jess's pistol and Bealing's shotgun faded away. Jess kept the ship covered as she scrambled to the dock, meeting Burke at the threshold between gravel and lumber and helping him pull Gillies to the clearing.

Gillies was alive, she saw, though he was hurt bad, bleeding through his county jacket through multiple wounds to the chest. Jess helped Burke lay him down, gasping, on the crushed gravel rock of the clearing, and before she could ask, Burke was slipping out of his own coat and tearing his shirt into strips, pressing it into Gillies's chest to try to staunch the bleeding.

Jess still wasn't sure what Burke was doing here, but there was no time to ask questions, not now.

"I have to call this in," she told Burke. "I need an ambulance, stat."

Burke looked up from tending to Gillies. Met her eyes. "Do it," he said. "He's not going to last if you don't."

She started, "But you—"

"I'll get out of here before they come," he said. "Don't worry about me."

She stared into his eyes a beat, mind racing, but she didn't say anything. And then Gillies gasped again and looked up, and his eyes saw Burke and went wide. "Burke?" he said, weak.

Jess stared at Gillies. Wondered if Burke had banked on this, on Gillies recognizing him. Wondered what he would do.

But Burke didn't react.

"Just hold on," he told Gillies. "Hold on, buddy. We've got help coming." He looked up at Jess again. "Call it in," he said. *"Hurry."*

He waited until Jess had called in the shooting. Until she'd put down her radio and set to helping Gillies. Until it seemed as though she had the situation under control.

Until she'd looked up and met his eyes over Gillies's prone form, told him softly, "Go," and he'd understood that whatever she thought of him, whatever she believed he'd done, she wasn't going to turn him in to the law.

Then Burke stood. He left Jess with Gillies, but he didn't run for the trees. Not right away.

He went back to the dock. Hurried down the length of it toward the wreck at the outer end, and it felt to Burke like crossing the Rubicon. He wanted to be with Jess. He was tired of being without her, tired of the death that had followed him since he'd arrived in this town. He didn't want to do what he believed must come next, but he'd come here for a reason that he needed to see through.

Burke reached the end of the dock and climbed the ladder quickly to the deck, where a pistol lay on the steel and a man lay beside it, flat on his back, struggling to breathe and bleeding from a hole in his chest. The man's hands were pressed to the red blossom on his shirt, and Mason knew he'd be dead within minutes.

Another man lay dead a few feet away, a big man with a scraggly beard clutching on to a shotgun. Mason looked at the men close and could tell the first man was Jordan, from the description Rengo had given him.

He knelt beside Jordan. The dying man watched him, expressionless, his hands bloodied.

"I need to know who killed Brock Boyd," Mason said softly. "I don't have much time, and neither do you."

Jordan stared up at him and struggled to breathe and said nothing.

"I know you knew Charlene Todd and I suspect it might have been you that killed her," Mason said.

Jordan still didn't answer, and Mason cast his eyes around the entryway for something he could use. He didn't want to hurt this man, but he didn't want to leave here and for this violence to have all been for nothing.

"You tell me who killed Boyd," Mason said. "Tell me why he's dead."

Jordan exhaled, shallow and ragged. Wincing at the effort. He blinked and his eyes shifted and he seemed to be seeing Mason clearer. He muttered something and it came out soundless, just spittle and blood flecked on his lips.

"What's that you say?" Mason leaned down closer as Jordan tried to find another breath, and it took some time and was obviously painful, but eventually Jordan found it.

He whispered, just barely loud enough for Mason to hear him, *"Broomstick."*

"Broomstick?" Mason repeated, hoping Jordan would find enough life left inside him to elaborate, but it was too late; the man's eyes went glassy and still, and he stared up past Mason and said nothing more.

And Mason waited, but Jordan didn't move again, or breathe or blink, just lay there in silence with the hint of a smile on his face. Mason could hear sirens on shore now, shouted voices and slamming doors, the rev of engines and the squeal of brakes, and he knew he'd got all he could out of Chris Jordan and it was well past time to leave.

He pulled himself to his feet and dropped down to the dock, and ran as fast and as quiet as he could to the shore and the junk piles and the safety of the darkness.

THIRTY-FIVE

Gillies was alive when Jess surrendered him to the ambulance, to the paramedics and the other deputies and the swarms of state patrolmen who'd descended onto the clearing after she'd called back to Deception that she had a deputy shot. He was alive but unconscious and there wasn't any time to ask would he survive, and Jess knew better than to ask, anyway.

Chaos overtook the clearing and the wrecked freighter just offshore, but Jess seemed to have no part in it. She was good at the shooting and the gunfire and the violence, but this part, the afterward, was the part she couldn't handle. This was why they'd kicked her out of the Corps.

She could feel herself withdraw from the commotion, urgent voices and men in motion, spotlights shining on the hull of the ship, the sound of machines as more vehicles arrived and departed. She crouched against the abandoned fish tote and stared across at the freighter and saw nothing. She could feel herself slipping away to her nightmares.

And then something crossed her face, warm and wet and slobbery, and Jess blinked and *over there* disappeared and she was back in the present with Lucy beside her, leaned in close and licking at her like she'd been trained to do, cutting off the nightmares before they could take hold.

Jess pulled Lucy close, and Lucy obliged her, nuzzled up good and tight and warm and solid, wouldn't stop licking her face until she couldn't breathe, until she had to push the dog away for a moment, take a gasp of fresh air.

"Okay, Luce," Jess said. "It's okay, girl. I'm all right."

Behind Jess was Sheriff Hart, holding Lucy's lead and looking down at his deputy and her dog with concern and relief writ all over his face.

"You're okay," he said. "Jess, thank God."

She petted Lucy one more time and pushed herself to her feet. Took the dog's lead from the sheriff and saw how his eyes lingered on her hands, stained with Gillies's blood and lots of it.

"What the hell happened?" he asked her.

She told him, as best she could. Felt the weight of the night pressing into her chest and fought through it, tried to explain. How Jordan had swung his weapon on them. How Gillies had put him down. How Bealing—and his shotgun—had caught them by surprise.

Through it all, Hart listened, but his eyes stayed on her hands. On Gillies's blood. When she was finished, he didn't say anything right away.

Then he met her eyes again. "You take care of them?" His voice was hard, but his eyes were wet, and Jess could see how the last week was starting to weigh heavily on the sheriff too.

That's Makah County. That's Deception Cove. Even the strongest get broken down eventually.

"Yeah, Sheriff," she told him. "I put them down."

Hart nodded. Looked out at the ship. The dock. "You're a hell of a deputy," he said. "If Gillies survives—God willing—it's thanks to you."

Jess hesitated. Heard her partner gasping, whispering Burke's name.

"No, Sheriff," she said. "I didn't save Gillies. That was Burke."

THIRTY-SIX

Rengo was waiting in the shadows on the turnoff to the loggers' main line. He had his little Toyota truck parked so deep in the forest that Mason wondered if the kid would be able to drive it out again, but before he could say anything, Rengo nodded up the logging road and shook his head, grim.

"We're fucked," he told Mason. "State police boys went up there about an hour back. Whole crew of them, everything four-wheel drive. Guess someone must have told them 'bout my hideout."

Mason followed Rengo's eyes up the main line, and he knew the troopers would have a hell of a time getting into Rengo's compound even with four-wheel drive, but it didn't matter. They'd get in there eventually, and that meant there was no going back.

Rengo was watching him. "I assume you all weren't setting off fireworks down there," he said. "So I guess things must've got heavy."

Mason filled him in. "I asked Jordan who killed Boyd," he said. "Before he died. Only thing he told me was 'Broomstick.' That make any sense to you?"

Rengo frowned. "I don't know nobody calls himself Broomstick," he said. "You sure you heard right?"

Mason didn't reply. It was late now, the wind blowing through the trees, bringing a chill from offshore. There was nowhere to go, and Mason was tired of running.

Beside him, Rengo paced the turnoff from the highway to the main line, glancing up the muddy road every so often as though he expected to see the state troopers come back down already.

Sooner or later, they'd come.

"Come on," he told Rengo. "Get that truck out of the bush and let's go."

Rengo looked at him and then dug in his pocket for the keys. "Where are we going?"

Mason wasn't sure yet. "Anywhere but here," he said.

They found themselves on Brock Boyd's property. A few miles east of Deception and at the end of another winding gravel road that Rengo said he'd never been down but he was sure was the right one.

They left the truck hidden as best they could in the scrub on the shoulder of Boyd's long driveway. It wasn't fifteen yards from the front gate that the wind had blown a tree over, crushing the fence inward and creating a nice little hole; Mason clambered over first, Rengo right behind him, and just like that they were on Bad Boyd's land, and nobody, as far as Mason could tell, was the wiser.

They pushed back through the forest to rejoin the driveway, the house still not visible down the curving declination. Rengo had dug out an old flashlight from somewhere in his truck, and he gave it to Mason to navigate by its anemic beam while he lit his own way with his cell phone.

The house must have been nearby, but Rengo tugged Mason's sleeve before they reached it, gestured into the woods with the light of his phone, and Mason shone his own light and saw that the forest opened up in a space to his right, a two-track trail through the trees, and in the distance, a building that might have been a barn.

Rengo led the way, and Mason followed. The trail was grown over, but there were signs it had been used, and used heavily, at some point in the past: felled trees lined its margins, mossed over now but with chainsaw marks still visible. Someone had put work into widening the trail, moving rocks to clear space, and where the trail opened up in front of the building, there were still signs of bare earth, mounds of dirt and gravel dug up and abandoned, neglected backhoe attachments and construction diggers. Almost like Boyd or whoever else had been looking for something here, and once they'd found it, left without repairing the land.

The building was two stories tall, bare wooden siding weathered gray by the elements. It was perhaps fifty feet wide and double that in length, and it looked as though it might collapse at any second. Mason didn't know why Rengo had brought him here, but when he slowed to glance back toward where Boyd's house would have been, Rengo pulled his arm again and urged him forward.

"Come on, Burke," he said. "You're going to need to see this."

The barn door wasn't locked, and it swung open limp from its hinges when Rengo pushed it inward. Inside was coal black and smelled of abandonment—must and some insidious organic damp. Something else too, something vague and coppery that lingered in the air but seemed to disappear whenever Mason tried to place it.

Ahead of him, Rengo aimed his cell phone at the walls of the building, and his light fell on a toggle shift covered in cobwebs. Mason watched the kid push the cobwebs away and try the switch, not believing Boyd would still have power running to this place, but when Rengo flipped the toggle, there came a low hum from somewhere above, and then, slowly, dim light, white and cold, began to illuminate the interior of the barn.

It took maybe a minute for the lights to warm up enough that

Mason could get a sense of what he was looking at, and even after he'd seen it, he still wasn't sure what it meant, not right away.

He'd expected a barn, and what he got instead was...an amphitheater? Bench bleachers, constructed crude and low and haphazard, lined two opposite walls of the barn. In between them was an enclosure maybe twenty feet by twenty, fenced in by low chain-link and surfaced with hard-packed dirt. Mason stared, and Rengo studied him, waiting.

And then Mason wished he *had* killed Bad Boyd, and he wished he'd done it slow.

THIRTY-SEVEN

"This is where they done it," Rengo said, walking Mason deeper into Boyd's barn as if he was selling the place, showing off the grounds. Mason followed on unwilling legs, his whole body rebelling, urging him to leave, as though he could erase the stain of evil just by turning around and walking out.

He could see now there were kennels in the back, beyond the fighting pit.

Mason could sense the ghosts in this space acutely, could hear the clamor of the dogs in their cages and the desperate, terrified violence within the pit, could hear the jeers and epithets and invocations that must have rung down from the bleachers, could smell the piss and shit and blood and human sweat that must have permeated this place on the nights when Boyd's dogs were fighting.

The dogs hadn't fought here in more than three and a half years, as far as Mason knew. They may well have fought yesterday, and his stomach churned just to think of it. He pictured Lucy in a space like this, consumed with fear in the kennels in back, waiting on her turn in the pits.

Lucy had been a runt. Bait. Her destiny had been as a blood sacrifice for the bigger dogs, the real fighters. Something to be torn apart to teach another dog how to kill. That she'd been saved made Mason grateful, but that didn't help him now. Not here, where other dogs had suffered as Lucy was meant to. Where living beings had killed each other for a rich man's pleasure.

Mason had known Bad Boyd was a dogfighter, but he hadn't really *known,* not until tonight. If he had, he suspected he might well have killed Boyd, like they all thought he did, and he wouldn't have felt guilty in the slightest. Nor would he have run.

They found nothing of use in the barn. The authorities would have taken anything they could use against Boyd when word of the fighting got out. That explained the unsettled nature of the land in front of the barn; someone must have dug the yard over in search of more evidence. Mason knew they'd have been digging for the dogs who'd fought and lost.

The bleachers remained, and the pit and the kennels, but there was nothing in the barn to point to Boyd's ownership. Mason was relieved when he and Rengo stepped outside again, through an empty doorway beside the kennels. He inhaled clean, cold air, gulped it down as though he'd been underwater and drowning, and his heart raced in his chest and his whole body shook.

"Give me a minute," he told Rengo, and the kid nodded and waited and paced off a few feet to give Mason his privacy. Mason wondered what the kid made of what they'd seen, if he knew how close Lucy had come to dying in some barn just like this one.

Mason caught his breath back and forced himself to stand square, caught Rengo's eye and gestured toward Boyd's house and the ocean. They walked down the trail and away from the barn, and Mason hoped he would never have to return.

The world seemed to open up when they reached the driveway again, the low canopy of overhanging trees receding and the sky above not the suffocating dark it had been inside the forest. Clouds scudded overhead, propelled by the wind, and beyond them Mason could see the dim light of the moon.

They walked the remaining distance to Boyd's house in silence. It wasn't far. Down a little ways and around a corner, and then the drive opened up in front of a low concrete structure that looked like a bunker but that Mason surmised was the garage. The structure was built into the forest, camouflaged ingeniously in the landscape, as though it had always been here with the rock and the trees and the water — which cascaded against the shoreline somewhere to Mason's right, far below the edge of an unseen cliff.

"Let's hope he turned off the burglar alarm," Rengo said, feeling around on the ground for a rock. Mason wandered toward the building's edge, toward the sound of the surf, using the thin beam of his flashlight to keep him from plummeting over the cliff. The house extended north from the garage doors, cantilevered over open space by a series of massive steel beams. From the glint of moonlight on glass, Mason could see how it was almost entirely windows, and he imagined the view from inside must have been astonishing.

He wondered how a man like Boyd could surround himself with such beauty, could have everything he ever needed or wanted, and still turn to blood sport for his pleasure. It didn't seem to make sense that a man who could build a house like this — so obviously in concert with the elements that surrounded it — could also own the barn behind it.

But there was plenty that Mason didn't understand about the human condition, and perhaps he never would.

His thoughts were interrupted by the sound of a window breaking, and he turned to see Rengo standing frozen by the house's front entryway, his head cocked, listening for an alarm.

No alarm sounded. That didn't necessarily mean none had been triggered, but Mason followed behind Rengo regardless as the kid reached inside the broken glass at the doorway, unlocked the door, and let them both into the house.

If Bad Boyd's barn had smelled of fear and death and human depravity, the man's house was the opposite. The still air in the front hall was laced with the barest hints of scents exotic and moneyed, some familiar to Mason—the smell of Boyd's cigars, for instance—and others completely foreign. Even with the glass broken behind them, the environment that greeted Mason and Rengo inside the house was largely silent, insulated from the wind in the trees and the water below, a tomb of empty space and luxury.

Beyond the hallway, the house opened vast and cavernous, more space than the feeble beams from their lights could penetrate. The night was dark outside the towering glass; the windows may as well have been walls, for all that Mason could see of the outdoors.

They found themselves in a sitting area dominated by a large fireplace and what Mason knew must have been very expensive furniture. Here and there were signs of the law: white fingerprint dust remained on armrests and lampshades, on a brass bucking-bronco sculpture sitting proud on an end table.

Mason couldn't remember ever being in a house this big; four or five of his prison cells would fit into the great room alone. He wondered how Boyd had coped with the space when he returned home at last, whether the emptiness had unnerved him as it sometimes did Mason, the absolute freedom where once had been total structure.

Boyd's bedroom had been similarly picked over by Sheriff Hart and his team; there were expensive-looking clothes in the closets, suits and shirts and ties, belts and cuff links and pristine rows of shoes. None of it would explain why Brock Boyd was dead.

Rengo had wandered away, no doubt already bored. Mason could see that Brock Boyd had been wealthy, and that he'd enjoyed the trappings of his success. But this house wasn't telling him anything he didn't already know or have cause to suspect about the man, and he wondered if there was a point to them being here at all, beyond simply hiding out from the elements and the inevitable, from Sheriff Hart and the state troopers who'd sooner or later catch up.

Then Mason heard Rengo shouting his name from somewhere deeper inside the house, and he pushed aside his worries and hurried out of Boyd's bedroom to seek out the kid.

Rengo had found himself in what must have been Boyd's recreation room, down a set of stairs from the kitchen, a basement level blasted out of the cliff face and boxed in by concrete, no windows but deep-pile carpeting and soft light, a pool table and another television, framed pictures of Boyd on the wall, trophies lined up on a shelf.

It was near the trophies that Rengo was standing, holding something in his hand as Mason entered the room.

"I think I maybe got something," Rengo told him. He'd turned on the lights, and his excitement was plainly visible; his eyes darted down to what he held in his hand and then back to Mason. "Check this out."

He held up what was in his hand, and from across the room, Mason saw it was a photograph, a hockey team's group picture.

"'Broomstick,' you said," Rengo said. "That's what Jordan told you, right?"

Mason nodded. "That's what he said."

Rengo looked down at the photograph. Smiled, self-satisfied. "Well, that's mighty good news, Burke," he said. "I think I figured it out."

THIRTY-EIGHT

The dog still wouldn't leave her side.

Jess sat in the office at the back of the Deception Cove detachment, where Aaron Hart studied her intently from behind the desk as she told him how Burke had come to surprise her at the derelict freighter, how he'd saved Tyner Gillies's life.

"Bealing had me pinned with the shotgun," she told the sheriff. "As far as Gillies was out on that dock, there was no way I could reach him without that boomstick cutting me down."

Lucy stood beside her, her snout resting in Jess's lap, chestnut-brown eyes gazing up at her worriedly, as though she was not yet convinced her owner wouldn't have another episode. The dog hated loud noises, generally spooked at the sound of gunfire, but the shoot-out at the shore didn't seem to have bothered her, at least not nearly as much as did the sight of Jess in trouble.

Hart regarded them both from across the desk. He'd closed the office door, and locked it, and though out in the main room of the detachment was bustle and commotion, none of it disturbed their conversation.

And none of what she told Hart in here, Jess knew, would be accidentally overheard by the lawmen out there.

"Burke told me to cover him," she told the sheriff. "I laid down fire toward the ship while Burke dragged Gillies to safety. While

174

he was exposed, I saw Bealing swing around with the shotgun, and I put him down."

She wouldn't lie to the sheriff. Gillies had seen Burke and he might yet survive, and Jess hoped like hell that he would. But even if her partner didn't one day betray Burke's presence at the shoot-out, Jess couldn't see how lying about it was going to do her or Burke any good.

Hart chewed his lip, and he thought for a while. "What the hell was Burke doing there?" he asked her. "Did you have any inkling he was following you?"

Jess shook her head. "No, sir," she said. "As best I could tell, he was there to see the men on the ship same as I was. He made sure I had Gillies in hand, and then he went back to the wreck."

Hart rubbed his eyes and stared down at his notepad, where he'd been transcribing Jess's account of the night's events.

"And you couldn't apprehend him," he said, his voice weary. "On account of how you were trying to keep Gillies alive."

Jess nodded. "Yes, sir," she said. She wondered if Hart had any update on her colleague, who'd been taken to Port Angeles, the major trauma center, wondered if he would make it through the night.

"By the time backup showed, Burke was gone," Jess told Hart. "I—honestly, Sheriff, it didn't cross my mind to arrest him. Not until afterward."

Hart mulled this over some more. Then he let out a long breath, and he shuffled the papers on his desk. Lucy shifted beside Jess, licked her lips. Looked up at Jess, sad and worried and ready to go.

"I gotta take your badge and your gun," Hart said at last. "Officer-involved shooting, it's standard procedure. I'm not saying you did anything wrong, mind, just that we have to be damn sure we play this by the book. The county's under enough scrutiny as it is, the Boyd thing and all."

She had her badge and her gun on the desk before he'd finished the thought, slid them across to the edge of the paperwork and leaned back again and let him study her and the dog where they sat across from him. He looked sorry too.

"You'll be okay," he said. "As best I can tell, you handled this thing fine. And maybe when morning comes, we'll hear Tyner's going to pull through and we all can breathe easy. It's just now I'm down two deputies, Jess, and that's the last thing I need in the world."

"Yes, sir," Jess said. She hesitated. "And Burke?"

Hart exhaled again. Glanced past her to the door, beyond which the state patrol waited. "I can't see as it would do any of us any good to let Shipps and his men know Burke was there tonight," he said. "Do you?"

Jess said, "No, sir."

"Fine," the sheriff said. "Then go home, Jess, and get some sleep. Hell, get some sleep for the rest of us too. God knows we're running on fumes."

The detachment was packed with the law, state troopers and crime scene technicians and any spare deputy Hart could call up. The troopers watched Jess, and Mitch Derry and Paul Monk watched too, eyes hollow and their shoulders slumped, as Sheriff Hart walked her to the detachment's front door, his hand on her arm at the bend in her elbow, as if he was escorting her down the aisle at a funeral.

Jess kept her eyes low and didn't look at anybody. Knew Derry and Monk must be hurting, looking for news about Gillies, but she had none to share, and she was too exhausted to pretend. She kept a grip on Lucy's lead and walked with the sheriff, and when they reached the front door, he leaned ahead and pushed it open for her and followed her and Lucy out into the empty street.

Hart told her, "Listen, you see Burke again, you tell him to turn himself in. We don't need more bodies around here, understand?"

Jess nodded and turned to go, but Hart laid his hand on her arm again. Firm, but not unfriendly.

"I'm talking about *him* too, Jess," he said. "I don't want to see that man killed, not before we've sorted this out. You tell him to turn himself in, and I swear I'll do my damndest to see he gets a fair shot. Okay?"

He kept his eyes on hers, not blinking, and Jess knew he meant what he said, that he'd do what he could for Burke, though whether because of Gillies or something else, she couldn't be sure.

She met Hart's eyes. "You know I think Burke is innocent," she said. "Of all of it, Sheriff, Bad Boyd *and* Charlene Todd. But if I see him again, I'll tell him that I think he ought to turn himself in regardless. I don't want to see him killed either."

Hart held her gaze a moment longer, searching her face for something that she wasn't sure she could give him. Finally, he nodded. Released her arm, wordless, and looked around, briefly, up and down Main Street—deserted at this hour—and then he squared his shoulders and bid her good night, and he turned and went back into the detachment again, where most of the law on the entire Olympic Peninsula waited for him.

Jess stood with Lucy outside the detachment. Her cruiser sat angled into a parking stall just a few feet away, but of course it wasn't her cruiser now; she wasn't the law anymore. The Blazer was still up at the motel, and there were no taxis in Deception Cove.

She was tired, bone tired, but there was no way to her bed but to walk. She tugged on Lucy's lead and turned south on Main Street, began trudging up the hill toward home.

THIRTY-NINE

The boys were just teenagers in hockey gear. Fourteen, fifteen years old, sixteen at the most. Lined up in two rows—first seated, second standing—facing the camera. They wore bulky hockey equipment and sweaters with a logo on the front that Rengo told Mason was the symbol of the Makah Screaming Eagles, the top team in the county. Some of the boys had the first wispy hints of beards, mustaches; they glowered at the camera and tried to look tough. But they were boys, all the same, twenty of them, frozen in time.

Brock Boyd had similar pictures for every year he'd played hockey, displayed on a shelf in the corner of his man cave, beside framed newspaper articles and magazine covers, trophies he'd won and jerseys he'd worn.

Mason studied the picture that Rengo had handed him and wondered what he was supposed to be seeing. Boyd sat in the first row, dead center, the *C* on his chest denoting he was the team's captain. His blond hair was long but unruly; he sneered out of the photograph as though he could see Mason looking at him, as though he was challenging Mason, even now, even then.

Mason recognized no one else in the photograph. He made to tell this to Rengo, ask him what the point was, but the kid had more pictures to show him.

More team pictures, younger boys now. Most of the faces the same, year by year, stretching back through early adolescence into childhood. In every picture, Brock Boyd was the centerpiece. In every picture, Boyd wore the captain's C.

"Okay, so Boyd was real good," Mason told Rengo when they'd worked their way back to about age six or seven. "What are you trying to tell me?"

Rengo shook his head. "It's not about Boyd."

He picked up the first photograph, the teenagers, and he handed it to Mason. Kept his finger on another face, in the back row: a tall boy, acne scarred and ungainly in his youth.

"You recognize this guy from the other pictures?" Rengo asked Mason.

Mason scanned through the older photos, looking for the boy. He had dark hair, almost black, a lock hanging over his forehead, nearly obscuring his eyes. He stared at the camera with a somber expression—no manufactured bravado, like most of his team-mates, or cocky self-confidence, like Boyd. He looked serious, almost resigned.

He looked as though he'd rather have been anywhere else.

Mason couldn't find him in the older photographs. He recognized most of the boys as they aged through the years, but not this one. "I don't see him," he told Rengo, shrugging.

Rengo smirked. Handed over another couple of photographs, team pictures from later years, the teenagers growing toward adulthood.

"Boyd only played a year or two more with the Eagles," he told Mason. "But you get the idea."

The faces, by and large, were the same. A little older. Slightly more facial hair. Not as many smiles; at this age, hockey wasn't just a game anymore but a potential meal ticket. A free pass out of

Makah County and into a life of which these boys could have only ever dreamed.

The solemn, dark-haired teenager was in none of the other pictures.

"That," Rengo said, grinning with satisfaction, "is Broomstick."

FORTY

The boy was scared. He'd been dreading this trip throughout most of the season and now it was here: Olympia, Washington, for the state regional tournament, twenty hockey players and three coaches and one bus driver, all of them crammed onto the second floor of an interstate motel, four players to a room, two to each bed.

He'd been afraid of this trip. A weekend alone, without family or even a place to escape to, imprisoned by the side of the highway with nineteen other boys, all of whom knew each other and had grown up together, all of whom seemed to hate him with a passion that sometimes stole his breath away.

There was no running away, not here, and the boy knew that this was where things would finally come to their head.

It was not about hockey. The team had won their first game in the tournament tonight, and he'd played well and hard, and afterward Coach Hughes had tapped him on the shoulder and told him, "Good game," and, "Be ready for another tough one tomorrow." And he'd felt good on the ice and somehow free and without worry, but the moment he'd stepped off the ice he remembered where he was and what was likely to happen, and he'd wished he'd pretended to be ill and not come on this trip, that he could be anywhere else in the world.

It wasn't up to the coaches to save him, and they wouldn't. Hughes and his staff believed in the old school, that rookies were hazed and it made the team stronger. The team had elected Bad Boyd as its captain, and even Hughes seemed to know that Boyd was the best goddamn hockey player the county would ever produce, and if Boyd wanted something, it was more or less done.

Boyd made the rules. The boy was a rookie and it was his lot to follow them.

But this wasn't about hockey or team building anymore. This was about something else entirely, something deeper and darker and mean.

The team had returned to the motel after the game. They'd showered and dressed and dispersed in packs of three or four or more to scour the restaurants that lined the road from the interstate, searching for food and maybe someone to serve them liquor, and, if they got really lucky, for girls.

The boy's roommates hadn't invited him to go out and he hadn't gone, ate dinner from the vending machines down the hall and sat and watched television and relished the silence, all the while listening for the sounds of his roommates' return. His roommates weren't bad guys and sometimes could even be friendly, one-on-one, but they, like the rest of the county, lived in thrall to Bad Boyd. If Boyd was around, they danced to his tune.

The boy knew he couldn't rely on his roommates to save him, any more than the coaches who'd long ago left in search of a bar. He entertained the notion, briefly, of simply walking away, leaving the motel and the team and finding the bus station and buying a ticket, but the only place he could go was back to Makah, and if he did that and word got out that he'd abandoned Bad Boyd's team, that he was a quitter, then the boy knew Makah was no place he'd want to be either.

Anyway, he wasn't a quitter, and he tried not to be afraid. He tried to believe he could stand up to whatever was coming, take it without flinching or letting Boyd beat him, look Boyd in the eye afterward and tell him he wasn't really as good as he thought.

The boy tried to believe this, but he couldn't quite get there. And he lay on his bed and strained his ears for the noise of his roommates down the hall; he knew sooner or later they'd come.

When they did, he'd been dozing, half asleep, and it wasn't until he *heard the key in the door that the boy recognized what was happening. They piled into the room, more of them than the three who belonged here. Their breath stank of liquor, and they laughed and jeered at the boy, crowding the small space and dragging him from the bed, forcing him to stand and be held in their midst.*

Bad Boyd was the last to enter the room, and he held something in his hands, hidden, so the boy couldn't see what it was.

FORTY-ONE

"Broomstick Cody," **Rengo** told Mason. "First name was Levi, I think. I forgot all about him, until I saw that picture."

Rengo had found his way behind Bad Boyd's wet bar, was digging out a bottle of some no-doubt-expensive scotch with an unpronounceable name. Found a glass for himself and held up another for Mason, questioning. Mason shook his head.

"Broomstick," Rengo said again. He'd been smiling, proud of his own cleverness, but that smile had faded. "Only played one year in Makah."

Rengo poured himself a drink. A healthy pour. "Then he threw himself off a cliff," he said.

Rengo didn't know exactly how it happened.

"Not really a sports fan," he told Mason. He tried the scotch, tentative, grimaced as it went down. "But I guess I heard the story once or twice."

The Cody family had moved to Neah Bay, Rengo remembered, from somewhere over the mountains. Wenatchee or Spokane, the eastern part of the state. His dad had been a white-collar guy, insurance or accountant, something at a desk. His mom had been a schoolteacher and, as far as Rengo knew, might still be.

"They split up, after Broomstick took his leap," Rengo said. "Dad moved away, mom stuck around. Nobody was ever really sure why."

Levi Cody was a hockey player, the legend went, and a good one. He'd walked onto the Screaming Eagles tryouts at training camp, made the roster with ease, starting line, defenseman. Meant someone had to clear out to make space, and that someone was Fat Gerald Hemp, who wasn't much of a hockey player, but who everyone liked.

Rengo picked up a team picture, an older one. Pointed to a chubby kid in the front row, the only person in the photograph with a smile on his face.

"The way the story goes is some guys took it personally," Rengo told Mason. "Like it was Cody's fault Gerald Hemp was a sack of shit on two skates. They saw it as their responsibility to make life hard for him."

Mason was starting to get the picture. "And one of those guys was Brock Boyd."

Rengo nodded. "Listen, I never went in for team sports," he said. "I don't play well with others. Plus it never rubbed me right, the way some guys would force you to do things. Like if you were new to the team and they didn't know you."

"Hazing." Mason hadn't ever been one for sports either, could never afford the equipment or the dues. But he knew well enough how men form communities, how they deal with outsiders and those they believe to be weak.

"I guess it happens in every sport, with every player," Rengo said, "and that's what the coach said when the whole thing came to light. 'Team building,' he called it. 'Boys being boys.'"

Rengo took another sip of scotch. Winced as he swallowed, and then he met Mason's eye. "You can probably figure out why they called Cody 'Broomstick,'" he told Mason. "Came from one of those *team-building* exercises."

Mason said nothing.

"It was Boyd who took charge of it," Rengo said. "On a road trip, down somewhere inland. Brought a few other guys and cornered Levi Cody in his hotel room, between games. And Boyd happened to be carrying with him a length of sawed-off broomstick."

Mason had known men like Brock Boyd, inside. He'd known men like Levi Cody too. In prison, it was the Boyds of the world who ruled. The Codys, in his experience, never lasted long. You could try to protect them, try to help them out, but you couldn't try too hard, not while the other men were looking. You risked becoming a Cody yourself, and there wasn't ever any escaping that. Sooner or later, they'd get you.

Prison wasn't exactly like being a teenaged hockey player. But Mason suspected there were more similarities than anyone would care to admit.

"Word got out," Rengo said. "Wasn't long before the whole county knew the whole fucked-up tale. Hockey rink to high school, girls to grown men. I reckon Levi didn't hear his first name spoke outside his folks' house the rest of the season. Hell, even his teachers must have known him that way."

There'd been moments, early in Mason's sentence, when he'd wondered if he would wind up like that. One of the broken, shrunken men who lingered on the margins, trying desperately not to be seen. The laughingstocks and worse, bruised and bloodied and black eyed, toothless.

He'd heard them cry in their bunks at night. He knew what happened when the guards weren't around. He'd pretended not to notice, not to care.

He'd pretended not to hear them when they called out for help.

"He didn't last the summer," Rengo said. "That nickname followed him after hockey season ended. Makah's a small county, and Boyd was the big man in it, and from what I heard, everyone was more or less happy to let Boyd have his way. And that meant Broomstick Cody had to suffer."

They died, the broken men. They hanged themselves in their cells or they tried to fight back and were beaten to death.

"They found him in the water off Cape Flattery," Rengo said. "Western edge of the county. He'd left a note, explained everything. His folks raised a stink, and some people made noise, but it never really changed anything. Boyd went away and got drafted, made the pros. And they still put his picture on a goddamn billboard at the county line."

Sometimes families would ask questions. The warden would catch heat. Sometimes changes were made, symbolic and always temporary. Token gestures—more guards, more supervision. A reporting system in place. Weeks would turn into months, and those changes were scaled back. Life returned to normal. The Boyds of the world chose a new Cody, and you hoped and prayed it wasn't you. You tried to keep your head down and serve your sentence in silence. You watched as another guy suffered.

Rengo drained his glass. Set it down, heavy, and looked across the room at Mason. "So that's the only Broomstick I can think of," he said. "And I reckon he'd be a hell of a suspect for killing Bad Boyd. Only problem is, Burke, he's been dead near fifteen years."

FORTY-TWO

After Chris Jordan's murder, Dax Pruitt saw how the reckoning would have to come to pass.

Logger Fetridge met Pruitt at his trailer in Deception Cove. As yet neither man had any reason to believe the law suspected their involvement in any of the recent chaos, but that didn't matter anymore. Not now that Fetridge's sister's only child was dead.

Fetridge looked tired when he showed up at Pruitt's trailer. The two men sat and drank bourbon and didn't speak much about what had happened to Jordan and Bealing. Neither could say whether it was that the law had traced Jordan back to the murder of Charlene Todd or it was just stupid blind luck that had led the deputies to the abandoned freighter, but the answer to that question was moot anyhow. Jordan was dead and he was family to Fetridge.

What Pruitt believed, though he'd never say to his friend, was that Jordan had earned what had come to him, and more of it besides. Logger Fetridge's nephew was a pervert and a murderer, and though Pruitt's own hands were far from bloodless, he drew a distinction between the things that he'd done and what Jordan had done to Charlene Todd.

The man Pruitt and Fetridge had killed had deserved it; he'd made his own bed long ago. Charlene Todd had done nothing more than what Jordan had asked of her.

But it made no difference. Logic rarely did, not in Makah County when blood relations were involved and grudges had to be settled. And though Dax Pruitt was no kin to Jordan or Bealing, he owed Logger Fetridge and would owe him for the rest of his life. And so there was no question that whatever Fetridge decided, Pruitt would walk beside him, no matter how tangled the road turned from here.

"It was that bitch cop who done it," Fetridge told Pruitt. "Winslow. The other one's as likely to die in the hospital as he is to live."

"Winslow." Pruitt had no quarrel with the young deputy. In fact, he mostly admired her, respected her for having fought for her country and then come back with her demons and still sought to do something right for her hometown. He'd have liked her even more if she'd kept her head down after clearing out Kirby Harwood, if she'd turned down the new sheriff's offer to sign on as a deputy and instead just focused on, say, wood carving or basket weaving, but she'd sworn the oath, and that made her an adversary to men like Pruitt and Fetridge, no matter how either of them felt about her personally.

"She's law, Floyd," Pruitt told Fetridge. "If you act on this, there's bound to be trouble. This, all of it, could come crashing down on us."

Pruitt knew there was still a good chance they could skate, on Boyd and the boss lady and everything else. Knew if Mason Burke just turned up and wore the coat Fetridge had cut for him that nobody in the sheriff's office would ever think to look beyond the ex-con, think to sniff out the grand conspiracy. He knew that once he and Fetridge turned down this next road, there was a fair chance they wouldn't come back.

Fetridge knew it too; Pruitt could tell by his eyes. But that didn't seem to be slowing him down.

"My sister ain't stopped crying since she heard the news," he told Pruitt. "Chris was her only child, Daxon. You want me to tell her I didn't do what I'm meant to?"

There was the crux of it, and there was no saying no. In Makah County, you stood up for your kin. You fought for them, to the death if need be.

"Bring Winslow to the mountain," Fetridge told Pruitt. "We'll deal with her up Lone Jack Trail."

FORTY-THREE

Jess could feel them coming back. Helpless, bitter memories. Violent dreams and resignation. Numbness.

Afia.

She could feel her mind slipping, all the work she'd put in, the foundation she thought she'd built solid starting to crack beneath her like ice, exposing the dark depths below.

They'd taken her badge and they'd taken her gun; they'd taken the man she loved, and they'd thrown her entire world into some new kind of chaos, the likes of which she wasn't equipped to deal with, not even with Lucy beside her and a VA doc waiting in Port Angeles to tell her how to breathe.

Jess could feel the numbness creeping back in, a numb born of trauma and surrender, of seeing horrible things done to people you loved, so many times and so often that you reached a point where you broke and you just couldn't feel anymore.

She might have been happy if she could have just died among other Marines.

But the Marines didn't want her, and so she'd come back. Come back to Makah County and Deception Cove and civilization, to her husband's ghost and Kirby Harwood's stupid games, to Lucy and Burke and some attempt at a normal life. Jess could feel it all slipping away again.

She could feel how she had nothing to offer this world but her violence.

Jess spent a short, sleepless night alone in her motel room, clutching Lucy close to her until the dog groaned and squirmed away to lie in a tight pretzel at the foot of the bed, her eyes on Jess and ears perked for any sign of a flashback. By then the light of dawn was beginning to filter in around the edges of the blackout curtain, and Jess could hear cars and trucks passing periodically on the highway outside, but she stayed in bed, tangled in her sheets and in the thoughts that raced, incessantly, through her mind.

She went to the beach. It was the same beach that Brock Boyd had washed up onto, but before Boyd, it had always been the beach she'd gone to walk when she needed comfort, or clarity, or just a breath of fresh air. She took the dog, got in the Blazer, and drove west on the highway to Shipwreck Point, parking in the lot where Cable Proudfoot had pointed her to Boyd's body, and she unclipped Lucy from her leash and followed the dog down to the rough, pebbly shingle, where the tide had gone out and there was nobody else she could see for miles.

Lucy ran. She dug in the sand, chased driftwood, and ran in great, loping circles as though she'd never been allowed to run before in her life. This wasn't true, but Jess *had* been too distracted to give Lucy a proper walk these last few days, and even then, she preferred to keep Lucy on her leash when other people were around.

Now, here, the dog could run as she pleased, and she did, down the beach onto the damp, dark sand below the tide line, mucking about in the pools left behind, chasing the gulls who stood here and there like sentinels, sending the birds squawking high into the air as she leaped for them, her whole body outstretched and her tongue lolling from her mouth as though she believed she, too, could fly.

Jess walked above the tide line, amid the rows of drying kelp and the great logs that had broken free of booms out in the strait and washed ashore here. She walked to where Cable Proudfoot had found Bad Boyd's body, or somewhere close to it. The ocean and the elements had erased any trace that Boyd had lain here, that he'd ever existed.

If only it were so easy, Jess thought. Because Brock Boyd *had* existed, and like a stone dropped into water whose ripples endure long after it sinks, he was still wreaking his peculiar havoc on his hometown, and the county unfortunate enough to call him its son.

Jess stood at the spot where she'd stood over Boyd's body, looking out over the gray, featureless water of the strait as she considered the sheriff's hypothesis, that Mason Burke had killed Boyd in the boat basin, then fired up Joe Clifford's old boat to dump the body out in the strait.

Jess knew enough about the water from Ty to know it was folly to try to draw any conclusions from where Boyd had washed up. Men who drowned off Deception Cove sometimes appeared on the rocks at Cape Flattery, or farther inland toward Clallam Bay. Sometimes they even turned up in Canada, and sometimes they didn't turn up at all. There was undoubtedly a science to the way the currents moved a body, but Jess didn't need any of it. What she *did* know plain and clear was that Mason Burke wasn't much of a sailor, and Joe Clifford's old troller wasn't much of a boat.

Burke had hung around Deception Cove even when the whole county wanted him caught. He'd told Ernie Saint Louis about Charlene Todd's murder. He'd helped Jess save Gillies's life. He wasn't behaving like a man who'd killed another, and he'd sworn to Jess he was innocent.

Burke wasn't the killer. But she would never convince Hart — or the state police — without proof.

Lucy came trotting over. She'd worn herself out with the running, and now she panted happily, nuzzled up to Jess and then caught scent of something, put her nose to the ground and tracked it to a pile of dead kelp a few feet away.

"Come on, girl," Jess said, clapping her hands. "Let's get you some water."

Lucy came back to her easily, that big panting pit-bull smile on her face, and together they walked back up the beach to where the trees parted at the trail to the parking lot, and Lucy led the way up to the Blazer.

The tires on the Blazer were flat. All of them. Jess felt something cold and ugly work its way down her spine. She looked around the parking lot, but there were no other vehicles, was no sign of anyone, and she shook her head and looked at the truck again as though it must be some mistake. She walked to the front driver's-side tire and leaned down and studied it as her brain struggled to process what exactly had happened.

But this tire had been slashed. Behind her, Lucy growled, and then Jess sensed movement, and she turned and found herself face-to-face with a gun.

FORTY-FOUR

Behind the gun was Dax Pruitt.

It was a pistol, somebody's take on a 1911, and Pruitt held it like he knew what he was doing. He stood far enough from her that she couldn't lunge at him, surprise him, not without him putting a hole in her before she got there.

"Hi, Jess," he said. "Awfully sorry about your tires."

She'd given Hart her service weapon. She owned a shotgun, a Remington 870 Express, but it was back at the motel, locked in Hank Moss's safe. Wouldn't do her a lick of good now.

Lucy stood ten feet behind Pruitt's right shoulder, her hackles raised and a growl in her throat, low and steady. She shifted her weight slightly, her muscles tensed and taut. Jess knew the dog could sense Pruitt's intentions, knew it wouldn't be long before she took it on herself to change them.

"What's this about, Dax?" Jess asked, as calm as she could.

Pruitt glanced at Lucy. There was no fear in his eyes, just acknowledgment. Another threat. He wouldn't let the dog surprise him. "Logger Fetridge wants to see you," he told Jess. "Talk about what you done."

She supposed she should have known this was coming. "I guess this is about Jordan," she said. "What happened on that ship. He pulled a gun, Dax. It was simple self-defense—"

"Logger wants to see you," Pruitt said again. "You going to come along easy or do we have to get mean with each other?"

"I'm an officer of the law, Dax," she said. "You sure you and Logger know what you're doing?"

"He knows," Pruitt said.

Jess didn't reply. That settled it; she could see how this was going to go. Lucy would jump at Pruitt, sometime soon and getting sooner. Pruitt would be ready for it, and he would spin and put a bullet in the dog before Jess could stop him. Jess would leap at Pruitt herself, try to protect Lucy, but Pruitt had the handgun and he'd probably get a bullet in her too before she could wrestle the weapon away.

She could die here on this gravel parking lot beside Lucy or she could take her chances somewhere else with Logger Fetridge.

"Lucy," she said. "Look at me, girl. It's okay. Calm down."

Lucy glanced at her, whimpered once, her ears flattened. She shifted her weight and she growled again at Pruitt and took a step toward him.

"I'll go with you, Dax," Jess told Pruitt. "Just don't hurt the dog."

Pruitt snorted. "Won't have a choice if she jumps me, Jess," he said. "I don't *want* to hurt her, but that dog's looking at me like I'm lunch."

He gestured her away from the Blazer, toward the turnoff from the highway, and now Jess could see where he'd hidden his Silverado, half blocked by the tree line that separated the lot from the highway.

"Stay there, Lucy," Jess said, holding up her hand to the dog. "You *stay*, okay?"

Lucy whimpered again, her paws tattooing the ground, indecisive and scared. Pruitt held the gun at Jess and motioned for her to walk to the pickup, eyeing the dog from his peripheral with every other step.

He was still too far away for Jess to disarm him. She slowed, and he outright stopped. "Problem?"

He was good. Good enough, anyway.

"If we have a problem, Jess, I *will* put one in your dog," Pruitt said. "I consider myself a pretty humane person, but you see how I've got to keep you motivated."

She walked.

"Don't hurt the dog," she said. "I'm going."

The dog had been trained, and trained well. First by Burke and then by professionals. But she'd been trained to forge a bond with her owner, and her owner was Jess, and there was no way Lucy was going to just sit there and watch some man she didn't trust haul Jess away from her.

Jess and Pruitt were about at the Silverado when Lucy made her move. Pruitt was distracted, fumbling in the bed of the truck for a length of rope, the gun still aimed square at the back of Jess's head. Pruitt didn't see Lucy coming, and neither did Jess or she'd have called the dog off, but by the time she saw Lucy, it was too late to matter.

The dog let out a growl, loud and vicious, and the next thing Jess knew, Pruitt was staggering backward, Lucy hanging from his arm with her teeth tearing through his jacket, gripping tight to the flesh beneath as he tried to swing around with his other arm, his gun arm, as he tried to aim the pistol and just blast the dog off of him.

Pruitt screamed, *"What the fuck?"* and Jess screamed too, word-lessly, knowing how this had to end. She pushed off the truck and tried to get between Pruitt and Lucy, tried to make a play for the gun, but Pruitt saw her coming.

He swung the pistol around and made solid contact with the

side of her head, as hard a hit as she'd ever taken; it knocked her nearly to the ground and sent stars through her vision. He hit her again and shoved her full to the ground, and she couldn't see much of anything then, couldn't make herself move. She heard Lucy growling and heard Pruitt swearing, and then the dog hit the ground somewhere not far away from her and she heard the gun roar and heard Lucy yelp, high-pitched and frantic.

Then Pruitt fired again and Jess didn't hear Lucy, and she wanted to scream but she couldn't make her mouth work, her thoughts sluggish and her limbs going some kind of numb. She lay there and heard Pruitt swearing as he set down the gun and examined his wound, as he picked up the length of rope from the bed of his truck and knelt down beside her.

"Goddamn you," he said, his mouth close and his breath a cesspool of chewing tobacco and rot. "Goddamn you for making me do that, Jess."

Then he bound her arms, and she didn't struggle, and he lifted her up as though she weighed nothing, dropped her in the bed of the truck. She couldn't hear Lucy and she didn't see her anywhere, and she lay in the bed of the truck, knowing that whatever Logger Fetridge aimed to do to her, it wouldn't amount to anything next to what Pruitt had just done to Lucy.

In the cab of the truck, Pruitt started the engine, and the Silverado drove slowly out onto the highway.

FORTY-FIVE

Levi Cody's mother was named Linda, and she still lived in Neah Bay. It only took seeing her the once before Mason was sure she hadn't killed Brock Boyd.

Linda Cody was a wheelchair user. Her house had a ramp up to the front door.

"Drunk driver," she'd told Rengo matter-of-factly when he knocked on her door like a Girl Scout selling cookies, told her how he was a writer doing a story about Bad Boyd and his days playing hockey in the county, said he understood her son had been a teammate.

Mason had been watching the encounter from across the street, sitting low in the driver's seat of Rengo's little Toyota, key in the ignition, foot poised to mash the gas at the first hint of trouble.

But then Linda Cody had invited Rengo inside, and Rengo had glanced back at the truck and shrugged, kind of helpless, and disappeared after her.

He related the rest to Mason later, once he'd come out again, excitement in his voice and a scrap of paper in his palm.

"Said she got a good settlement when the drunk hit her," Rengo told him. "But it messed up her memory something awful. Never mind how she couldn't use her legs anymore."

Linda Cody's house was outfitted with grab bars and low tables, not many chairs. The entire kitchen had been redone so she could cook from a seated position. Rengo had sat in her living room in one of the only chairs he could see in the house, while Linda sat across from him in her wheelchair.

"I have a nurse who comes twice a day," she told Rengo as they made small talk. "So I'm not entirely alone."

He asked when the nurse was due next, and she'd glanced at the clock on the wall and said not for a couple of hours. So Rengo relaxed and sat back in his chair, asked her was she aware that Brock Boyd was dead.

She nodded; she'd heard something about it. "Wasn't he supposed to be murdered?"

"That's what they're saying at the sheriff's detachment," Rengo told her. "You have any thought as to who'd do something like that?"

Linda Cody paused before she answered, a hitch in her breath. She was older, Rengo told Mason, but it was hard to tell her exact age. Like, she might be fifty or she might be sixty or she might be seventy, for all he could tell. Her body was thin and it was frail, her wrists all delicate tendons and translucent skin. She was a small woman, he believed, would be barely more than five feet tall standing up.

"She might have been faking the wheelchair stuff, but I don't think so," Rengo told Mason. "And even if she wasn't, she didn't look like she'd have the strength to *move* Boyd even if she had shot him."

She didn't drive either—couldn't, considering her spinal injury and how it had cost her the use of her legs.

"I saw that movie where the handicapped guy did it," Rengo told Mason. "Like, he was faking the whole time and then he walked away clean at the end. But this lady, Linda? She ain't it."

All the same, she'd paused a little before she'd told Rengo how she had no idea who might have killed Boyd. So he asked her did she still harbor a grudge, given what Boyd had done to her son. She closed her eyes and said nothing for a long time, and it was obvious she still hurt pretty bad over the whole situation.

"That man took my boy, Mr. Rengo," she said finally, opening her eyes to fix them on his. "He didn't push Levi, but he brought him to the edge. So if you're asking if I'm sorry Boyd's dead, well, I'm not; I won't ever be. But his being dead won't ever bring Levi back, and I'm not fool enough to think otherwise."

Rengo couldn't see how she *could* have done it, even if she'd wanted to. Moreover, he believed her that she wouldn't have if she could. And so he'd thanked her, and was standing to leave, and that's when he caught sight of the scrap of paper sticking halfway out of a paperback novel somebody had left on the mantel above the fireplace, far out of Linda Cody's reach.

Rengo kind of ambled over to the mantel, glanced at the book and the paper sticking out of it so he could see what it was, and then he looked back around the living room and saw the family snapshots on the wall, and he looked at the scrap of paper again, and eased it as stealthily as he could from the book, folded it up into his palm, and thanked Linda Cody again and got the hell out of her house, lickety-split.

Mason was dozing in the driver's seat, trying not to fall asleep but losing a battle with the exhaustion that tugged down on his body like a concrete block. He woke up fast, though, when Rengo came running down Linda Cody's front ramp, bounding across the road to the truck.

"It's the sister," he told Mason, half breathless, as he hurled himself into the car. "Levi Cody's sister—it's got to be her."

The scrap of paper in his hand was a ticket, good for one

passenger and one vehicle, for the ferry that ran across the strait between Port Angeles and Victoria, Canada. The ticket was dated just before Brock Boyd's murder. It was made out to a woman named Jana M—

"Jana Marsh," Rengo told Mason as he studied the ticket. "She must've got married and given up her last name. But she was Jana Cody when Levi was alive. That's his younger sister."

"You didn't ask her?" Mason said, gesturing back toward the house. "About her daughter?"

Rengo shook his head. "I didn't think of it, Burke. I was too busy trying to get the hell out of there without the old lady seeing how I was stealing the clue."

Mason looked over the ticket again. It might be something, or it might be nothing. It certainly wasn't enough to convince Sheriff Hart to drop the charges against him, go investigate some mystery woman. But, Mason figured, it was worth checking out all the same.

"I don't suppose you have a passport," he said to Rengo, who laughed outright, sharp and incredulous, before he realized Mason was serious.

"What, so I can fly off to *gay Paree* for the weekend?" he said. "Nah, Burke, I don't have a passport. Do you?"

Mason didn't have a passport. Odds were he would never have one. There weren't many countries eager to let men of his pedigree across their borders.

"No," he told Rengo. "I don't."

FORTY-SIX

Jess woke in the back of the truck, and the truck wasn't moving. Above her was nothing but forest and sky, the faint hint of blue beyond the clouds. She lifted her head and felt groggy and nauseated, her temple throbbing where Pruitt had pistol-whipped her. The rope chafed at her wrists, and her arms were sore from being bent behind her. Her whole body ached, and she supposed it was the bed of the truck that had done it, no creature comforts and what must have been one hell of a rough ride up into the hills.

She could hear birds singing. Movement, somewhere in the trees, but it was delicate, precise, not the ponderous, thrashing noises human beings made when they ventured out into nature. She shivered. It was colder here; they'd gained some altitude. May was still early spring in the high country of Makah County, and when the sun went down, the temperature might yet dip toward freezing.

There was no sign of Pruitt. The cab of the Silverado was empty, and he wasn't anywhere she could see nearby. Behind the bed of the truck, the road dropped down an uneven, precipitous grade into more forest, and Jess had no way of knowing how far they'd come. By the width of the road and its deteriorated condition, she supposed it was a logging spur line, half forgotten and never charted, up the contours of the low mountains south of Deception. There were hundreds of such roads on the Olympic Peninsula, remnants of loggers and miners, now mostly invisible, dying slow deaths as the forest claimed back its ground.

The truck was parked in a clearing, Jess saw, just wide enough to turn a Silverado around in a five- or maybe eight-point turn. Ahead of the truck, the road continued as a steep trail through mature alder and young pine, impassable by anything wider than an all-terrain vehicle.

She rested her chin on the rim of the truck bed and looked out at the forest and listened. It was, objectively speaking, a beautiful day.

Her head ached. For once, it was almost *too* bright. Her thinking was foggy, and she probably had a concussion, but she remembered the noise Lucy had made when Pruitt shot her, and she leaned over and vomited in the bed of the truck until her stomach was empty and nothing else would come up.

And then she pushed herself to her feet.

Pruitt was gone, but he would come back soon, and Jess wanted to kill him for what he'd done to Lucy. Her wrists were tied behind her back and her vision blacked out for a moment or two when she struggled up from her knees to stand in the bed of the truck; she swayed a little bit and had to close her eyes, and she thought she might fall, but she didn't.

She looked around again and suspected that Pruitt had parked his truck as far up the trail as he could get it, but he must have needed some smaller vehicle to bring her up the last distance to where Logger Fetridge waited. Carefully, she stepped over the Silverado's tailgate and down onto the bumper, and then, as her balance shifted, she jumped to the mud rather than fall, landing without grace but unhurt. Pruitt still hadn't come back.

She needed to get her wrists untied somehow. She circled the truck, looking for a rusted edge somewhere, some bare metal, some kind of sharpness she could use to cut the rope. But there was nothing on the Silverado that suited her needs, and no jagged rock on the trail or in the margin of the forest that would suffice.

She was screwed.

And she was weak. Her vision blacked out again, and she leaned against the side of the truck and waited for the nausea to pass. She needed to free her arms, and she needed to find a weapon, but hell, she could barely stand up on her own, and she was suddenly very thirsty.

From somewhere in the forest above came the sound of high-revving small motors, at least two of them, and they were coming her way. Jess kept her eyes closed and felt the hint of sun on her face and listened for the sound of the birds in the trees, but the birds were gone.

It was Mason who saw the dog first.

Shipwreck Point or just a little ways east, just past the parking lot at the beach. She was running along the side of the road toward Deception, half on the macadam and half on the shoulder, her ears flattened back and her gait awkward, hopping on three feet and favoring the fourth.

"Pull over," Mason told Rengo, and the kid saw the dog and did as instructed, slowed the truck just behind Lucy, who didn't look back and didn't stop running, not even when Mason stepped out of the car and whistled for her.

"Lucy."

At the sound of her name, the dog stiffened. She stopped, at last, and turned around, slow, stared back at Mason with her eyes wide and the whites visible, her right front paw still dangling above the ground. Mason called to her again, took a step forward, but as soon as he moved, the dog spooked and started running again.

What on earth? Mason thought, starting after her. *Where the hell is Jess?*

There was no answer that was a good one, he knew. He jogged down the shoulder toward the dog, and Rengo followed behind in the truck. Every moment they were out here on the highway was a danger, the whole county looking for them and this the most well-traveled road east of Clallam County.

They'd been trying to get inland when they spotted the dog, to find somewhere east of Makah to hole up and get rest before they drove the truck north to the Canadian line. Mason had heard the border wasn't fenced or too heavily patrolled; it was a gamble, but he was hoping to get across somehow, somewhere there weren't eyes on him, work his way back to the coast and the island across the strait, find Jana Marsh in Victoria.

Truthfully, it wasn't a plan with a very high probability of success, but Mason couldn't see what else to do. He needed to keep moving, if only to stay sane. If only to remind himself that he hadn't killed Bad Boyd, that he wasn't the cold-blooded murderer this county thought he was.

Now, though, Mason had other priorities. He caught up to Lucy around thirty yards down the road, the dog half limping, half running along, until he was almost on top of her, at which point she ducked down and cowered, hunched over like a paper clip with her tail between her legs, and Mason could see how she was shaking. There was blood on her paw.

"The hell happened to you, girl?" he asked her, but his voice only made her shake harder, and he scooped her up, walked back to the truck, and hoisted her into the cab beside Rengo, then climbed in after her.

"She okay?" Rengo's eyes were wide, and he looked damn scared himself; the kid loved the dog almost as much as Mason and Jess did. "Where's she coming from, Burke?"

Mason held Lucy tight against the seat and picked up her hurt paw. Saw blood from a wound midway up her foreleg, a deep cut but small, something lodged in there tight that Lucy wasn't about to let him remove.

She squirmed and whined and licked at his face and her paw, and she settled and shook some more when he released her.

"I think she's okay," Mason told Rengo. "Cut herself somehow. As for where she came from..." He twisted in his seat, glanced back down the highway. "Closest thing around here's the beach."

FORTY-SEVEN

They found the Blazer in the parking lot shortly thereafter. Even from a distance, Mason could see something was wrong.

"Shit," Rengo said, pulling the Toyota up beside it. "All four tires are flat, Burke."

Not just flat but slashed well and good and unfixable, Mason discovered as he circled the Blazer with his hands on his knees. He could feel something cold in the pit of his stomach, some sense of all-encompassing wrong, and it made his knees weak and constricted his breathing.

Where is Jess?

"Stay in the truck," he told Rengo. "Look after the dog." Then he hurried down the path toward the beach.

But Jess wasn't on the beach. The shingle was deserted, about a mile in either direction, just the wind whipping in off the water and further agitating his thoughts.

Mason ran the beach anyway. Had a nightmarish vision of Jess in the water, rolling facedown somewhere in the violent margin between the surf and shore. He thought she might be dead already, that whoever had found her here had killed her and dumped her body, and he ran west along the tide line as far as he could, until the beach turned to rock and there still wasn't any sign of her. Then he ran back, past the parking lot and east toward Deception Cove, but she wasn't anywhere. He was breathing hard when he slowed, and it wasn't just exertion, and there were tears in his eyes, and it wasn't just the wind.

Where are you? he thought, and wanted to scream it. *Where the hell are you, Jess?*

———————

She was in no shape to fight, and though she hated to run, Jess had no other option.

The motors were close now, little Japanese engines strapped to dirt bikes or all-terrain vehicles, probably at least one of the latter. Pruitt was armed, and whoever he'd bring with him was bound to be carrying too, and here was Jess, tied up and most likely concussed, no weapon but her wits, and she hardly had those.

She hated to run. She wanted to stay and confront Pruitt, bash his head in for what he'd done to Lucy, but staying here was a death wish, and she wasn't ready to die yet, not at least until she was sure she could take Dax Pruitt with her.

She crashed into the forest beside the Silverado, leading with her shoulder and tucking her head down, trying to avoid the thin, tangled branches that raked at her skin and tugged through her hair. She was making noise, and lots of it, but that didn't matter; Pruitt and his buddy were making noise too, and right now all that was important was putting in distance.

The slope of the mountain was steep and her balance precarious. She didn't dare follow the road, for fear they'd see her running and be on top of her quickly. She was banking on a few minutes of confusion back at the Silverado, hoping the men would scour the little clearing before they started their descent.

Anyway, if she stayed in the woods, there was no way they would find her. The forest was thick and it was vast and the men were bound to be impatient; they would stick to the trails, at least at first. The highway lay somewhere below her, stretched out like a ribbon along the coastline, and Jess knew if she could just keep dropping altitude, she would find it in time. Assuming she didn't break her neck.

Jess bulled her way down the slope. Crashing, careening into tree trunks, losing her balance, and slipping in the mud. The angle was severe and if she fell wrong she'd topple into a minefield of stumps and root systems and rock, all waiting to arrest her fall at the expense of her bones, or her life.

She tried to switchback down the grade as best she could, leaning upslope and scrambling behind her with her bound wrists for handholds, anything she could find to slow down the drop. She couldn't hear motors up above her anymore, but she was breathing too hard and making too much noise to hear anything anyway.

She couldn't worry about the men. What mattered was that she keep moving. Keep dropping in altitude.

And then she did fall.

She'd glanced back, upslope—that was her mistake. There was no point to looking back, but she'd done it anyway, and she'd stepped forward without planning that step and touched down on a thick, wizened root, gnarled and slippery. The sole of her shoe skidded and her ass flew out from under her, and she landed hard on her back and those wrists bound behind her, and then she was sliding down a steep, muddy wall and there was no way she could stop herself.

It might have been fifty feet or it might have been more. God knows how fast she was going when she hit. But she saw the tree coming and she knew it would hurt, and reflexively she shifted her balance and tumbled onto her side, and then she was racing past the tree and continuing to fall.

It would have been smarter, she realized instantly, to have let the tree stop her. Because beyond the tree was more open ground, a slope of mountainside too steep and too slippery to permit any growth, and beyond *that* was a shallow gulch and a riverbed, and Jess could sense water, but she could see only rock, a low, jagged line of boulders, immovable and unforgiving, lying in her path as she careened downward at speed.

Jess tried to dig her heels into the dirt. Clawed with her fingers at the mud underneath them. She succeeded not at all; she continued to plummet. There was nothing to do but close her eyes and brace for impact, try to shield her head and hope against hope she survived.

The impact seemed to steal her consciousness before her mind could process the pain.

FORTY-EIGHT

The dog was okay. Mason had found a tiny shard of bloody stone lodged in her foreleg, which must have been painful for Lucy, but it wasn't going to kill her. So that was a good thing at least.

The shard looked like it matched the gravel in the Shipwreck Point parking lot, like it had chipped off of something and gone ricocheting up into Lucy's leg. Like someone had been jackhammering in the middle of the lot. But Mason found a bullet casing, up toward where the parking lot narrowed for the exit to the highway. It gleamed in the intermittent sunlight peeking down through the clouds, and he spied it from about twenty paces, shiny and pristine amid the dusty lot.

Someone had been shooting, and Lucy had been close.

There was only the one casing, though. There might have been blood on the ground, but Mason couldn't see it. Mason hoped that meant that whoever'd slashed Jess's tires hadn't shot her, that she was still alive somewhere.

But he knew the clock was ticking.

"This is not good, Burke; I know you love that woman, but this is really not good."

Rengo was starting to panic. They'd been out in the daylight too long, too visible, and sooner or later some state patrolman or

212

a sheriff's deputy was going to recognize the truck and light them both up, and then the game would be over.

But Mason wasn't so focused on that right now.

"Who'd come for Jess?" he asked as Rengo pulled out onto the highway and drove slow toward Deception. "Who stands to gain from snatching up a sheriff's deputy?"

Rengo glanced at him. "She killed Chris Jordan," he said. "And Dougie Bealing. Those guys both had people; maybe they're pissed."

"Who?" Mason said.

"I don't *know*, Burke," the kid replied. "Jordan's kin to Logger Fetridge, so it might have been him. But it could well be anyone."

"Take me to Fetridge," Mason said. "Wherever he lives. Take me now."

Rengo sighed, frustrated. "That's all the way back in Neah Bay. We don't have time for this. We need to get out of this county."

"Just *take* me," Mason told him, thinking he might have to push Rengo out the driver's door and scour the county himself.

But Rengo set his jaw and slowed the truck. Glanced quick in the rearview and pulled a U-turn on the narrow highway.

"You're thinking we'll just run up on Logger Fetridge and his people unarmed?" he asked. "Sounds like a pretty smart way to get dead, Burke, you ask me."

Mason didn't know what he was thinking, except there'd been shooting and Jess was involved, and this Fetridge might know something about it. It was better than nothing, but just barely.

Probably it was all they had.

Jess came to, and kept running.

Her head throbbed, and there was blood all over, and it felt like knives when she shifted position, but Jess forced herself to her feet, forced herself to keep moving until the adrenaline and the old training kicked back in and she couldn't feel the pain anymore. Wasn't sure how long she'd been out, but it couldn't have been too long; the sky was still blue behind the clouds up above, the forest not yet that encompassing blackness of twilight.

She found a jagged, sharp piece of rock, sheared off from something much larger and left here, in the path of the gully in which water flowed steadily toward the ocean. She leaned her back against the rock's edge and rubbed the rope against it as hard as she could, the exertion straining her muscles and her dwindling energy, the movement so painful it made her want to cry out.

She didn't cry out and she didn't slow, not until she'd cut through the rope with the knife-edge of the rock and her wrists were unbound. Then she clambered down into the narrow gully and ducked her head into the stream of water at the bottom, cleaned the blood from her face and drank, greedily, until she felt sick.

She was tired and she was weak and she was sore. She couldn't hear the sound of the men and their machines over the rush of the water. They might have been close or they might have given up; Jess had no way of knowing.

She drank one more time and then stood and climbed atop a large rock and looked down the river's path through the forest, trying to pick out a trail along the side of the gully. The descent was steep and the rocks were slippery and loose and uneven. Jess knew one wrong step could trigger another fall, break her ankle or worse. But the river was the surest way she knew to find tidewater; she couldn't risk going back and looking for the road.

So she began to climb down the rocks, the work maddeningly

slow, sweat on her brow and streaming down her back, collecting with the blood and the dirt she'd accumulated already.

Above her, the day's light was already on the wane.

"We've got to bring this to the sheriff," Mason said as Rengo drove the little Toyota back toward Neah Bay. "We can't just hope to find Jess on our own."

Rengo didn't reply right away. He glanced at Mason. "They'll lock us up," he said. "Both of us."

"Better than we let anyone hurt Jess," Mason said. "Give me your phone."

Rengo didn't move. Between them, Lucy lifted her head as though to cast the deciding vote. She tilted back and studied Mason, licked at his face and then looked across the cab, solemn, at Rengo.

"Shit," Rengo said. "Even the dog's on board, huh?"

He steered with his left hand and dug in his pocket with his right, pulled out his cell phone and held it across the cab to Mason. "You know what they do to guys like me in prison, right?" he said.

Mason took the phone. "I'll watch your back. Best as I can."

"Yeah," Rengo said. "Okay."

Mason flipped the phone open and studied the screen, looking for bars and not seeing any. No service, not here, way out between Deception and Neah Bay, a cellular dead zone that would extend all the way to the town limits.

Shit.

"Drive faster," Mason told Rengo, hoping that Jess had it in her to survive, to fend off whichever asshole had thought to threaten her. Hoping she could buy them some time.

She's a combat-decorated Marine. She's more than these bumpkins can handle, you bet.

Beside Mason, Rengo pressed the gas pedal down farther and the little truck surged forward—and then, suddenly, Rengo yanked the wheel over, jerking Mason from his thoughts, and before he knew what was happening, the truck was dropping off the highway, down some uneven path at a speed beyond sane, the dog bouncing beside him and up into his lap, cowering and whimpering as the violent action of the truck brought fresh pain to her paw.

"The hell are you doing?" Mason asked just as Rengo slammed the truck to a stop, hitting the brakes so hard the dog would have crashed into the glove box had Mason not been holding on to her tight. They'd followed a fishing trail down to where a river passed under the highway; on the other side of the bridge, Mason saw, the water widened into an abbreviated delta, and beyond that the ocean.

Rengo gestured out the truck to the river, gestured inland, to where the water came spilling down the slope of the land, its banks wide and tall and ringed by boulders and scree. "Thought I saw something moving," he said, leaning forward to peer out through the windshield. "Up there—you see it?"

Mason squinted up the line of the river, following Rengo's gaze. Wondering what the kid had seen, knowing it must have been nothing, and precious time was wasting—but something made him want to be sure, anyway.

He stared and saw nothing, and then he did see it, small and dark in the growing shadows of the late afternoon. It was descending the bank of the river, following the water toward them, moving cautious, deliberate. He thought it might be a bear, but it didn't move like he believed a bear would.

Rengo craned his neck, a smile slowly spreading on his face. "Tell me that isn't her," he said. "Just try and tell me, Burke."

Mason didn't answer. Didn't want to jinx it, not even when he knew. Not even when he saw that it was human, a woman. That she was wearing Jess's jacket.

The woman moved slowly and didn't seem to see them, focused only on her feet and where they landed on the rocks. Her coat was torn and her face was dirty, and she carried her left arm as though it had been hurt.

Mason waited. He waited until the woman stepped off the last rock at the edge of their little clearing, came up from the water's edge to where he stood by the truck, and stared at him, her eyes empty and her expression numb.

"Burke," Jess said, her voice hollowed by fatigue and something else besides. "How the hell'd you find me?"

Mason laughed, sharp and outright, a great wave of relief crashing over him, immersing him, pounding him senseless.

"Well, shit, Jess," he replied. "I didn't find you. Rengo did."

FORTY-NINE

Jess climbed up from the riverbank toward Burke, drenched with sweat and blood and grime, exhausted and in pain. She didn't know how Burke had come to be waiting at the bottom of the mountain for her, but she doubted she had the capacity to ask right now, or the energy to process how he answered.

It didn't matter anyway.

Lucy was alive.

Behind Burke was a truck, a little rusty Toyota, and there was Rengo standing beside the open driver's-side door, and Jess was glad to see him and the truck, but they didn't matter either.

Lucy was alive.

Climbing down from that driver's seat, tentative but alive, was Lucy. The dog dropped to the ground, favoring her right forepaw, and Jess could see blood on the white patch of fur she'd always thought of as Lucy's socks, but there wasn't much blood, and the paw was still there, so Dax Pruitt hadn't shot her, or if he had he'd just glanced her.

Lucy's tail wagged helicopter-strong. She ducked her head and came trotting over toward Jess, happy but cautious and still residually scared, and Jess knelt down as best she could and let the dog come to her, wash her face with kisses, and leap at her and turn and wriggle her body against her, that tail whipping back and forth, but Jess barely felt it.

Her dog was alive.

Jess was aware, suddenly, of the magnitude of her fatigue. Lucy was safe, and she, too, was safe, and there was nothing left, no rocks to climb or men to run from; she was allowed to feel things again, and she did. She felt sore and she felt tired. She sensed her vision start to cloud, narrow in on the dog and the rough ground of the clearing, and she swayed a little and would have toppled over had Burke not been watching and right there to hold her.

"All right," he said, gripping her, strong. "All right, Jess. Let's find somewhere and get you fixed up."

She let him pull her upright and guide her to the truck, Lucy swirling around her legs, looking up at her, worried, as though she might run off again.

"I'm not going anywhere, Luce," she told the dog as Burke piled her into the passenger seat and helped the dog up into the footwell in front of her. "I'm right here."

———

Hank Moss was a friend of both Jess's and Mason's; he'd treated Mason with kindness and courtesy when he'd arrived in Deception Cove, stood protective of Jess throughout the entire Harwood ordeal, and, in the end, played his own role in ridding the county of the corrupt deputy. Aside from Chris Rengo, Moss was about the only man Mason figured he fully trusted in all of Makah County. He drove Rengo's truck to Moss's motel.

Rengo sat squished in between Mason and Jess, the dog at Jess's feet, and it was a tight squeeze in the little truck, but nobody complained, and they made good time back into Deception. Moss's motel was laid out in a single level of maybe ten units, all of them facing the highway, but Moss kept his own apartment in the back.

Mason drove the truck around to the rear of the motel and parked outside Moss's door. It was just about dark when he killed the engine, climbed out, and told Rengo to wait with Jess. A couple of minutes later, he was coming back with Hank in tow, the motelkeeper fumbling with his keys for the front door to the apartment, walking quickly, seeing the truck parked nearby but not breaking stride.

Moss was about in his fifties, a member of the Makah tribe who'd fought with the 41st Infantry in Desert Storm. He was a good man, and Mason knew he would house them as long as they needed.

They bustled Jess and Lucy out of the truck and into the apartment, a modest sitting area and a kitchen, a bedroom hidden somewhere down a hallway.

"Got a first-aid kit in the bathroom," Moss told Mason. "Looks like they both could use a little touching up."

Mason and Moss installed Jess on the couch, sat her down nice and comfortable, and set to examining her wounds. She'd been hit in the side of the head, and there was dried blood where it had happened. Mason saw the blood and went rigid, felt his muscles tense and his hands clench into fists, wanted to hit something or someone and felt helpless that he couldn't.

"Fetridge?" he asked Jess.

"Pruitt," she replied, wincing with the effort. "But he was doing it on Fetridge's say-so."

Mason still wasn't sure he understood the politics of the situation, how Jess had come to be embroiled with both men in the first place, but Jess told him the story, how she'd heard Pruitt shoot the dog and how she'd thought Lucy was dead, how she'd run, her wrists tied, down the side of the mountain.

There were scratches and scrapes on her face, and bruises. Holes in her clothes where branches had torn at her and sharp rocks had cut. She was mostly lucid now, though; she'd eaten, ravenously, a candy bar and some cold cuts liberated from Moss's kitchen, as Mason dabbed at her wounds with hydrogen peroxide.

"Gonna have to get these clothes off of you," Mason told her once he'd done all he could to clean the cuts on her face. "Get the rest of you tidied up as well."

Behind him, Rengo coughed, awkward, and Mason turned to see the kid blushing.

Meanwhile, Hank Moss was pushing himself to his feet. "I'd best get back out front," he told them. "Keep an eye on things. You all can manage without me?"

Mason nodded. "I think so."

"I'll go with you," Rengo said quickly. "Sure this dog could use a quick pee, or maybe you need some company?"

Moss grinned. "I got HBO on the TV in the lobby," he told Rengo. "And you look like you could use a cold beer."

Burke held her like she was something precious and breakable, like he was afraid she'd fall apart if he handled her rough. He helped her out of her chair and guided her to the bathroom, and she could sense in how he looked at her that he was scared for her, scared she was hurt somewhere he couldn't see.

And maybe she was, but it didn't feel like it now. Not with Burke beside her and Lucy out of trouble.

She waited while he ran the water for a shower, and as the water ran and the bathroom filled up with steam, he helped her pull the sweater over her head, and then he knelt down in front of her and slipped the button free on the front of her jeans, worked them slowly down her legs to the floor. He was trying to be gentle, she could tell. He was trying to be good.

But she'd missed him so much.

She leaned down and tugged him up to meet her lips, kissed him and could tell how he was holding back, still.

"I'm not made of glass, Burke," she told him, reaching for his belt. "You're not going to break me."

She kissed him again, hungrier, felt his body respond.

He said, "You're hurt."

"Scratches," she told him. "I need something different than first aid right now."

Maybe she ought to have been embarrassed, but she wasn't, and Burke didn't seem to mind. He unhooked her bra and slipped it off of her shoulders as she unbuckled his pants and slid her hand inside, and he was hard already and kissing her back, both of them breathing heavy, hands all over each other.

They'd been apart for so long, but they were together now. Burke had been waiting at the bottom of the mountain for her, and maybe it was coincidence or just dumb luck, or maybe it was something else, some kind of cosmic sign that they were in this together, the two of them, until the very end.

Jess didn't know yet, but she did know that she loved Burke, and she missed him, and she wanted him now.

She peeled off her underwear and kicked it to the corner of Hank Moss's little bathroom. Then she slid back the shower curtain and stepped under the spray, hot and breathtaking and relentless. She looked out from under the water at Burke, to where he stood watching her. He wasn't looking at her like he was afraid he would hurt her now.

"What are you waiting for, Burke?" she asked him. "Or are you going to make me do this alone?"

Afterward, when they'd showered long enough for the hot water to run out and made up for those many nights they'd been apart from each other, Rengo—still blushing—delivered fresh clothes for them both from Jess's room around front. They gathered again in Hank's living room. Lucy sat curled up on the couch with Jess and Burke on either side of her, Hank in an easy chair, and Rengo by the window while Burke filled in his side of the story. Why he'd come to the *Amy Usen* the night Tyner Gillies was shot. What he'd discovered about Brock Boyd and a boy named Levi Cody, known as Broomstick.

"I won't ask you for help," he told her, daring to meet her eyes over the top of Lucy's broad back. "Not unless you believe in it. And not until you're ready, those cuts and bruises healed up."

She didn't hesitate. "I'll go tomorrow," she said. "No sense waiting any longer."

He searched her eyes as though he was looking for some telltale sign she believed him. "It's a lot to ask."

"I've been asked to do worse," she replied. "Ordered, in fact. But what the hell are you going to do, Burke, while I'm running down this lead?"

Burke broke her gaze. He exhaled and shifted his weight and looked down at the floor. Chuckled a little. "I'm going to do what I'm supposed to," he said. "What the whole county's looking at me to do."

He shrugged. Grinned at her.

"I'm going to go see the sheriff."

FIFTY

They didn't stop searching until nightfall, but Dax Pruitt knew they'd lost Jess Winslow long before dark. Pruitt drove his Yamaha and Fetridge a four-wheeler ATV with enough of a flatbed platform on the back that he could have carried Jess up to where they wanted to carry her, if they'd found her again.

The narrow track up the mountain was steep and muddy, half washed out by the rain and overgrown by alder trees, whose branches clawed and tugged at Pruitt's jacket as he rode his dirt bike up the grade. The forest was pitch-black and quiet save the sound of his engine and that of Logger Fetridge's motor behind him, lapping at him, urging him higher and higher through the forest.

Pruitt had been careless. He'd known as he left Winslow in the back of the Silverado that he ought to have tied her up better. Found more rope somewhere and bound her legs too, anchored her well and good to the tie-down holes in the bed of his truck. He'd known by the time he was halfway to where Fetridge waited that he'd fucked up, that there was a fair chance Jess wouldn't be waiting for him when he came back down with Fetridge and the four-wheeler to ferry her up to the mine.

He'd been distracted. Preoccupied. Hell, he'd been in a kind of daze, thinking about the dog and how he'd had to shoot it, wishing like hell it hadn't come down to that. He'd been picturing the dog bleeding out somewhere, been feeling right guilty and miserable about the whole situation, and he hadn't done his job like he should.

He'd given Winslow an out, and she'd taken it and disappeared. If they were lucky, she was dead somewhere, broke her neck in a fall and died quick, or fractured a leg and was settling in for a long, slow starvation.

Either way, it didn't solve the issue. Fetridge didn't get to have his revenge, take out his anger on Winslow for killing his sister's son, which was the whole point of hauling her up the mountain in the first place. Fetridge wasn't happy.

And that's not even considering if Jess Winslow made it down off the mountain alive.

When they reconvened at the top of the mountain, they agreed that the cause was lost.

The place where they wound up was where Logger Fetridge had intended to punish Jess Winslow: the abandoned shaft to a forgotten mine, the old Lone Jack claim, sunk deep in the side of the mountain in search of copper, manganese, gold. The mine was little more than a hole in the hillside now, held open by rotten lumber crossbeams, the remains of a narrow-gauge railroad disappearing into the gloom. Surrounding the shaft were piles of tailings and rusted, tangled cable, uneven stacks of moss-covered board wood, what Pruitt supposed had once been the camp. The forest had reclaimed most of the ground the miners had taken, and it wouldn't be long before it overran what was left.

Pruitt had never been told how Logger Fetridge had come to discover the place, but he did know his friend sometimes cooked a couple hundred feet down the main shaft, where a ventilation chimney had been cut through the mountain for the miners. And he knew Fetridge came up here for other purposes too, and that

Jess Winslow would not have been the first problem Fetridge had solved high atop the mountain, away from curious eyes and anyone who might think to tell about what he'd done.

Pruitt was half deaf from a day's worth of high-octane riding. The night sky above them was clear and carpeted with stars, but it was too dark to see the expression on Fetridge's face. Even so, he could see plain and sure that his friend was unhappy. The men lit cigarettes and stood in front of the open shaft of the mine.

There was still time to run, if Pruitt wanted it. He could ride back down the trail, pack a couple of bags hasty, drive out through Clallam Bay, and be well on his way anywhere else in the country by morning. He had a brother in North Dakota, fracking shale, swore it was good money and steady work. Kept bugging Pruitt to come out and give it a try. He could do it, if he wanted. Still plenty of time, dawn at least and then some.

Jess Winslow would raise all kinds of hell if she did happen to walk down off the mountain. She'd tell the sheriff how it was Pruitt who'd tried to kidnap her, and the sheriff would come looking, and he'd probably look for Fetridge too, and somebody was bound to make the connection between Fetridge and Pruitt and Jordan and Bealing, and Charlene fucking Todd and Bad Boyd. Pruitt could see how, sooner or later, the whole house of cards would come tumbling down.

But he could see, also, that Fetridge didn't care anymore. His nephew was dead, and that meant that someone had to be punished. That code was more important than Fetridge's life or freedom.

And Pruitt wasn't a runner either. Not when it meant abandoning the people who'd stood by him when he needed them. Pruitt owed Logger Fetridge his life, and he still walked with a limp that proved it, and he would walk with that limp for the rest of his life, no matter how far he ran away from Deception Cove. He would carry that reminder of what Logger Fetridge had done for him, and what he'd failed to do in return.

Dax Pruitt couldn't stomach the thought of it.

Fetridge lit another cigarette, and in the flare of the lighter, Pruitt could see the determination etched into his friend's face.

"Best we entrench up here for a couple of days," he told Pruitt. "See if that Winslow makes it down off the mountain. See what happens next."

He passed the lighter to Pruitt, who lit his own cigarette, and they smoked and said nothing and stared up at the stars. Pruitt wondered about Jess Winslow and just wished he'd been good enough to do what Fetridge had asked.

And he wondered if he would ever make it down off this mountain, and he expected that the odds didn't favor him.

FIFTY-ONE

The little sheriff's detachment in Deception Cove felt deserted when Mason walked in the next morning, empty save for the rookie Paul Monk, who sat at the reception desk by the front door and whose eyes went as wide as sand dollars when he saw Mason come in.

"You'd better handcuff me, Monk," Mason told the rookie after a couple of seconds of awkward silence. "I think the sheriff would be choked if you didn't."

Still gaping, Monk stood and rounded the desk. Removed the handcuffs from his duty belt and locked them on Mason's wrists, his body skewed back as far away from Mason as he was able, as though he imagined the ex-con was playing a trick on him, that this was just a precursor to some strange and unforeseen ambush.

"Good," Mason told him when his wrists were secure. "You're doing fine. Now go ahead and give Sheriff Hart a call."

Monk looked back at the phone on his desk, then at Mason. Didn't seem inclined to move.

"I'm not going anywhere," Mason told him. "Go ahead and call."

So Monk made the call. Leaned over his desk and pulled the phone across and punched in the numbers for the Neah Bay detachment.

"Uh, Sheriff?" he said, the receiver to his ear. "It's Monk here in Deception. I, uh, have Burke — Mason Burke — at the detachment."

Monk listened.

"Uh, yes, sir. In custody. Well, he just walked in."

He listened some more.

"Yes, sir," he said. "Okay. We'll see you shortly."

Monk ended the call. He looked around the detachment like it was the first time he was seeing the place.

Mason watched him.

"Think you ought to put me in a cell?" he asked.

Monk stiffened and reached for the key ring on his belt. Turned to Mason, a stricken look on his face.

"Relax, Monk," Mason reassured him, leading the way toward the back of the detachment. "You're doing fine."

A short while later, Mason heard the front door open and Hart walk in. Heard the sheriff ask Monk, "Where is he?" and Monk tell him, "Back in the holding cell," and Mason sat on his little bench and waited, and after a moment the sheriff appeared. He took in the sight of Mason behind bars, and then he glanced toward Monk at the front desk.

"The kid did fine, Sheriff," Mason told him. "He'll make a solid cop someday."

Hart squinted in Monk's direction. "Still pretty green," he said.

"Hell," Mason said. "We were all green once."

Slowly, Hart turned back to look at Mason. Frowned and worked his jaw. "You're turning yourself in," he said.

Mason nodded. "Yes, sir."

"You're ready to confess to the murder of Brock Boyd," Hart said. "And Charlene Todd."

"No, sir," Mason replied.

The lines on Hart's forehead grew deeper. "You're *not* ready to confess."

"I'm still not ready to lie to you, Sheriff," Mason told him. "I know you consider me a suspect in both murders, and I'm here as a show of good faith."

This was the part of the plan where he'd nearly lost Jess, back in Hank Moss's living room. She'd been worried, at first, and then she'd been mad. "This whole county's hungry for you," she'd warned him. "You walk into that detachment, you won't ever come out again, not a free man."

"Sure I will," he'd told her, and tried to sound confident. "I didn't kill anybody, and you're going to prove it."

She hadn't talked to him much the rest of the night. Mason could tell there was at least a part of Jess that still wondered if he *had* killed Brock Boyd. He suspected that, partially, was why she didn't want him to turn himself in.

Hart stroked his chin and stared in at Mason through the bars. "You're here as a show of good faith," he said.

"Yes, sir," Mason replied. "Faith in your powers of investigation and, if need be, in the county's court system. And in whatever higher power's carried me this far. I didn't kill Brock Boyd or Charlene Todd, but I'm willing to wait here while you all work out who did."

Hart didn't answer for a beat. Just watched him, incredulous. Then he scratched his head, and paced a bit. "Where's Jess?" he asked finally.

Mason looked Hart in the eye. "Jess is out of town, Sheriff," he said. "Working vacation."

Jana Marsh had done well for herself.

It hadn't taken much sleuthing for Jess to find the house. Jana was on Facebook, and her husband, Ronnie, was too. They were living in Victoria, British Columbia, in a tidy suburb east of downtown, a couple of blocks to the beach. The peaks of the Olympic range visible over the strait.

Rengo had driven Jess into Port Angeles early that morning, in time for the first ferry crossing of the day. Burke seemed confident that Sheriff Hart would call off the search for the kid once he'd seen Burke was locked up and heard Burke's version of events, but Jess still watched the passenger-side mirror more than she watched the road, an hour's drive east with the sun coming up ahead of them, what looked to be a beautiful day in its infancy.

Jess hoped it was a good omen.

The ferry terminal sat square in downtown Port Angeles, and the waiting ferry was smaller than Jess remembered, gray with black and red trim, already loading cars through a massive doorway in its stern. Jess double-checked she had her passport as Rengo pulled over in the drop-off lane, and then she swapped a look with Rengo that seemed to convey enough for the both of them. Neither spoke as she pushed the door open and stepped from the car, turning back only to tell Lucy goodbye and scratch behind her ears, promise she'd try to be home by nightfall.

Then she was walking away and into the little terminal and buying her ticket, wondering what the hell she was doing and hoping Burke and Rengo were right about Jana Marsh. Knowing that whatever she was able to accomplish in the Great White North could make the difference between Burke dying in prison or ever breathing free air again in his life.

No pressure.

Jess spent the ferry ride—an hour and a half—gazing out the window, the ocean an impossible blue and not even the barest trace of a cloud in the sky.

It was still midmorning by the time Jess cleared Canadian customs, walked out of the terminal into downtown Victoria, and hailed a taxi for the neighboring community of Oak Bay. She'd never been to Victoria before, but she'd seen Jana's Facebook posts, and she knew to expect wealth. The streets were wide and tree-lined, with generous-sized lots and large houses, almost mansions but without the pretense that word would suggest. The community was quiet; kids played in yards and parks; cars drove slowly. It seemed to Jess like a lovely place to be, if you could somehow find the money to afford the cost of entry.

Jess had learned that Ronnie Marsh worked in some kind of technical industry. Computers—the specifics didn't make much sense to Jess, and she supposed they didn't matter. What mattered was that he would be at an office today and not at his home. The kids—two boys, beaming and blond, from what she'd seen on Facebook—would be at school.

The home in question was tucked into an odd-shaped lot at the end of a cul-de-sac, isolated from the neighbors by tall trees and a hedgerow and a wrought-iron gate. Jess unlatched the gate, pushed it open. Found herself in a front garden: a fishpond, a hidden waterfall burbling, a curved path of raw stone leading up to the front door.

The house was another one of those Pacific Northwest fantasies that seemed to have missed Makah County, Brock Boyd's estate notwithstanding. It was low and boxy, expanses of glass and steel and wood, not so much a part of the landscape as it was built on top of it. Maybe there was a symmetry between this house and Boyd's. Or maybe Jess and Burke and the rest of Makah County had simply been caught up in some rich people's deadly game.

She climbed to the front door and rang the doorbell and waited. After a minute or two, she heard the lock disengage, and the door swung open. And Jana Marsh stood behind it, smiling out at Jess vaguely, as though she recognized Jess but just couldn't quite place her.

"Jana Marsh," Jess said. "I'm Jess Winslow. Makah County sheriff's deputy. Can I come in?"

FIFTY-TWO

Jana Marsh was beautiful, in a way that spoke to wealth of both money and time. She wore a cream-colored sweater that looked as soft as a cloud, form-fitting jeans that might well have cost as much as Jess's entire wardrobe. Her makeup and hair were flawless, though she was home alone in the middle of the day. She ought to have radiated serenity, the same calming vibe of her garden, with its babbling waterfall and artful seclusion.

But Jana Marsh was scared, Jess could tell. She watched the woman's features harden at the mention of Makah County, her grip tighten on the frame of the door.

"You're a long way from home, Deputy," Jana said.

She was striving for an attitude that Jess knew well, that comfortable kind of airiness that money brought to the equation. But the tremor in her voice betrayed her; she just couldn't pull it off, and Jess knew in that instant that Burke had been right to ask her to come here. This woman knew something about Brock Boyd's demise that very few others did.

Jess looked Jana Marsh in the eye. "Brock Boyd," she said, trying to sound more in control than she felt. "I have a feeling you just might be able to tell me who killed him."

The other woman didn't reply, not at first. She stayed stiff in the doorway and looked away from Jess's eyes, stared out into the front yard beyond her as if there might be any kind of absolution there. She seemed to be weighing her options, and Jess knew that this moment was pivotal; she wasn't here on behalf of Sheriff Hart or any other arm of the law, and Jana Marsh would be well within her rights to kick her off the porch.

But Jess hoped she could bluff her way into the house. Into this woman's story. "Invite me in, Mrs. Marsh," she said. "You'll find it easier to talk to me than the Mounties."

Jana stared out at the trees for another moment. The hedgerow, the blue skies. The burbling pond. Then her shoulders seemed to slump, and she turned, wordless, and led Jess into the house.

———

The house had never quite felt like home. Not in all of the years Jana Marsh had lived here.

It was beautiful, of course; it had cost Ronnie a fortune when they bought it and was worth even more now. She'd come to appreciate the way the sun filled the kitchen with light and streamed down through the skylights above the living room and the master bedroom. She appreciated the calm that came with living in secret, behind hedgerows and gates and double-locked front doors. She liked that nobody knew her name here, except as Ronnie's wife, and that nobody here had ever heard of Levi "Broomstick" Cody and the things that had been done to him.

But she'd never felt at home here, and perhaps it was that this wasn't her hometown and wasn't even her country, that it wasn't her money that had purchased this place. Perhaps it was Ronnie and how he'd always been good enough, but no better. Perhaps it was her children and how when she looked at them she saw only the men like Brock Boyd who waited for them, out in the world.

Or perhaps it was that Jana could walk a couple of blocks to the beach in the morning and gaze out over the ocean and see the mountains in the distance, and know that if you followed those mountains west about as far as you were able, you'd come to Makah County and the ghosts that still haunted it, ghosts of a brother and of the sister who'd once idolized him, loved him more than just about anything else she could think of.

A sister who'd died almost as sure as her brother had when he'd jumped from that cliff. Who'd been replaced by a young woman defined at first by her grief and then later by her anger.

Who would only go back to Makah not to visit her ghosts but to avenge them.

She led the young sheriff's deputy through the house to the kitchen, where that bright midday sun shone in through oversized windows and the sliding door to the backyard, a tidy manicured lawn and Ronnie's putting green, a tipped-over tricycle, a soccer ball and a net.

Jana saw the house, the whole property, through the deputy's eyes, as though she'd never before in her life set foot in here. "How did you find me?" she asked.

She expected to hear that the men had ratted her out, the men she'd hired to help her and dispose of Brock Boyd, that they'd turned on her as she'd been afraid they would, but the deputy shrugged and said instead, "Your lipstick."

She explained how the investigators had searched Boyd's house, how they'd found the place immaculate, pristine, everything in its right place. Except—

"In his garbage can," Deputy Winslow said. "In the kitchen, sitting on top of his trash. A broken wineglass, Mrs. Marsh, about the only indication we had that he'd been entertaining a woman before he died."

It felt something like relief. Jana turned again, to look out through the windows at the sun and the lush green beyond, but it wasn't her backyard she was seeing.

FIFTY-THREE

He poured the wine in front of the fireplace. The house was beautiful, of course, but Jana had known that already, and she supposed there was something beautiful about Boyd too; she could certainly see he was an attractive man, how it might not be so unusual to him that a woman from a bar — a stranger — would be willing to come home with him, to sleep with him.

She'd followed him long enough that she felt confident she knew his movements. His routines, his predilections. She knew that he liked to drink at the Cobalt, raise hell in a back-corner booth with a rotating collection of acolytes and hangers-on, drink until near closing, and then stagger out to his fancy Cadillac truck and try his damndest to navigate the couple of miles back to his house without swerving into a tree or running anyone over.

It was in the parking lot of the Cobalt that she'd found him, bourbon on his breath a testament to another good night, the lot half filled with cars but devoid of humanity, Boyd just zipping up his fly after pissing nearly all over his truck and his boots besides.

His eyes swam some when he saw her; he leered and reached for the hood of his truck for balance. She'd come out of the shadows and pretended to just recognize him, pretended she was on her way somewhere else. Let him succeed, in his clumsy, near incoherence, to believe he'd seduced her.

He'd seemed to sober up some by the time they reached his house, and to his credit, he didn't rush her. He asked for her coat and hung it away for her, *made no secret of his appreciation of her figure as he followed her into the great room, built a fire for them, and poured wine.*

He asked her to sit on the couch, and she sat, and he sat near her but not too near, patient despite the clear hunger in his eyes.

She wondered then if the men she had paid had followed her as they'd promised, if they'd managed to sneak around the gate in Boyd's driveway, if they were outside right now and preparing for what must come next.

She wondered if she was dreaming, if this was really going to happen.

She'd waited such a long time to do this.

She had watched her brother die over time, gradually, like how sometimes the tide came in and you weren't aware until it was lapping at your toes. She wondered, often, later, if there was something she would have done if she'd realized what she was seeing. If there was any way she could have saved him.

She was never sure what had marked the tipping point, but she knew it had started with that trip to Olympia. If she thought back on it, he might have been paler when he came home, might have seemed a little more hollow when she looked in his eyes, but she'd had her own life to contend with and hadn't paid much attention. It was only when the nickname started to spread that she noticed how worn down he looked.

"Broomstick."

Her brother couldn't go anywhere without hearing it. Certainly not school, and nowhere after, either. At home, he stopped eating; even she noticed that. He spent long hours in his room, and he pretended to be sick so he wouldn't have to go to school. Still, he never missed a hockey game, never a practice. He never let the boys on the team see how they'd hurt him.

The Makah Screaming Eagles won the state championship that year. Brock Boyd was named the most valuable player, as he had been every year since he first laced up skates. Levi played well in the finals; she was there. She cheered for him even as the crowd jeered whenever he touched the puck, as mockery and ridicule rained down from the stands. She flushed bright red and nearly burst into tears; frustrated, she wanted to storm out of the arena.

When he came home, he told her he didn't hear the catcalls, that it didn't matter. They'd won the game and were champions, the whole team.

She didn't understand the nickname. Not until afterward, when she read the note. She knew only that Levi was somehow different and that it seemed like the entire county was laughing at him.

Afterward, she understood.

She believed that what her brother had written, and what he did after, would mean that Bad Boyd wouldn't play hockey anymore. She imagined there would be some reverberation, the county looking inward and confronting its failings.

She screamed for justice, but her voice was weak. Boyd continued to play hockey, and continued to win. The county continued to idolize him.

He went away and became famous, the pride of Makah. She stayed behind and remembered how her brother had faded. How he'd come home from Olympia and wasted away. How the nickname Boyd had given him had followed him everywhere, a chorus, a constant reminder of what must have been the most terrifying and traumatic moment of his life.

She stayed and grew older until there weren't more than two or three people in the whole county who could recall Levi's name.

She grew, and she expected the pain to dull. She expected the anger to cool. But the pain didn't dull, and the anger burned hot. She remembered her brother, and she remembered Brock Boyd.

She'd been waiting for this night in front of the fireplace since the moment Levi jumped.

Finally, there she was, sharing a couch and a bottle of wine with the man who'd been the focal point of her hate for years, and she felt her pulse racing and her thoughts racing too, her whole body rebelling at the prospect of what she'd come here to do, while her mind urged her onward at a dizzying speed.

She hoped the men were outside and she hoped they would come soon. And at the same time, she wished she had never come back to Makah County at all.

Boyd offered her wine, which she drank, hoping the alcohol would calm her, give her strength. And then of course she dropped the glass, after barely a sip; sent it crashing to the floor and spilling wine everywhere.

If Boyd was angry, he didn't show it. He laughed and went off for some paper towels, tidied up the mess and brought the broken glass to the kitchen, and when he returned, Jana was standing, purse in hand, and she asked him if he would show her the balcony, if they could stand above the cliff face and look out at the sea.

FIFTY-FOUR

In the kitchen, Jess watched Jana Marsh blink, shake her head clear, come back from wherever it was she'd gone. Jess could see how her hands were shaking, how the skin on her knuckles got whiter and whiter as she gripped the countertop.

"You know what Boyd did to my brother?" Jana asked.

Jess nodded. "I heard the stories."

"They weren't just *stories*." Jana's eyes flashed. "Stories are what you tell your friends around the campfire. This was..." She trailed off, lost something for a moment and then seemed to find it again. "What Boyd did to Levi, that killed him. Sure as if he'd pushed him off that cliff himself."

"It was a horrible thing, what he did," Jess replied. "Unimaginable."

"You don't think Boyd deserved it?" Jana asked. "What he did to my brother, what he did to those dogs, you don't think the world's better off without someone like that?"

Jess leaned against the countertop beside Jana. "Of course I do," she said. "I'm not losing any sleep over Brock Boyd being dead. If circumstances were different, I'd be applauding you. It's just—"

Jess dug into her jeans for her phone. Swiped to a photo she'd saved: Burke, smiling, on the breakwater that protected the Deception Cove boat basin, Lucy beside him, and the sun shining on the water. It hurt Jess to look too hard at it, knowing how he was back in Deception, in her jail, waiting on her to get him freed.

"You see this guy here?" she asked Jana. "He's in jail right now because they think he's the killer. And that's the man I love."

She looked at the phone some more, the picture, and she could smell the low-tide brine and hear the gulls call, see Burke smiling about the happiest smile she'd ever seen from him, like everything he'd ever wanted in the world was before him and there was nothing else he could ever think of needing.

You. Me. Lucy. That's it.

Jess could hear Burke saying it, every time she saw the picture. She wondered how Jana Marsh could look at the photograph and not see who Burke was and what he meant to the world, to Jess and to Lucy. How she could not want to go back to Makah and set things right.

Jana studied the phone but didn't take it from Jess. "They told me he was just some nobody," she said. "Just some greasy ex-con from back east. They said nobody would care if it came out like he'd done it."

" 'They,' " Jess said.

"The men who killed Boyd," Jana said. "Because I didn't do it." Then her expression turned hard, and she looked away again.

"I didn't shoot Boyd," she said, "and that's the honest truth. And I swore I'd never tell who did."

FIFTY-FIVE

At first, Jana was too torn with grief, too young and heartbroken. She was younger than Levi; she was twelve when he jumped, and barely understood what had happened.

But the stories lingered, after he'd gone. The punch lines. The nickname. Even after her brother was dead, there were still people in Makah who called him "Broomstick." Who still laughed about Levi, when they thought she couldn't hear. And Bad Boyd kept playing, and the county celebrated him.

Of course there were plenty in Makah who regretted what Boyd and his teammates had done, how far the hazing had been allowed to go. A few of Levi's teammates showed up at the Cody house, tearful; they tried to apologize, tried to explain themselves. And even young Jana could see their suffering, how they were lost. How they would carry with them what they'd done for the rest of their lives.

But not Boyd.

She hoped the dogfighting and the trouble that followed would lead to some karmic retribution. She read about the proceedings with interest, the grisly details and the public indignation. She expected that someone—a dog lover, an angry anonymous angel—might do to Boyd what she knew he deserved. Maybe in prison, a fight. It wouldn't matter if his death had no tie to Levi. Just so long as he suffered.

But Boyd survived prison, and by many accounts he'd been as much a celebrity on the inside as he'd been on the outside. Even the fact that he'd

*murdered dogs didn't hurt him. As far as Jana could tell, Bad Boyd was
going to coast through life bringing harm and unhappiness to others, and
profiting without consequence while he did.*

*It was when she learned that Boyd was to be released from prison,
that he planned to return to Makah County, that Jana realized she
couldn't wait for someone else to administer the punishment she knew
he deserved.*

It was then that she began to formulate her plan.

Now Jana could see how there was still a chance she might make
it out clean.

The law didn't seem to know about the men she'd hired. They
had tracked her here by the lipstick she'd left on Boyd's wineglass,
not by the testimony of the killers. The men she'd paid, who'd
taken her money and promised to make things right, and followed
her to Boyd's house.

As long as they didn't know about the men, Jana thought, she
might still survive.

She regarded the young deputy across the kitchen countertop.
"You don't have jurisdiction here," she said, with renewed strength
in her voice. "You can't prove I was involved with anything more
than a glass of wine. Everything else is circumstantial."

She swiped back through the phone to the picture of the
handsome, rugged man whom the deputy claimed to love.

The deputy took the phone and studied it for a beat, and then—
reluctantly, it seemed—she slid the phone back into the pocket
of her jeans.

"Jana—" she began.

Jana cut her off. "It's time for you to go, Deputy," she said,
pushing away from the countertop. "My children will be home
soon, and I don't want you here when they come."

The deputy straightened too. At her full height, she was taller than Jana by a couple of inches. It wasn't much, but it was something, and Jana tried to hold the other woman's gaze and prayed she would leave.

Finally, Winslow nodded. "Fine," she said.

FIFTY-SIX

"**One more question:** Do you know who Charlene Todd is?" Jess asked Jana Marsh as they reached the front door.

"I don't," Jana replied, "and I mean that. So whatever else you're thinking of accusing me of, I can promise you, you're wrong."

She was still scared; Jess could tell. She was afraid but trying to hide it behind bluster and aggression. But Jess wasn't intimidated. Nor was she convinced that Jana Marsh hadn't killed Brock Boyd.

The only thing Jess could think of was to keep Jana talking. Hopefully pry some more information out of her. She pulled out her phone again. Swiped to a new picture, and handed it to Jana.

Jana looked at the picture and her eyes went wide. "What are you—" she said. "Why are you showing me this?"

She tried to turn away. Jess wouldn't let her. Held the phone up, the autopsy photo, held it steady in front of Jana's eyes so she could see, really see, what had happened to Charlene Todd.

"You ought to look at it, and look close, if you ask me," she told Jana. "If you choose to kill a man, you'd better be prepared for the ramifications."

"I told you," Jana said. "I didn't kill Boyd. And you'll never prove—"

"I don't believe you," Jess said. "Take a look."

The photographs were horrifying. Jess knew that. Charlene Todd's throat was slashed wide open, and the lighting in Doc

Trimble's autopsy room didn't conceal any details. Jana Marsh looked like she wanted to be sick.

"That's Charlene Todd," Jess told her. "She lied and told the sheriff a story about how she heard my friend Mason Burke kill Brock Boyd. And then somebody cut her throat."

Jana pushed the phone away. This time Jess didn't press it. "The law thinks Burke killed her," she said. "Retribution or something. But Burke's a good man, no matter what your accomplices think. I know Charlene was killed so she wouldn't change her story, and I know it was someone named Chris Jordan who did it.

"And I know Jordan did it," Jess told Jana, "to protect *you*."

Jana Marsh didn't say anything. She looked back toward the kitchen, the sunlight through the windows. Finally she shook her head.

"I have a life here," she said softly. "A husband." She let out a breath, and then she looked up and met Jess's eyes, and her gaze was as hard as steel, something fierce and determined. "I'm sorry about your friend. I really am. And I'm sorry about . . . Charlene."

"You can't get out of this," Jess said. "It's too——"

"You can't prove anything," Jana interrupted. "All you have is a wineglass and some half-cocked theories. That's not nearly enough to sway a judge and jury, and if you think you can guilt me with your pictures into confessing, you're fooling yourself. Brock Boyd deserved what happened to him. Hell, he deserved more."

The posh, put-on affectations were gone. She was Jana Cody now, speaking direct from Makah County.

Jess let it sit there. Let Jana stew in what she'd said, let her words echo around this big fancy house, this tidy life. There was no appealing to her sympathy, not as it related to Burke or even Charlene Todd. Jess knew she'd played it wrong, trying to key on the other woman's remorse.

Remorse wouldn't turn Jana Marsh; her anger had burned too hot, for too long, to let sympathy cool her. But Jess had one more bullet to fire.

"Well, I want you to think about something," she said.

Jana sighed, impatient, shifted her weight as if to shuffle Jess out the door.

Jess held up her hand. "No, hear me out," she said. "This is something you'll care about."

Jana looked at her.

"Chris Jordan is dead," Jess told her. She hadn't talked this part over with Burke and Rengo and Hank Moss.

"But *I* know neither Jordan nor that joker he ran with, Bealing, was smart enough to pull off a scheme like this on their own. And I know you wouldn't trust a couple of no-account hillbillies with a job so big."

Jana Marsh said nothing. Her eyes drifted to the pictures on the walls, two beautiful boys. Cherubs, bright and beaming and innocent.

"A man named Logger Fetridge tried to kill me the other day," Jess told Jana. "Him and his buddy, a guy called Dax Pruitt. They're the type I could make for an operation like this one, you know?" She paused. "And the real funny thing is, Logger Fetridge is Chris Jordan's kin."

Jana still didn't say anything, kept studying the pictures on the wall.

"Wake up," Jess told her. "You're either ahead of this thing or behind it. It won't be long before we're hauling in Pruitt and Fetridge on charges that have nothing to do with Bad Boyd or your brother. But how long do you think, Jana, before they start looking to bargain? You think they won't sell you out to save their own asses? You want to spend the next twenty years watching your boys grow up from behind prison glass, Jana? Is that what you want?"

The other woman still hadn't responded. But her attitude shifted, her posture. The defiance that had been there a moment ago was defeated, the confidence gone.

"Now," Jess said, pushing forward, "you want to tell me who really killed Brock Boyd? Or you want to wait until someone tries to make you for the whole sorry affair?"

FIFTY-SEVEN

On the balcony, Boyd put his arm around her. It was cold out, and Jana was shivering, but the wine was working or maybe she was just getting used to the idea that this was the man she would help to kill tonight.

Maybe it was the balcony, the view, knowing that her brother would have seen something similar, although in daylight and a few miles farther west, before he'd jumped. Maybe it was the feeling that Boyd had pushed Levi there, and appreciation of the irresistible symmetrical possibility of ending Boyd's life in a similar spot.

Or maybe it was just how Boyd reached for her and held her, self-assured and without hesitation. He'd always been given what he wanted. He assumed Jana was yet more of the same.

She sensed movement behind her, and she pulled Boyd closer. He smelled of sandalwood, bourbon, and cigar smoke, of sweat and the dank, mildewed Cobalt; his hands reached for her and slid across her body over her dress. She could sense the hunger in his touch, and the entitlement, which made her hate him more.

Then she felt Boyd go rigid against her. He'd been touching her, pulling her closer, mumbling something in her ear that was supposed to be seductive. As he tensed, she pulled away from him and knew this was the moment she'd planned for.

Boyd was looking over her shoulder, and Jana knew that if she turned to follow his gaze she would see the man she'd paid to be here.

She moved fully away, left Boyd alone on the edge of the balcony as the man with the gun stepped neatly around her, aiming the revolver at Boyd's head and staying far enough back that Boyd couldn't make a move against him.

The dogfighter stood in half shadow, only partway lit from the light inside his house. What she could see of his features betrayed confusion, then anger; never fear. His lip curled and his eyes glinted steel and he looked at the gun and the man holding it, and he seemed to have forgotten she was there.

"What the fuck is this?" Boyd asked. "Are you trying to fucking rob me?"

The man with the gun didn't say anything, but he nodded slightly in Jana's direction, and Boyd slowly turned to follow. He glared at her, and she could see how he saw her, how she was less than human in his eyes, just a toy to be played with, could imagine his frustration that he would never get the chance.

"What is this?" he asked her. "What the fuck?"

She exhaled, knowing this was the moment she would replay in her head for as long as she lived.

"Levi Cody," she said.

Boyd's brow furrowed. There was no recognition in his eyes, no epiphany. He couldn't remember her brother's name.

She took a step forward and wanted to hit him. Didn't.

"Broomstick, you fucker," she said.

Then she nodded to the man with the gun, and the man with the gun pulled the trigger.

FIFTY-EIGHT

Jess helped Jana Marsh concoct a cover story. For her husband and her boys. For the after-school babysitter she called, last minute, in a rush.

There was an afternoon ferry that Jess wanted to catch. Back across to Port Angeles, then west into Makah County. They would take Jana's Land Rover, but Jess would be driving.

She'd listened to Jana's story. All of it. Watched how Jana had seemed to become lighter in the telling, physically and mentally both. She stood straighter and wore relief on her face after she'd finished, as plainly obvious as her lipstick.

Jana hadn't named the men who'd helped her kill Brock Boyd, but she'd agreed to come with Jess. She'd agreed to tell the sheriff her story, and she'd agreed to tell who it was she'd hired to kill Boyd, but only on conditions. She had to know that she'd still be charged, that she wouldn't ever walk away from this scot-free, but she must've known, too, that sooner or later the law was going to catch up to Logger Fetridge and Dax Pruitt, and that she'd be better off telling *her* story to the sheriff first, before the men had the opportunity to speak out against her.

Jess figured Sheriff Hart would have his own opinion about Jana's stipulations, but she knew that getting the suspect across the border was a good start in and of itself.

If nothing else, she might free Burke by doing this. And beyond that, nothing else really mattered.

There was a cafeteria on the ferry, but Jess spent the entire ride on the afterdeck beside Jana Marsh, keeping an eye on the woman in case she decided she'd rather jump off the stern than let Jess take her home to Makah County.

But Jana didn't move. She stood stoic at the railing and stared out at the water, and did not say much to Jess as they waited. Jess wondered what she was thinking, whether she knew this was probably the last ferry ride she'd be taking for a while. Whether she even cared, now that Bad Boyd was dead.

The Land Rover was a nice truck. Leather seats, heated steering wheel, a GPS-based navigational map in the center of the dashboard. It was dark by the time they drove off the ship in Port Angeles. Jess's stomach growled. She knew Port Angeles pretty well, but she still followed the lines on the map as she drove the SUV away from the ferry terminal toward the state road, headed west.

There was apparently satellite radio in the Land Rover too, but Jess kept that turned off. She and Jana rode in silence.

They drove out of Port Angeles on empty highway and passed through Clallam Bay a short time later, and then they were nearing Makah County and the spot where the billboard with Brock Boyd's face would have been. Jess slowed the Land Rover and peered into the trees at the edge of the road until she found her turn, a little dirt path cut through the pines to a clearing on the opposite side.

The Land Rover made short work of the dirt and the bumps; Jess could tell it had been built for the hard stuff, heated steering wheel notwithstanding. In the clearing sat an old wooden gillnetter, all faded paint and rotten wood like everything else in this part of the world.

The boat was called *Esperanza,* "hope" in Spanish. Jess couldn't decide if that was an omen. Certainly the boat itself looked like it had run through its fill of hope, and then some.

Jess parked the Land Rover and checked her phone, but there was no reception here. She killed the engine and sat and looked out at the boat, and listened through the trees for the sound of cars on the highway, waiting for the sheriff to arrive.

They didn't have to wait long. Hart pulled into the clearing in his Makah County Super Duty, parked behind the Land Rover as Jess reached for her door handle.

"Come on," she told Jana, and if there was the slightest bit of hesitation before Jana followed, it wasn't much. She kept her head high as she exited the truck, chin forward and her expression blank.

The sheriff climbed from his truck and took in the Land Rover. Made a noise in his throat like he was impressed. He came up to meet Jess and Jana at the front of his truck, looked Jana over.

"You want to tell me what we're doing out here, Jess?" he asked. "Why you called me all the way out of my jurisdiction with the whole county going to hell?"

"Sheriff, this is Jana Marsh," she told Hart. "Maiden name's Cody."

Hart looked at Jana some more.

"Cody," he said. "I seem to recall we've got a Linda Cody out in Neah Bay. You're related?"

"My mother," Jana said. "Levi Cody was my brother."

She said it as though Hart might know who he was, and from the look on his face, Hart didn't, and it was how Jana'd said it that made Jess feel rotten.

"Sheriff," she said, "Jana's got a story to tell you. And she'll come back to Makah County and confess to her role in Brock Boyd's murder, but I told her you'd listen to her first."

Hart looked from Jana to Jess and back again. His eyes goggled.

"She?" he said to Jess. Then, to Jana: "You're going to tell me, once and for all, how it was Bad Boyd was murdered?"

Jana barely tilted her head: *Yes.*

"Well, heck," Hart said. "If that's the case, then sure; I'd be glad to listen to your story, Mrs. Marsh."

FIFTY-NINE

"I want immunity," Jana said. "I'll give you as much as I can on the men who killed Bad Boyd, but I don't want to go to jail."

Hart snorted. "You're not getting immunity," he said.

They'd reconvened in Hart's county truck. Hart at the wheel, Jana riding shotgun. Jess perched on the middle seat in the back, listening to the conversation. Trying to keep from wondering about Burke.

"You set up Boyd to be killed, and you'll have to do your time for it," Hart said. "But I'd be willing to go to bat for you with the prosecutor if you can give me the names of the men who pulled the trigger."

Jana didn't reply. Hart met Jess's eyes in the rearview.

"That's all I can offer you, Mrs. Marsh," Hart said. "But whether or not you want to help me, you've still got to know you can't walk away from this now."

Jana sat stone-still for a minute or two, and Jess wondered what was going through her head, whether she regretted letting Jess bring her back here, whether she'd always kind of known it was going to end this way.

Then Jana cleared her throat. "That's fine," she said. And before Hart could say anything else, she told him in a clear, calm voice how she'd come to find the men who would murder Brock Boyd for her.

She'd been waiting in the pick-up line outside her sons' school when she learned how Boyd was to be released from prison, how he planned to return to Makah County, to the house where the dogs had been made to fight, the house that looked out over the water. The article was small, two or three paragraphs, but Jana read it maybe fifty times, sitting behind the steering wheel of that Land Rover, oblivious to the children who'd piled into her car, to the horns blaring outside, behind her.

She tried to keep her anger hidden. From her husband, her children. From her new friends in Victoria, who knew her only as another mom, an American transplant, a reliable carpool with a handsome husband and a beautiful home, a weakness for Italian reds. She took pains not to mention her brother's name around them, lest her eyes or the tremor in her voice betray how she still grieved. How the anger burned in her, a fire that seemed only to grow with time.

She went back to Deception Cove intent on killing Boyd herself. Rode the ferry over from Canada on the pretense that she was visiting her mother, and spent her time instead looking for Boyd.

He was easy to find. That gaudy truck, and the crowd that seemed to follow him everywhere. He stopped her dead-cold, the first time she saw him: tall and rugged and lean, those sharp, cruel eyes, the mocking smile.

She hung back from Boyd, always out of his line of sight. Always a few steps away from the athlete and his entourage, always hidden in a doorway, behind someone's parked car. She didn't know how she would kill him, didn't own a weapon, but she knew she had to do it.

After she'd followed him around for a few days, she drove back to Port Angeles. Bought a ten-inch carving knife from the Super K, paid cash. Then she drove back to Deception Cove, got drunk at the Cobalt, and waited for Boyd.

———————

"So that's what I did," Jana told Jess and the sheriff. "I got a booth in the corner, and I drank until all I could see was my brother's face in the bottom of the glass. And Boyd came in like he always did, got drunk and raised hell like he owned the place, and when he was good and shit-faced, he left to drive home, and I paid my tab and I followed him out."

"Boyd was shot," Hart replied. "You said you didn't have a gun."

Jana said, "I'm getting to that, Sheriff." And then she told him how she'd followed Boyd to the parking lot, out to that Cadillac truck. How she'd slipped the knife out as she approached him, nobody else around. How she'd hoped he would turn around, see her, look into her eyes.

How she'd hoped he would recognize her, but he didn't.

He never turned around.

"I couldn't do it," Jana said. "He was bigger than I'd expected he'd be, up close like that. Stronger. I knew there was a chance I wouldn't actually kill him, not with that knife. And I wanted to be sure, when I did it."

"So you let him go," Hart said.

Jana nodded. "I let him go," she said. "Boyd never even knew I was there."

———————

She wound up inside the Cobalt again. Couldn't remember walking back through the door, couldn't remember much more than the back of Boyd's head and his brake lights, disappearing into the night.

It was Dax Pruitt who found her. Pruitt, who ambled up to the bar beside her, three fingers raised to the bartender, another round. Who met her eyes in the mirror behind the bar and then kept looking at her, even after she turned back to her whiskey.

She ignored him, knowing he was waiting for her to look up again, knowing he had some stupid line he was itching to try, hating to give him the satisfaction.

Wishing he would just leave her alone with the knowledge that she could have killed Boyd, but she didn't even try.

"Say," he said finally, after he'd figured out that she wasn't aching for eye contact, "aren't you Jana Cody?"

She might have lied to him, or she might have just told him to go ahead and fuck off, but she didn't do either; she looked up, slow, and met his eyes in the mirror.

"Marsh," she said. "It's Jana Marsh now."

But she was lying. Her passport may have said Marsh, and her driver's license, but she was a Cody still. Just not a very good one, not tonight. Not with Bad Boyd yet breathing.

"Well, holy shit," Pruitt said, holding his hand outstretched. Introducing himself, telling her, in case she didn't remember, how she'd gone to high school with his youngest brother, how they'd maybe partied all together a couple of times. "What the hell are you doing in a place like this, Jana Marsh?" he asked. "Hell, what are you doing in Deception?"

She'd come back to the Cobalt, she remembered, to forget. What she could have done outside to Bad Boyd, and she didn't. What Boyd had done to her brother, to her family. She'd come back to drink until she couldn't see straight, until she remembered nothing. Until she didn't care whether she lived or died.

Instead, the drink had done the opposite. It had strengthened her memories and strengthened her courage, to do what she'd come to do the next time she saw Boyd. And Jana Cody was drunk enough at that point that it didn't seem to matter who knew about it; hell, they were all going to find out soon enough anyway. So when Pruitt asked her what she was doing in Deception, she met his eyes in the mirror and didn't shy away from it.

"I came here to kill a man," she told him, and when she spoke the words, she knew there was no going back.

SIXTY

"I'd come prepared to go to jail," Jana told Hart and Jess as they sat in Hart's truck beside the beached troller *Esperanza*. "When I came over from Victoria to kill him, I knew that was the end, and I believed I'd be okay with it. I'd have avenged my brother, and there was nothing else I needed to do in this world."

Jess said, "Your kids."

"My husband," Jana replied. "They love him, and he loves them. More than anything. I knew they'd be provided for." She paused, looked out through the windshield, and Jess wondered what she was thinking. "I'd made my peace with it."

"But Dax Pruitt and Logger Fetridge convinced you otherwise," Hart said. "They told you they could kill Boyd and you'd walk away clean."

"Twenty thousand dollars," Jana said. "Boyd would be dead and I'd get what I wanted. And nobody would ever know what we'd done."

She twisted in her seat, glanced back at Jess, who sat still in the darkness. "I didn't know they were going to frame your boyfriend for it," she said. "That wasn't part of the plan. Or that they would kill . . . that woman."

No, Jess thought. *You just expected you would pay your money and everything would be taken care of. You could just wipe your hands clean and never think about Brock Boyd — or Makah County — again.*

She didn't say anything, though, and neither did Hart, or Jana for that matter. The time stretched until it was almost tangible, a blanket laid over the top of the truck and enveloping all three who were inside it. And when Hart sighed and shifted, Jess knew that whatever he was about to say would break the spell and remove the blanket, that time would start to turn over again, and there was no way to stop it.

"I didn't know about your brother," Hart said to Jana. "I'm not from Makah County, and where I'm from, we didn't…" He paused. "The news didn't make it that far, I suppose."

Jana didn't say anything. She sat still, as she had done all afternoon. Like she was waiting for fate to reward her or punish her.

"I'm sorry that it happened," Hart continued. "I've known men to do things that way, whether schoolkids or deputies. I know how cruel we can be, and sometimes we don't recover."

Jess had never known Levi Cody, but she remembered the stories. Remembered how a boy from Neah Bay had died by suicide—not the first and certainly not the last. She'd known the nickname that had followed him even after he was gone.

"I guess what I'm saying is I understand why you did it," Hart told Jana. "But that doesn't mean I can just ignore that you did. You understand that, right?"

Wordless, Jana nodded.

Hart exhaled. "Okay," he said. "So how about you tell me something that'll help me track down Logger Fetridge and Dax Pruitt, and we'll see if that can't help your case a little bit."

———

Mason had been sitting in that holding cell all day, and he wondered how much longer he would have to sit here. Had Jess made it to

Canada, had she found Jana Marsh, had she made it back yet, had she convinced her to talk?

He wondered if this entire situation was going to land on his head after all.

Mason had had confidence in the plan when he walked into the Deception Cove detachment that morning. It was a Hail Mary, but he'd liked their odds, knew Jess was sharp and there was a good chance she'd find out something from Jana Marsh that might exonerate him.

But now?

Now, pushing twelve hours in this little box, a couple of tray meals of white-bread cheese sandwiches, baby carrots, and milk delivered with indifference by Paul Monk and Mitch Derry, the sound of a clock ticking somewhere, the intermittent squawk of a radio—now Mason had had plenty of time to rethink his decision. He'd had time enough to come up with more than a few reasons why turning himself in was the stupidest thing he'd done in a good long while.

But there was no changing what he'd done. He would sit here and hope that Jess could get him out of it. Hope that Hart had sense enough to listen to her. Hope, sometime soon, he'd be a free man again.

The door to the detachment opened, somewhere around the corner and out of sight of Mason's eyes. He'd been listening to it open and close all day, Monk and Derry ducking in and out, Hart, a couple of the state policemen. The troopers had come into the back here to look at him, studied Mason as if he were an insect pinned inside a display window, some kind of rare curiosity.

They were young men, and bored, and this case was a change for them. They looked in at Mason and pretended to be brave, kidded each other and jostled and told themselves he didn't look half as mean as he was supposed to be.

They spoke about Mason as though he wasn't there, and Mason ignored them, knowing they were young, as he'd been young too: desperate to prove his manhood, show the world he wasn't scared.

But this time when the detachment door opened, it wasn't the troopers returning for another look-see; it was Sheriff Hart. He carried a sheaf of papers in his hands, and when he looked at Mason, he looked at him thoughtfully. Waited for Mason to meet his eyes before he spoke.

"What I have here," he said, brandishing the papers, "is the autopsy report for Charlene Todd."

Mason watched Hart and wondered what this was about.

"Prevailing wisdom in these parts had you a slam dunk for Charlene's murder," Hart told him. "But I guess I just wasn't so sure. So I had Doc Trimble—that's the county coroner—really key in on the time of death, knowing that Ernie Saint Louis had watched you walk out of Charlene's room around quarter after eight in the evening."

Mason said nothing, though it seemed like Hart was waiting for some sort of reply. Finally Hart cleared his throat. Shuffled the papers.

"According to the good doctor," he said, "Charlene Todd had been dead nearly a full day before you walked out of her bedroom. And you don't seem like the kind of man, Burke, who'd stick around with a body that long."

"I figure you're probably right, Sheriff," Mason replied.

"We worked the crime scene pretty hard too," Hart continued. "Found fingerprints all over the room matching those belonging to a man named Chris Jordan. I believe you might have met him once or twice."

Jordan. Mason blinked and saw Jordan dying on the bare-steel deck of the *Amy Usen,* struggling for his breath and wheezing out the nickname that had sent Jess to Canada.

He kept his face noncommittal, for the sheriff's sake.

"What I'm saying, Mr. Burke, is that I don't think you killed Charlene Todd after all," Hart said.

Mason nodded. "Well, that's good. Because I don't think I killed her either." He studied the sheriff. "But that's not going to spring me for what happened to Bad Boyd, is it?"

Hart smiled, thin. "Not by itself," he said. "Yet."

Mason heard the detachment door swing open again. Heard a familiar jangle that he knew must be a dog collar, heard the hurricane *fwap* as Lucy shook out her ears. And then Lucy came around the corner, Rengo in tow, the dog straining on her leash and her tail going full helicopter as she saw Mason inside the cell. The dog leaped at the bars, straining and whining, and Mason stood and walked over to her, knelt and let her lick his face and paw at him.

Then he looked up and saw Jess behind Rengo, and behind her, Paul Monk and Mitch Derry leading a woman who must have been Jana Marsh toward the cells, her hands cuffed behind her back, but her chin high.

"I guess you talked to Jess already," Mason said.

Hart was already reaching for a key ring on his belt. "I guess I did," he replied. "And it seems to me she had a productive little vacation."

He unlocked the cell door, slid it open. Lucy was halfway inside before the door hit the wall. Rengo released the leash, and the dog bolted forward, jumped into Mason's arms and attacked him with slobbery kisses. Mason withstood the barrage, scratched Lucy plenty behind the ears, until finally the dog had calmed somewhat, and then he stood again and walked to the door, where Hart waited.

"No hard feelings, I hope," Hart said.

"None," Mason replied. "I'd have arrested me too, Sheriff."

"Good," Hart said. "Then come on out of there already. We'll be needing your cell."

The sheriff stepped aside so that Mason could exit, and Mason led the dog out just as Derry and Monk shepherded Jana Marsh inside in his place. Their eyes met briefly, Mason's and Jana's, and in the killer's eyes Mason saw nothing resembling remorse, saw acceptance of a kind he'd witnessed only rarely among the men he'd known inside, a kind of peace he'd never seen staring back at him in a mirror.

Then Jana Marsh was inside the cell and the sheriff was locking the door, and Mason was following Lucy toward where Jess waited, leaning against the wall in the hallway and watching him come near.

"You must be a hell of a cop," he told her. "And boy am I glad for it."

Jess smiled, but there was something behind it. "You did all the thinking," she said as the dog in between them scrambled for attention of her own. "I just put the pieces together."

SIXTY-ONE

But of course it wasn't over yet.

Burke was free to walk out of the detachment with his one hand in Jess's and his other holding Lucy's lead. By rights they could have turned toward the harbor and walked down to Joe Clifford's boat and spent the rest of their lives making love on the water, or they could have walked up the hill to Hank Moss's motel and done the same thing between the sheets of her bed.

And Jess wanted to do it.

But it wasn't ever going to be that easy.

There was still violence out there in Makah County. The men whom Jana Marsh had hired to kill Bad Boyd still lurked somewhere, at large, and neither Aaron Hart nor the state troopers had had any luck tracking them down.

"We started looking for Pruitt as soon as Burke told us what he'd done to you," Hart told Jess, with a helping of side-eye to tell her he wasn't entirely pleased that she hadn't reported the attempted kidnapping herself. "Best we can tell, though, Dax has flown the coop. His trailer's deserted, and his truck's missing too. Ditto for Logger Fetridge."

Jess was no longer a deputy; at least temporarily. Hart still had her badge and her gun, pending the investigation into the shooting deaths of Chris Jordan and Doug Bealing. But Hart still needed her help. She'd been up the mountains with Pruitt about farther than anyone, after all, and the sheriff was hoping she could point the way back.

They stood at a table in the center of the detachment, Jess and Sheriff Hart and Mason Burke and Lucy, Chris Rengo and Paul Monk and Mitch Derry and a couple of the troopers crowded in besides. On the table in front of them was a topographical map, Makah County, and Jess pointed to Shipwreck Point and told them how Pruitt had ambushed her there. Burke traced a line from the bridge where he'd found her, up Iron Creek, and into the low mountains.

"She came walking down from here," he told the sheriff. "So wherever we're looking, it ought to be close."

Hart pointed to a thin line on the map, winding south from the highway in line with the topography of the land.

"Pruitt likely took you up the number 12 line," the sheriff told Jess. "If it was Iron Creek you hiked down. You think?"

Jess didn't remember the ride, but she knew the 12 line well enough. "That road branches off pretty quick," she said. "Used to be about eight or nine spur trails running off the first five or so miles, logging tracks and mining runs. All of them abandoned now."

"So we figure they're holed up at the gnarly end of one of those trails," Hart said. "Now we've just got to figure out which one."

Easier said than done, Jess thought. The whole southern half of the county extended into those low mountains, and it was, all of it, crisscrossed with four-wheeler trails and abandoned roads, old timber camps and mine shafts and hermit emplacements, hundreds of miles and none of it well charted. If Fetridge and Pruitt were up there, Jess knew, they could be looking for months.

Paul Monk said, "Helicopter?"

But Hart shook his head. "Too much ground to cover," he said.

"Too much of a goose chase. We don't have the budget for a full-scale air assault, not if we don't know where they're hiding."

The room went silent. Men looked at each other. Jess caught Burke's eye, then quickly looked away. Not before she'd felt the spark, though, that bolt of painful electricity that reminded her how good they'd had it, and what they'd risked losing.

She could feel the heat rise in her face, and she hoped Burke and the other men weren't looking at her. Wished someone would say something, anything.

And then Jana Marsh spoke up from the holding cells.

"What's that you say, Mrs. Marsh?" Hart called.

A pause, and then Jana spoke up, louder.

"I said, Sheriff," her voice piercing the stillness of the detachment, "that if you're looking for Dax Pruitt and Logger Fetridge, you ought to try Lone Jack Trail."

SIXTY-TWO

Pruitt could sense the law coming. Still far down the mountain but climbing, steady and unrelenting, even as the light died above and the first stars began to show in the clear, moonless sky. A quiet night, and peaceful—it would have been almost pleasant were it not for the sense of foreboding that had settled over the camp.

The law was coming, and with it, the reckoning. Pruitt clutched his rifle tight, and listened and waited.

Fetridge had a fire going, at the mouth of the mine shaft. Apparently the old timber thief felt secure enough this far up the mountain to show an open flame to the world, and who could blame him? The county was vast and the sheriff's resources small. If anyone chanced upon them, it would be everyone's bad luck.

Fetridge was armed too; he kept a stockpile of weaponry in the old mine, long guns and small, and a mountain of ammunition. Pruitt wondered if his friend had always known this was coming, if he, perhaps, welcomed it. Certainly Fetridge didn't look scared as he contemplated the fire, slowly cleaning his rifle. He'd catch Pruitt looking now and then, flash him a smile, his eyes a maniac-wild in the glow of the flames.

"Just like old times," he told Pruitt. "Just you and me and the mountain."

Old times.

The old times, Pruitt figured, were why he was here. Why he

felt he owed something to Logger Fetridge he could never repay. Why he sat by the fire on this mountain instead of running to North Dakota, something better. Why he'd tried to kidnap Jess Winslow.

Old times, and the debt he'd accrued.

It had been one of Fetridge's timber-falling operations, years ago, dead-of-night stuff, outside the bounds of the law. Fetridge tended to operate alone when he poached, but sometimes he needed a hand. He asked Pruitt one night at the Cobalt if he needed a little cash and didn't mind getting dirty.

Pruitt had never minded getting dirty, and there wasn't a soul in Deception Cove who couldn't use a little more money. He agreed, and they met up later that night on some forestry road in the foot-hills, their trucks parked nose to nose outside a padlocked gate.

Pruitt never was really sure just whose timber Logger Fetridge had decided to poach that night, only that his friend seemed damned determined that it must be these particular trees, on this lot. He clipped the chain with a pair of strong bolt cutters, swung the gate open, and nosed his truck through, Pruitt riding shotgun, and they followed a rocky two-track along the contour of the land for maybe ten minutes, until they stopped, deep in the bush.

It was Pruitt's mistake, how it happened. He'd never felled trees before, and he wandered into the fall line, nearly got himself crushed when Fetridge made the cut, sent a beautiful old-growth cedar tumbling down almost on top of him.

He dived out of the way, but a branch knocked him down, pinned him to the earth, shattering his leg pretty bad in two spots, and left him howling and moaning and unable to move.

And it was about then that they heard the shotgun blast, some-where not too distant, and Pruitt could remember how Fetridge had looked stricken as his gaze shifted between Pruitt on the forest floor and the direction of the blast, and Pruitt could see how his friend was calculating, whether it didn't make more sense to just bail, save his own skin and leave Pruitt for the proverbial wolves.

Any man might have done it. Pruitt couldn't have even blamed him.

But Fetridge hadn't bailed. He stayed and turned the chainsaw on the branch that pinned Pruitt, worked feverishly to free him as the shotgun boomed again from the dark, and men's voices neared, shouting threats and warnings and punctuating every declaration with more buckshot.

Fetridge had stayed, and they'd fled from those woods together, Fetridge half carrying Pruitt to his truck, speeding them back down that two-track to the forestry road, the shotgun shooting off one more time behind them, a farewell and a final warning.

Pruitt had driven his own truck to the health center in Neah Bay, screaming in pain the entire twenty miles. And he and Logger Fetridge had never really talked about the mishap, except in that Pruitt believed Fetridge knew he could ask Pruitt for anything, that loyalty had been tested and found true on one side, and that one day it would come to Pruitt to return the favor.

Now, as Dax Pruitt sat by the fire high up Lone Jack Trail, he could feel the pain in his leg flaring up as it always did when he'd had a long day, and it throbbed in his thigh such that he could visualize the scar, jagged and angry and red, could imagine it glowing hot with implication. And he knew he was doing the right thing being up here with Fetridge.

Pruitt sat by the fire and held on to his rifle and thought about down the bottom of the trail, Deception Cove and the tidewater, and he wondered when the law would finally reach them.

Across the fire, Fetridge set the butt end of his rifle in the dirt and used it to push himself to his feet. His eyes met Pruitt's through the flames.

"They're coming," he told Pruitt, as if he'd read his mind. "But I don't reckon they're ready for the surprises we're about to give them when they get here."

He grinned at Pruitt. Circled the fire and reached down to Pruitt, his palm open. "Come on," he said. "Got us a few party favors for when they come roaring up that hill."

Pruitt looked at Fetridge's hand, dark with ash and dirt. At the gleam in the man's eye behind it. He hesitated, just a moment, but there was no sense in dawdling. You made your bed, and you slept in it.

He clasped Fetridge's hand in his own and let the poacher pull him to his feet.

SIXTY-THREE

She didn't sleep well.

Jess wished she could have spent the night cuddled up with Burke and Lucy, watching something mindless on the TV and making up for the time they'd lost. Better yet, she'd have liked to have joined Sheriff Hart and the other deputies.

It was Sheriff Hart himself who'd forbidden Jess from joining the raid, in the Deception Cove detachment the night previous, after Jana Marsh had called out the name of the Lone Jack mine, where she swore Logger Fetridge and Dax Pruitt were hiding.

"Too dark to go up there tonight," Hart had told the assembled, Mitch Derry already on the phone with Neah Bay, and the state troopers calling for backup of their own. "We'll have to get up there first thing tomorrow."

Then he'd turned to Jess.

"And by 'we,' I mean me and my deputies, Jess. Those of them who still carry a badge in good standing."

She'd stared at him, thinking that what they were planning was just about the only thing in the world she was good at, an early-morning hike through forbidding terrain, a sneak attack on an entrenched enemy position.

"In case you forgot, Sheriff," she said, "I was a US Marine. This is exactly the kind of stuff I was trained for."

Hart nodded. "And I'd love to have you, Jess. But if I let you walk into this while you're still on leave, it's your career on the line, and mine. Don't forget how those state boys are involved too."

"So what?" she said. "I'm better up there in those mountains than anyone else you've got, Sheriff, and you know it."

Hart sucked his teeth, and he looked at her. "Go home," he told her. "I mean it. You've got a real bright future in this county, Jess. Don't throw it away over a couple of bumpkin outlaws."

She wanted to fight him, her whole being screaming that this was the showdown, the climax, that she deserved to be here for it, that it just wasn't fair that she had to sit on the sidelines for the grand finale.

She wanted to tell him about Tyner Gillies and Chris Jordan and Doug Bealing. About the welt on her temple she bore from Dax Pruitt. About how she'd brought in Jana Marsh and how she'd made the connection between her and Jordan and Fetridge.

About how this was *her* goddamned bust.

But she didn't, and maybe it was because she knew the sheriff was right, or maybe it was just how Burke touched her arm just then, and Lucy nuzzled up beside her and found the palm of her hand with the top of her head. Jess closed her eyes and forced herself to understand that it didn't matter who put the handcuffs on Fetridge and Pruitt in the end. She'd proven herself a damn good deputy, and she'd cuff a good many more of these backwoods assholes before her career was through.

She'd exhaled through clenched teeth.

"Fine," she'd told the sheriff. "But I'm only standing down under protest."

By dawn, Jess had given up on trying to sleep. She kicked her legs free of the covers and swung her legs over and pulled on yesterday's jeans as Lucy stirred at the foot of the bed, looked up, sleepy, those ears perked.

She was listening for trouble, Jess knew. Studying Jess, her senses attuned to any sign of a panic attack, any hint of an episode. Waiting to see if she was needed.

She was a good dog, and she cared about Jess deeply.

Stretched out around Lucy, Burke lay asleep, his head tilted back, one arm stretched over his head. He was snoring softly, oblivious to her movement. She wondered what he was dreaming about, if he was content.

She watched him sleep, and she knew he was a good man, and that if he woke up and saw her awake, he would come and hold her and listen to her worries, and never think to burden her by telling her his own.

She didn't want to be held now, or comforted. It wasn't yet the time.

Jess walked instead. She slipped out of the motel room and into the parking lot as the daylight came and brought with it fog from out over the strait. To the east, the sun was shining and the world was still by and large bright, but the fog lent a chill and a muteness to the air. As Jess walked across the parking lot, it seemed as though she could be the only person alive in the world.

She walked west on the highway, away from the intersection with Main Street that led down into town, and toward the lights of the ARCO gas station a quarter mile up the road. The fog seemed alive when it touched her, icy fingers trailing the bare skin of her cheeks and her hands, cold as death. The sun was behind her and it barely warmed her, still too weak this early. Jess huddled in her jacket and kept walking, watching her breath chuff out in front of her.

To the right was the ocean and to the left were the hills, and beyond the hills were the low mountains, and somewhere in the mountains were Logger Fetridge and Dax Pruitt, and Sheriff Hart and Mitch Derry and Paul Monk and all of the other actors, the entirety of the cast to which she, too, rightfully belonged, climbing the mountain toward the Lone Jack mine, setting themselves in harm's way.

She'd left friends to die before.

Afia, her best friend, abandoned in some village in some other mountain valley, abandoned to an agonizing end. Her death Jess had seen; it was the agony she'd missed, days of torture before the insurgents had let Afia walk free, to stagger bloody and maimed back to the OP in which they knew Jess waited.

They'd let Jess see her friend, just a glimpse. Then they'd felled her with sniper fire from some hidden roost. And Jess had been left to cry over the body.

It was when she heard the sound of gunfire wafting down from the mountain that Jess knew she couldn't stay out of the fight. The sounds were faint but unmissable, muted staccato drifting with the fog. They were gunshots, and many of them, and then something else, deeper: the kind of low rumble that seemed to shift her insides, made her stomach clench tight. An explosion.

She couldn't just wait down here. Not while men she knew were up top, in the teeth of it. She'd led Tyner Gillies almost to his death, and there was still a chance Gillies could succumb to his wounds. Then she'd pointed more men into trouble, and she'd be damned if she was going to wait down here, warm and comfortable, while they fought.

Jess turned around and walked back to the motel, retracing her steps as the sun rose in her face, causing her to squint and see nothing but silhouettes as she walked. She made the motel and the door to her room, and she unlocked it and slipped inside again, and Burke hadn't moved, and Lucy lay on the bed with her head between her paws, playing coy while her tail thump-thump-thumped its betrayal.

Jess patted the dog on the head and gave her a belly rub, absent and rushed. She loved the dog, but it was best if Lucy stayed here with Burke. She knew how Burke would argue and ask her to stay and how he wouldn't understand—not at first—that she needed to go.

And she knew that if he did understand, he would try to go with her.

She still kept the shotgun she'd bought to scare Kirby Harwood last year, a Remington 870 Express with a twelve-round capacity, and she dug it out slowly from its soft case underneath the bed, and shells too, taking care not to wake Burke or disturb Lucy too much as she filled her pockets with ammunition.

She went to the bathroom and filled a canteen with water from the tap, then came out again and stood at the foot of the bed, cradling the shotgun and regarding Burke and the dog one more time. The dog's tail wasn't wagging, and she looked back at Jess concerned, like she knew Jess was planning to do something stupid and she knew, also, there was no way to stop her from doing it.

Jess took the shotgun and went to the door again, glanced at Burke to make sure he was still sleeping, and also just to look at him.

Then she opened the door and set out for the mountain.

SIXTY-FOUR

Mason Burke woke to sirens. Woke, groggy, in an empty bed, sunlight filtering in around the blackout curtain, the dog lying awake by the door. No sign of Jess, and he assumed, first, that she was in the bathroom, but he could hear nothing moving, no water running, and from the way Lucy was watching him as he rubbed his eyes clear of sleep, Mason could tell something had gone wrong.

He'd been afraid of this.

He'd been afraid that the events of the last couple of weeks might have knocked Jess back a step or two, that the whole fiasco with Boyd and then the shoot-out with Jordan and Bealing might have hit her somewhere, dislodged something inside her that she'd been working to stop up. He'd been afraid that she couldn't—or wouldn't—keep away from this fight, and from the look on the dog's face and the soft-shell case lying half open, half underneath the bed, Mason knew he'd been right to be afraid.

He just hadn't been sure what to do about it.

Sirens outside, and lots of them, screaming down the highway one way or the other, and Mason hadn't lived in Deception Cove very long, but he'd been here long enough to know there was usually only one disaster happening at a time. And that meant the sirens had to do with the sheriff and his apprehension of Logger Fetridge. And that was bad news if Jess was trying to get involved.

Mason swung his legs over the side of the bed and reached for his pants as he pulled on his shirt. At the door, Lucy pushed herself to her feet with a look back at him as if to ask him why the hell he'd made her wait so long.

"I'm sorry, girl," he told her, lacing his boots. "I should have been more on the ball."

He didn't have a vehicle, but Hank Moss did, an old F-100 pickup with a canopy on the back. Hank was awake and in the lobby, and he tossed Mason the keys without complaint or additional questions, except to ask whether Mason needed company, and Mason told him no.

"Plenty of lawmen up the trail already," he told the motelkeeper. "I just have to see for myself she's all right."

More sirens outside as Mason unlocked the truck and helped Lucy inside, an ambulance screaming by headed east on the highway, away from the mountain and Neah Bay, toward Clallam Bay and the trauma center in Port Angeles, where Tyner Gillies still struggled for life. A couple of state patrol cruisers raising hell in the other direction, lights on and engines roaring, blowing past the motel and Mason in the truck as he nosed out of the parking lot to the highway.

None of this was any good.

Mason drove west in the wake of the state patrol cruisers, Lucy sitting rigid in the passenger seat, staring out through the front windshield like she was searching for Jess. Mason watched the road shoulders too, daring to hope, though he knew Jess was likely long gone by now, somewhere off the main highway and climbing up toward the action.

The state cops had the 12 line blocked off at the outlet, two cruisers nose to nose and men with long guns standing guard. A small cluster of bystanders already, pickup trucks and rusted hatchbacks parked along the shoulder up and down from the turnoff, men and women in oilskin jackets and hooded sweatshirts milling about a few paces from the cruisers, talking among themselves and casting suspicious glances at the men with the guns.

A news van too, a reporter and a camerawoman. Likely more of those on the way.

Mason nosed the truck to a halt behind someone's old Pontiac, twenty or twenty-five yards from the crowd. He took Lucy's lead and clucked his teeth, and she jumped down from the truck and looked around and immediately set to sniffing, nose to the ground and her ears perked. But Jess wasn't here, and as far as Mason knew, the dog wasn't much of a tracker. Not from this distance, anyway.

He recognized faces as he walked up the shoulder to the state patrol blockade, folks he'd seen in Deception, or at the stores in Neah Bay. From the looks on their faces, they recognized him too, but they didn't speak to him, or even bother to nod. Those who didn't turn away quickly just glared at him, muttered to each other, wouldn't even look down to pet Lucy as she sniffed their hands.

The county didn't like Mason, and he supposed it might never.

But it was Jess's home and she loved it, and Mason had come to feel an affection for it as well, the rainforest and the ocean and the misty, brooding hills. He could understand why the people here hadn't cared for him at first, but he'd hoped to change their minds, somehow, prove he was decent. This mess with Brock Boyd had likely washed away his hard work; he knew he'd be starting over from scratch when it ended, if he had the chance to start over at all.

The state patrolmen at the barricade eyed him blankly as he approached. If they recognized him from the manhunt, they didn't let on.

"Wondering if you fellows saw a woman come up this way," Mason asked them. "Deputy Winslow, out of Deception Cove. She would have been alone and she would have been armed."

Neither patrolman changed his expression.

"Hasn't been up this way," one of them said. "We're under orders; nobody in or out without checking with us first."

The second of them said, "No one named Winslow's been through here all morning."

The troopers regarded Mason, looked closer, at Lucy too, like they were starting to wonder who he was and what he was doing here, why he was asking after the deputy.

But before they could say anything more, another ambulance came barreling around a highway curve, PORT ANGELES TRAUMA emblazoned on its flanks, and slammed to a stop beside the blockade and the crowd. The troopers set to work moving people aside, making space for the ambulance to park near their cruisers.

At approximately the same time, Mason became aware of the sound of an engine working hard through the trees, descending the 12 line toward the blockade. Within a few seconds he saw the headlights of a Ford Super Duty pickup appear at the crest of the closest hill, blinkers and police lights flashing, hauling ass down the grade with its big diesel chugging.

Mason stepped back as the truck came near, pulled Lucy away from the cruisers and the blockade and the ambulance. For an instant it looked like the truck wouldn't slow, like maybe the driver didn't see the cruisers or he just didn't care.

The troopers tensed, and the crowd, and the young paramedics inside the ambulance, but at the last moment the driver of the truck hit his brakes and the truck careened to a halt in a cloud of gravel dust, not more than a couple of feet from the doors of the cruisers.

Mason watched as Sheriff Hart hurried out of the driver's seat, circled the nose of the truck, and pulled the passenger door open.

"Medic," the sheriff called over his shoulder, as if this were a battle zone, and the paramedics rushed between the cruisers to help Hart as he pulled a young man from the truck.

The young man was bleeding, and he'd been burned too. Hart was bleeding as well, a cut on his forehead leaking a thin river of blood down his face. The paramedics took the young man from the sheriff, shouldered him aside, half carried and half dragged the victim to the back of the ambulance and a stretcher. As the victim passed by the cruisers, Mason got a good look and saw that it was Paul Monk who was injured, and badly.

The paramedics slammed the doors of the ambulance and it took off, siren wailing as it tried to turn around on the highway amid the mess of onlookers.

Mason called out to Hart. *"Sheriff."*

Hart scanned the crowd for a moment before he found Mason, his eyes not quite focused, even when they'd landed on him.

"Sheriff," Mason called again, and Hart gestured to the troopers that they should let Mason through.

Mason took Lucy and navigated between the cruisers. "You got Jess up there with you?" he asked.

Hart blinked, like it was taking a minute for him to comprehend the question.

"She ducked out of the motel room this morning," Mason explained. "Took her shotgun. I'm afraid she might have gone up there to try and pitch in."

Hart still said nothing, just stared at Mason, the look on his face like those of men who'd just come through a riot, who'd been beaten and gassed and somehow barely survived. "She's not with us," he said finally. "Not that I saw."

"Not yet," Mason said.

Hart stared out at the barricade. At the troopers and the crowd beyond, the crowd staring back in at him and some of them shouting epithets, calling for the sheriff to tell his men to stand down.

Logger Fetridge's people, or Dax Pruitt's, or just wilderness people who resented the law. Mason thought of Paul Monk in the back of that ambulance, and he wondered how Hart couldn't think the whole world was going to hell.

The sheriff looked out at them, his constituents, opened his mouth and worked his jaw like he wanted to find something to say to them. And the crowd stared back and jeered and shouted and shifted, uneasy, and Mason saw the two troopers exchange glances as if they were preparing for trouble.

Finally Hart glanced back at his truck. "Get in," he told Mason. "If she's headed up that mountain, you'd better come too."

Mason piled Lucy into the passenger seat and climbed in after. Waited as Hart shifted the truck into gear, pulled a three-point turn, and pointed the vehicle back into the hills. The sheriff stepped on the gas pedal without ceremony or preamble, and the truck chugged forward up the grade, and Hart drove in silence for the first little while, and then when he talked, he told Mason what had happened.

SIXTY-FIVE

The outlaws had been ready for them. They'd been waiting. And no number of lawmen—not even Hart's army—would persuade them to surrender easily.

"We moved on them at dawn," Hart told Mason. "Just as I'd planned. Surrounded that Lone Jack mine shaft and hoped they'd be sleeping."

The sheriff gunned his engine as the grade outside the truck steepened.

"But they weren't sleeping," he said. "They were waiting for us."

They'd booby-trapped the clearing in front of the shaft opening, improvised explosive devices of a style and ingenuity that would make the Taliban proud. Trip wires and punji sticks surrounding the property, fishing line strung at eye level between trees, rusty fishhooks hanging from it at intervals.

"We managed to duck most of the traps," Hart said. "The primitive ones, anyway. Once things started to blow up, though, it threw us."

Logger Fetridge had turned the Lone Jack shaft into a fortress, and the clearing around it his moat. Mitch Derry had been hit right away, stepped into a bear trap that might have claimed his foot. Derry's screams drew a mess of state troopers toward him, and that's about the time either Fetridge or Pruitt threw the first Molotov, a bottle of hooch and a rag and some gas.

"They opened up with their long guns pretty shortly thereafter," Hart explained. "Had decent position on us too, entrenched in that shaft."

The sheriff had called for patience, knew his men had the outlaws surrounded, outmanned and outgunned, knew if it came to a siege that his side would win, and in the meantime it boiled down to just keeping out of Fetridge's range, avoiding the booby traps and ducking the shells that whizzed past overhead.

But the siege didn't last long. Little by little, Hart and his men had tightened the noose, reclaimed, inch by inch, the ground in front of the mine shaft. The shaft was dug into the mountainside, and he'd sent men above to look down and hurl gas canisters into the hole, aimed to incapacitate the outlaws, coax them out peacefully and without further violence.

It hadn't quite worked out that way.

"Something exploded inside," Hart told Mason. "Bigger than a Molotov. Those boys must have cooked in there, and they'd left flammables handy. As soon as those gas grenades exploded, the whole shaft turned into a fireball and it blew out toward us."

Hart and Mason had reached a clearing now, where the road petered off at the top of a steep grade, and a narrow four-by trail continued higher up the slope. Mason knew this must have been where Dax Pruitt had parked his Silverado and let Jess escape. Here now was a collection of lawmen all wearing the same dazed expression as Hart had.

The sheriff parked his truck and climbed out, and Mason followed with Lucy, and the sheriff led them to a pair of four-wheelers parked at the foot of the trail, gesturing that Mason should take one and he would take the other.

Lucy shied away from the machine almost immediately, but there was no way that Mason was leaving her. His machine had a basket in the back and he hoisted her into it, tied her leash to the rail good and tight, and by then Hart had already started his machine and was aiming toward the foot of the trail.

Mason turned the key in his ignition and followed, shouting to Lucy over the howl of the motor, telling her not to be scared and knowing it was a futile effort. The dog wouldn't easily forgive him when this was all said and done, but Mason had a suspicion he would need her.

Jess is out here, girl, he thought. *Just bear with me until we find her.*

Lone Jack Trail must have once been a road, but it hadn't been for decades, and even before, it would have been a rough one. It rose steep and uneven, hemmed in by encroaching forest, and as Mason gunned his engine to keep pace with the sheriff, he was afraid he might tip the four-wheeler, roll it, or maybe just slam into a tree. He knew the dog must be hating her life right now, and he couldn't blame her, but it took all of his focus just to keep the machine climbing steadily in the sheriff's wake.

He could not have guessed how long they followed that trail, but it must have been thirty minutes of climbing flat out. They reached a point where the forest seemed to shrink away and the trees were stunted and it was more and more bare rock and low brush. There were no further lawmen on the trail, coming down or going up, and above the forest the sky was a deep, flawless blue. The sheriff hadn't finished telling Mason what had happened up at the shaft, and Mason wasn't sure who was still alive and who wasn't, if the bad guys were caught or they weren't.

Then the trail leveled out some, and ahead of Mason, the sheriff slowed his machine, and Mason pulled in tight behind him and found they'd reached a clearing, a great gouge in the side of the mountain. Beyond the clearing, yawning open and still pouring smoke, was the Lone Jack mine shaft.

Mason had never been to war or even entered a war zone, but he imagined the clearing in front of the mine shaft more or less fit the description. Charred ground and smoke rising, empty shell casings and mangled machinery, a patrol's worth of deputies and state troopers moving around the margins with urgency, their heads ducked low and their weapons at the ready.

"Try and find yourself some cover," Hart told Mason as the men dismounted. "We're still not sure if Fetridge and Pruitt are dead yet."

They took shelter behind a boulder thirty feet from the cave mouth, and Hart explained the rest, how his men had rushed the entrance to the shaft after the explosion, how they'd found no sign of the outlaws, but then Paul Monk had gotten curious and poked his head into the shaft a little deeper, and someone had thrown out another Molotov and then shot him for good measure.

Another shoot-out had transpired, this one in tight quarters and near darkness, a hellish confusion on uncertain terrain, punctuated by muzzle flashes and the deafening roar of gunfire at close range.

"That's when I decided we'd fall back and wait," Hart told Mason. "I've got four or five men shot or burned or otherwise injured, and I'll lose double that if we opt to play tag in that mine shaft.

"We'll wait them out," Hart continued. "What I know of that mine, there's only one entrance or exit. Sooner or later, they're going to have to try a jailbreak."

"And no sign of Jess," Mason said. He assumed she would come up here to where her friends were, and if she hadn't made it yet, she would arrive sooner or later.

"No sign of her," Hart said, looking back from the boulder and scanning the surrounding forest with concern. "Not yet, anyway."

SIXTY-SIX

Dax Pruitt still half expected to die on this mountain, but he hoped he could taste one more breath of fresh air first, before it all ended.

He felt like he was suffocating. The air claustrophobic and warm and dark as a tomb, lit only by the weak flashlight Logger Fetridge carried ahead of him. The walls of the shaft seemed to close in around Pruitt, hugging him tight in some smothering death embrace, though sometimes when he reached his arms out, he found nothing beyond his fingertips but stale air. Other times the rock seemed to squeeze at him, intent on crushing the life out of him. And ahead, Fetridge staggered forward and didn't slow down. There was nothing for Pruitt but to follow, lest he find himself alone in the black.

Fetridge breathed heavy and his walk was unsteady, and Pruitt suspected his friend had been shot at least once, or maybe more. Pruitt, for his part, was burned and felt broken; he'd been hit by a rock or shrapnel knocked loose by the blast, may well have fractured a rib.

Shot or not, though, Fetridge remained on his feet and kept moving. The poacher swore there was a second way out of this literal hellhole, another path broken through the skin of the earth, a secret escape they could find and be free.

Pruitt wasn't sure he believed his friend, suspected Fetridge might have been addled by the concussive effect of the vicious, tight-quarter shoot-out they'd just survived—not to mention the explosion that had nearly killed them both, all of Fetridge's cook supplies turned to heat and flame.

They'd sought cover in a secondary shaft dug off the main tunnel, watched the lawmen enter the cave, cautious, drew them in until there were four or five of them sitting plum, silhouetted in the daylight that filtered in from outside, off-balance and blinded as they peered into the darkness.

At Fetridge's signal, Pruitt had opened fire, knocked two or three of the men to the ground before Fetridge hurled another Molotov cocktail and hollered at Pruitt to fall back.

So Pruitt fell back, following his friend through a labyrinth of rusted rail and rotting timber, past the chimney and the still-smoldering remains of the poacher's lab, breathing fumes that were acrid and toxic and nearly overwhelming, choking and coughing and staggering as they passed.

They ran. Deeper and deeper into the earth until the voices of the lawmen faded behind them and there was no light but what Fetridge carried, no sound but their breathing and their boots in the rubble.

Ahead of Pruitt, Fetridge staggered onward, tripping on loose scree and larger cannonball rocks. Pruitt didn't know how far they'd come, just that they'd taken a tunnel that Fetridge swore was the right one, and as the trail alternately dropped deeper underground or climbed higher, as it narrowed and widened, Pruitt tried not to think about the tons upon tons of rock above his head, about what little it would take to send it all crashing down atop him.

Fetridge stank of chemicals, and Pruitt knew he must smell fairly awful himself. The poacher was wheezing as he breathed, his feet slipping and his hands scrabbling at the walls to keep himself upright. Pruitt wondered if his friend would die in this cave, and where would that leave him but to die also. He wasn't sure he could find his way out the way they'd come.

"Almost there," Fetridge said, as though reading his thoughts. "Not too much longer to go now, old boy."

The trail underneath Pruitt's feet had started to climb again. The walls tapered in so narrow that he had to turn sideways to slip through, holding his rifle ahead of him and sucking in his belly— afraid for a terrifying instant that he'd wedge himself so tight he could never escape.

On the other side of the tunnel, Fetridge waited. He grinned at Pruitt as Pruitt squeezed through.

"Bet you're glad we been on tight rations lately," he said, and then he turned and continued down the tunnel before Pruitt could answer. Before he'd even fully freed himself.

Pruitt squeezed out of the narrows and hurried to follow. Tripped on a boulder and nearly fell flat, pushed himself up and kept going—and then he felt it: a coolness to the air that hadn't been there before, seconds earlier. It wasn't much, but it was noticeable in the oven-hot tunnel, and Fetridge's pace seemed to quicken, and Pruitt's behind him.

The air continued to cool and grew fresher, the smell of rain and the forest. Perhaps the tunnel grew lighter too, or maybe that was just Pruitt's imagination. It didn't matter. The end was near.

The end, as it was, was a small shallow cave, an overhang of rock so low it forced Pruitt and Fetridge to their knees to crawl beneath it, but Pruitt didn't care; he could see again, more than the beam of Fetridge's weak light, could hear birds in the trees and smell earth and life, and he emerged from the cave and stood tall and stretched, blinking in the sudden sunlight.

And he felt, immediately, as though he'd been returned from the dead.

As though he'd died in that tunnel with those lawmen, walked this tortuous path and been given new life.

Beside him, Fetridge stood doubled over, clutching at a wound in his stomach that oozed black with blood. The poacher coughed and wiped his mouth and his hand came back bloody too, and Pruitt knew his friend was dying, but Fetridge didn't seem to care.

"Told you we'd get out," the poacher said, and he straightened himself using his rifle as a cane. Surveyed the forest and began to walk again.

The forest was overgrown and featureless, but there was a narrow trail leading away from the cave, leading down the natural declination of the land, though to where, Pruitt had no idea.

But Fetridge was following the trail and seemed confident in its direction, so Pruitt shouldered his rifle and followed. He didn't look back at the cave as he walked; what had happened back there was no part of him now.

SIXTY-SEVEN

This was where she belonged. And perhaps it was the only place, but she was here now, and there was no point in thinking about anything else.

The gunfire had stopped. It could have just been that the mountain was baffling it from her, that she'd hiked up the wrong side of a finger ridge that the sounds of the shoot-out couldn't traverse, but Jess didn't think so. She could hear sirens somewhere below, and sometimes the sound of cars and trucks on the highway through Deception. Faint, but she could hear them.

Anyway, the forest seemed to have relaxed now. It was hard to explain, but in Jess's experience, the land knew when there was violence nearby; the birds stilled and even the wind sometimes seemed to hold its breath, waiting for the anger to subside. Jess could hear birds above her, and the rustle of leaves. The forest had reclaimed its peace.

Jess was drenched in sweat. She'd climbed up the mountain the way she'd come down, clambering mossy boulders along the path of Iron Creek. Her body wasn't as broken as when she'd made the descent, but it was harder to climb anyway, even with the twelve gauge as a walking stick.

The road was blocked off, the 12 line; she'd seen it. Twin state patrol cruisers and twin state patrol troopers, installed to keep out the looky-loos and the innocent. She'd watched ambulances scream past on the highway and the dark, unmarked state patrol trucks with their lights blaring, the few Makah County vehicles that weren't parked somewhere up the mountain already.

Jess didn't know how far up Iron Creek extended, but she aimed to follow it at least to the point where she'd found it the first time. Then she intended to skirt up through the forest where Dax Pruitt had left her in his Silverado, follow the ATV trail to the mine shaft.

She didn't know what she would do when she got there, aside from pitch in and try to keep Pruitt and Fetridge from killing her friends. She knew the sheriff would be angry and that he probably wouldn't give her badge back, but so be it. She wasn't going to sit idle as more of her friends died.

The hike was exhausting, and her muscles ached as she climbed, but she didn't slow except to drink from her canteen and to strain her ears for the sounds of the battle. But the forest was silent, aside from the burble of the river and the birds in the trees and the drone of a helicopter, somewhere high above. Jess hiked up the boulders and gained altitude steadily, and when she stopped to rest, the air was cooler, and raw.

Time passed. She didn't know how far she'd come, but then, she'd had no idea how far she'd descended that first go-around. The forest looked familiar and unfamiliar at the same time, the boulders blending into one another. She couldn't see the summit of the mountain, but she could see a spot high above where the forest gave way to bare rock and alpine terrain, and beyond which the sun traversed the sky.

Jess climbed, and with purpose. Stopped to catch her breath one more time at the top of a rock formation, set down the shotgun, and dipped her head into the water, a shallow pool at the top of a small waterfall, drenched her head in the bracing cold, ran her fingers through her hair, and straightened again, refreshed, invigorated.

Damn it, she was almost having fun.

Then something hit her—hard—a kick to the chest, and a split second later, Jess heard the shot ring out from somewhere above her. She staggered backward, fell, as the riverbank exploded around her, more shots and whizzing bullets and chipped, razor-sharp rock, as if she'd walked onto a battlefield without knowing.

She lay back on a slab of rock, and she didn't feel the pain yet, but she knew, dumbly, that she had to find cover. The shotgun lay beside her, and she reached for it and grabbed it and used it to push herself to her feet, stumbling away from the open ground of the river, toward the relative protection of the rainforest alongside.

The shots echoed behind her, and Jess couldn't know if they hit her or not, her adrenaline pumping and her survival instinct not letting her slow. She reached the forest and hurled herself into the trees and ducked low and just stayed there, unmoving, and the gunman or gunmen stopped firing, and the sounds of their shots reverberated down the mountain and then faded away, so that there was only the burble of the river and the drone of that helicopter somewhere that remained.

It was as though, in that sudden silence, the gunfire hadn't happened at all. But Jess knew better. First was in how the birds had stopped singing, and the wind seemed to have died.

Second was in the hole in her chest, steadily staining her T-shirt with blood.

SIXTY-EIGHT

Fetridge had seen the woman first. He and Pruitt had followed the trail from the cave to where it met this creek, trickling down between two finger ridges toward the base of the mountain and the ocean. Fetridge was shot and he was struggling, blood soaking both the front of his jacket and the exit wound in the back; he stopped often to catch his breath and rest his legs, leaning against trees or rock or his rifle, his breathing labored and liquid and sickly.

But there was no slowing down. They continued on the trail until it reached the creek, and Pruitt could see that if you followed the boulders that studded the cascading water, you could pick a tenuous path down the mountain.

And that seemed to be Fetridge's goal, though the poacher slowed even more when the men began their descent. Pruitt watched his friend struggle and saw the futility of the effort, knowing there was no way Fetridge would survive to the bottom, knowing all the same that he owed it to Fetridge to stay beside him until the man dropped.

And that's what Pruitt did. He descended ahead of Fetridge, and below every boulder he stopped and waited and let Fetridge lean on him as he made his own drop. And at every boulder they would stop and Fetridge could catch his breath, and at every boulder Fetridge's breath seemed that much harder to catch, and the bloodstains on his jacket grew larger and darker.

"There's money hid down there," Fetridge told Pruitt, gesturing in a vague way toward the base of the mountain. "The Cody woman's money, ten thousand dollars."

He paused again for breath, and Pruitt waited, and Fetridge grinned at him with teeth stained too, by blood.

"Stashed it in the spare tire," he said. "My cousin Thumps's van."

Pruitt worked his jaw and he thought about this, tried to catch his own breath, his thoughts dizzy now from exertion and lack of water and food. He could picture where Thumps King kept his trailer, could picture the old Dodge Caravan beside it. And he could picture the money, Fetridge's share of the twenty thousand dollars Jana Cody had given so that they would kill Bad Boyd for her, dispose of the body, and keep her name out of it.

Pruitt could see now how Fetridge aimed to play it. How he hoped to make his getaway when he walked off of this mountain.

But Pruitt watched his friend struggle and knew there was no hope that he'd ever see that money. "You'll never make it," he told Fetridge. "Not in your state. We ought to just set and rest awhile."

But Fetridge shook his head. Fixed Pruitt with a stare that seemed to encompass all of what they'd done, the history they'd created and the violence they'd wrought. "That cash ain't for me, old boy," he told Pruitt. "It's yours now."

Pruitt looked for an answer and couldn't find one, and before he could, Fetridge stiffened. Pointed down the chute of the river. "Shit," he said, his voice raspy. "There's the law."

Pruitt turned, slowly. Weary, wondering if his friend was hallucinating now, not expecting there was anyone at all within a mile of where they stood. But down the mountain, climbing toward them, maybe a hundred feet lower: Jess Winslow. Alone, with a gun.

Fetridge was already steadying his rifle on the edge of a slab of granite. Muttering under his breath, taking aim at the woman. His finger tensed on the trigger, and then he glanced over at Pruitt. "Well, hell, come on, son," he said. "Help me cut her down."

It didn't seem right to Pruitt to just shoot the Winslow woman, not without at least giving her warning first, but Fetridge was already drawing a bead on the young deputy, and Pruitt told himself that Jess Winslow was armed and climbing toward them, and that if she'd seen them first she'd have opened fire too, and maybe that was true and maybe it wasn't. Then Fetridge pulled his trigger and there was no time to think anymore; the shot went out and Jess Winslow staggered backward and went down, and Pruitt opened up too, not aiming to kill Jess but keeping his shots close, chasing her out of the open and into the trees somewhere, hoping that would be enough to scare her off and at worst incapacitate her. Let him and Fetridge continue their descent, and maybe they'd make it to Thumps King's minivan, that ten thousand dollars stashed away.

But Fetridge had a different plan.

"That's the bitch killed my nephew," he told Pruitt, and in his eyes there was new life and energy. "Let's get on down there and pay her back for it."

SIXTY-NINE

It was Lucy who first heard the shots.

She'd been cowering more or less since Mason had untied her from the back of the four-wheeler, dragged her to cover at the edge of the clearing overlooking the Lone Jack mine. She'd curled tight around herself, her back hunched and her spine turned and wrapped in a paper-clip shape, her ears back and her tail tucked, refusing to make eye contact with Mason or anyone else, like she was hoping if she just sat still and waited, all of this would fade away.

But then she moved—she'd heard something. The dog hated loud noises, from fireworks to slamming doors, tended to duck and cover whenever anyone so much as revved an engine. And she could hear from a distance too, knew instantly when kids from the high school were setting off firecrackers on Shipwreck Point Beach, or the freighters out on the strait were sounding their foghorns.

Now Mason watched her ears perk, felt her start to shiver beside him again. He stilled his own movements and strained to hear over the drone of the state patrol helicopter high above.

At first, he heard nothing. Then Lucy flinched again, and the sound reached his ears, distant but unmistakably gunfire, rapid and angry. Mason looked to the sheriff. "You hear that?"

Hart cocked his head, frowning. "My ears are shot, son," he told Mason. "Been a day of loud noises. What do you hear?"

Mason said, "Guns, Sheriff. Someone's firing off somewhere. Lucy's getting it too."

Hart listened some more. Stuck his head above the rock they were hiding behind, looked in toward the mouth of the mine. "What," he said, "in there?"

Mason shook his head. Best he could tell, the sounds were coming from elsewhere. From down the mountain, far away.

Then the gunfire stopped, though Lucy kept shivering. Mason listened and heard nothing, and tried to figure out what it meant.

"You're sure there's no other way out that cave," he said.

"Far as anyone's ever heard, there's just the one exit," Hart replied. "And we're parked on it. Could be what you're hearing is something unrelated."

There was no way to be sure, but Mason didn't think so. He stayed behind that boulder and watched Lucy try to curl herself tighter, and he felt restless and urgent and aware of time wasting, as if he was dreaming and late for an obligation, couldn't find the car keys or the right pair of shoes. He didn't know Logger Fetridge, but he suspected the man wouldn't simply just dig in and hide, not knowing what awaited him outside in daylight. If there was another way out of that mine, Mason expected the outlaw would find it.

And if Fetridge found an exit, then he'd sure as hell take it.

"Give me a flashlight," Mason told the sheriff.

Hart stared at him. "Now, hold up a minute—"

"You can come if you want, or don't; that's your choice," Mason said. "But Jess is still unaccounted for, and I'm hearing gunfire."

"Those outlaws will kill you," Hart said. "I can't let you do it."

Mason stood. "I'm going, Sheriff," he said. "You hang back if you want. But if Fetridge and Pruitt made it out of that cave somehow, I need to know about it."

Hart studied his face and then looked toward the mine shaft

again. Opened his mouth to argue. But then another gun sounded, somewhere far away, a resonant *boom* that even Hart could hear clearly, that seemed to rumble the earth beneath them.

Jess's shotgun.

Mason stood and was running before the sound had died away, pulling Lucy behind him, the sheriff calling his name. Mason ignored him. He reached the mouth of the mine shaft and didn't break stride. Pulled the dog into the darkness and kept running.

SEVENTY

Jess could hear the men coming. They didn't exactly make a secret of their approach.

She was shot bad, but not fatally, she didn't think. The bullet had caught her high, but it hadn't hit anything vital. She would never throw a ninety-mile-an-hour fastball, but if she could find her way down the mountain, she would probably live.

Jess set her back against a pine tree and wedged herself into the earth so she was looking out from the forest toward the river chute and the rocks, and she listened to the sound of scree kicked down the mountain as the men who'd fired on her made their way toward her.

Upslope and blocking her view was a huge slab of mountainside completely bare of dirt; it rose at least twenty feet in a sheer, immediate climb, forcing the trees of the forest to skirt around it, away from the river. As it was, it made for decent cover, and Jess stayed beneath it and tried to make out by the sounds of the men how many of them were coming.

It was Logger Fetridge who poked his head around the side of the face first. Jess had just enough time to recognize him before she pulled the trigger on her shotgun, sent him flying backward into the sunlight and the river. The sound of the shotgun echoed with an intensity that might have brought down the mountain; she braced herself for either landslide or counterattack, but neither was coming.

Directly ahead of her lay Fetridge, flat on his back now and staring up at the sky, and she could see his chest moving and hear his labored breathing, and she knew he was dying and she didn't feel remorse.

According to Jana Marsh, it was Fetridge who'd done it, murdered Brock Boyd with that .38 revolver. He'd pulled the trigger and then he and Dax Pruitt had wrapped up the body in the back of Pruitt's Silverado, tidied up Boyd's house as best they were able. They'd taken Jana's money and told her to go home, which she'd done, and they'd driven off and tried and somehow failed to make Boyd disappear.

Twenty thousand dollars, Jana'd said.

Jess thought about the other casualties: Charlene Todd, who'd had her throat cut by Fetridge's men; Chris Jordan and Dougie Bealing, who'd played their own roles in this tragedy and died for it too. And Tyner Gillies, who still clung to life in that Port Angeles hospital. And who else had been claimed by the violence on this mountain this morning?

Jana Marsh maintained that she hadn't killed Bad Boyd, that it was Fetridge and Dax Pruitt who were responsible, but Jess knew that Jana was wrong. Jana's money had killed Boyd, and the others too, and Boyd may have deserved it, but the others surely didn't. Maybe not even Logger Fetridge.

But there was no time for reflection, not now. Jess could hear the second gunman out there somewhere, could sense him in how the birds and the air remained still while pebbles shuffled on dirt above her head. She could sense the man as she'd sensed the insurgents who'd waited to ambush her team on patrols in the Hindu Kush; after a while, you tended to get pretty good at reading the land, picking out what belonged and what didn't.

Jess knew this second gunman wouldn't be so careless as to leave himself open as Logger Fetridge had.

She pushed herself to her feet—her wound hurt now, a hot poker of fire through her breastbone, but she stifled any complaint—and tried to move as stealthily as she could, back farther into the forest, to where the slope of the mountain outflanked the bare face, where she could pull herself higher using trees and exposed roots and handholds and footholds.

She heard the man call out her name. *"Jess?"*

It was Pruitt; she recognized his voice. She kept her mouth shut and didn't reveal her position, climbed the slope of the mountain until she'd gained enough ground that she stood level with the lip of the bare face.

"Jess, I don't want to hurt you; I swear it," Pruitt called. "You let me get past you, and I'll be on my way. We'll forget we ever saw each other, okay?"

She couldn't see Pruitt yet, and she didn't answer. Didn't know if the man was telling the truth or trying to game her and didn't suppose it mattered. He'd tried to kill Lucy, after all, and brought violence on her friends and fellow lawmen farther up the mountain. She wouldn't let him walk off of this mountain, not without confrontation.

She edged out from the forest toward the rocky chute of the river path, swinging the shotgun left to right, slowly, in case Pruitt appeared. The forest ended in rocky spill, and she couldn't see her target; he'd dropped, she surmised, while she'd climbed, and now he must be near the base of the cliff face, where she'd shot Fetridge.

Jess edged out toward the lip of the face, intending to lean over the side and rain buckshot down on Pruitt from above. But then she slipped, slightly, her boot losing traction in the dirt and the dust, and she nearly bailed out and toppled over the edge, when Pruitt surprised her.

He poked his head up from the other side of the outcrop, not down below as she'd figured but hiding just alongside it. Jess watched in slow motion as he swung his rifle around. She fought to regain her balance and turn the shotgun on him too.

Pruitt fired first. Jess fired back. Heard Pruitt cry out and go down, and then she was falling too.

SEVENTY-ONE

Mason slowed only when he was sure the sheriff was following. He'd reached about the limit of daylight in the mine shaft, stumbling over the rusted iron rails set into the ground, the remains of tools and fallen timber and the detritus that Logger Fetridge and Dax Pruitt had left behind.

There was nowhere to go but deeper into the dark, and Mason might have done it alone, though he knew it'd be foolish and futile. Fortunately, Hart was catching up to him, panting, gripping a flashlight in one hand and his rifle in the other.

"Careful," he told Mason. "These boys seem to have a fondness for booby traps."

The sheriff let Mason lead. Mason let Lucy lead. She may have been scared, but her natural curiosity seemed to win out, and she pulled at the leash at the edge of the flashlight beam, urging the men deeper into the abyss.

And the mine *was* abyssal. Beyond a high chimney about a hundred feet in, Mason could sense no light or fresh air, though the narrow-gauge rails on the main shaft continued, and auxiliary shafts cut away in both directions every fifty-odd feet. The air was smoky and acrid and chemical, hazy even in the beam of the sheriff's light. Mason scanned the ground ahead of him for footprints but saw nothing; the floor of the shaft was loose rock too coarse to keep an imprint of a man's boot.

"Where's Jess?" he asked Lucy, and the dog glanced back at him with those ears on high alert, then scanned the dark beyond the flashlight beam. "Where's your mom, Luce? Where's Jess?"

He'd never know if the dog understood, if she could somehow sense Jess or if it was simply dumb luck that set her and him and the sheriff down the right path. But Lucy came to a particular branch from the main shaft and turned down it without hesitation, and Mason didn't argue but followed and let her lead, and behind them the sheriff followed too.

The branch shaft narrowed and dug itself into the earth, and at points Mason felt sure that Lucy had led them to a dead end. But there was always a way forward, the dog nosing through, slipping between the tight confines of rock with a grace the men behind her could never match. At times Mason found himself ducking nearly doubled over; other times he had to turn sideways, make himself as lean and tall as he could, try and inch through the crevices with rock pressing into him, front and behind.

It was at one of these narrows that Hart fell back. The sheriff was a wider man than Mason and the rock was unyielding, and there was no way the lawman could squeeze through. Mason stopped and looked back, kept the beam of the flashlight out of Hart's eyes. Heard the sheriff mutter an epithet as he tried, one last time, to force his way through.

Mason said, "We'll go back."

Hart didn't answer.

"We've got some idea which way they headed," Mason said. "If we hurry back, we can try and trace this tunnel aboveground, see if we can't track where it comes out."

The sheriff grunted and backed out of the narrows, and Mason started to follow, tugging on Lucy's leash to turn her around. The dog resisted, dug in her feet and bucked against the lead.

"Come on, girl," Mason said.

But then Hart said, *"Burke."*

Mason looked, and the sheriff was holding out his rifle. Mason stared at it, dumb, for a moment.

"We're losing time on those boys," Hart said. "If Jess is up here, then she'll need us to get to her, fast."

"I can't leave you alone in a cave in the dark," Mason said, but Hart dug into his pocket and came out with a cell phone, an old one, a flip model.

"It'll do me," the sheriff said. "But my battery's low. So take the rifle and try not to kill anyone, Burke. Just find Jess and make sure she's safe."

There was no time to argue, and Mason wasn't really inclined anyway. He took Hart's rifle. "Thanks," he said.

"Jess told me what you did," Hart told him. "For Gillies. That man owes you his life, and I'm glad you were there to save it for him."

Mason shook his head. "It was mostly Jess's doing, Sheriff, to be honest."

"Not the way she tells it," Hart replied. "And somehow I suspect that she's right." He motioned Mason forward, deeper into the black. "Go," he said. "I'll try to circle around to you up top, if I can."

Then the sheriff turned and started back through the darkness, lit by the sickly green tint from his phone. Mason listened to the man find his footing, waited until his light had disappeared. Then he turned back to the way he was going, the way Lucy wanted to lead him. He slung the rifle over his shoulder and clicked his teeth for the dog.

"Go, Lucy," he said. "Find your mama."

SEVENTY-TWO

Jess hurt. She still wasn't sure if Pruitt had hit her when he'd shot at her, but she was in pain nonetheless. She lay in the scree at the bottom of that bare face of rock and tried to stand up and couldn't quite make it work.

She'd toppled over the side of the face as she'd tried to duck away from where Pruitt was swinging his rifle. Squeezed off an answering shot with her Remington, and then it was like the whole lip of the face gave out, and she was sliding off the edge and then falling and hitting hard, twenty feet below, the shotgun falling away somewhere and her body coming to rest against a piece of jagged rock.

Jess could hear Pruitt groaning somewhere, out of sight. So maybe she'd hit him, or maybe he'd just fallen, same as she had. She supposed it didn't matter. None of this mattered. She was probably going to die on this mountain, and that didn't matter either.

The violence, the unending violence. The only thing she'd ever been good at. Afia. Ty. Scores of nameless Taliban. Kirby Harwood and both Whitmer brothers and their accomplice, Mr. Joy. Shelby Walker and her mother. Charlene Todd and Chris Jordan and Doug Bealing. Logger Fetridge and Dax Pruitt.

Mason Burke.

A noise from around the side of the rock face, the tumble of pebbles and baseball-sized rocks, and then Dax Pruitt appeared, sliding on his ass, kicking up a sturdy cloud of dust. Jess looked around for her shotgun, found it lying a few feet away, leaned over and grabbed for it, everything seeming to move in slow motion again, like in some kind of bad dream.

"Relax," Pruitt said. He coughed, wet. "I ain't going to shoot you."

Jess gripped the shotgun anyway, lifted it and labored to swing it around in his direction. Pruitt lay on his back where he'd come to rest at the base of the cliff face, propped up slightly on his right arm to look across at her. He was bloody, his face and chest, and he was covered in dirt, and she could see how the buckshot she'd thrown at him had perforated his clothing in multiple places, how he was hurt bad enough to no longer pose a threat, and maybe even worse than that.

His eyes were wide open, though, and a startling blue she didn't think she remembered from seeing him before, his hair a tangle of mud and more dirt and matted blood besides, everything about him dirty and injured and worn.

"I'm sorry," Pruitt said, every word an effort. "What I did to your dog."

She didn't know what he meant at first. Thought he was referring to some new evil, something he and Logger Fetridge had somehow done while up on this mountain, after she'd left Burke and Lucy in the motel room this morning. She felt her heart clench and her finger tense on the Remington's trigger, and Pruitt watched her and didn't say anything.

Then Jess remembered the ambush at the beach, how he'd shot at Lucy.

"She survived," Jess told him. "You didn't get her."

Pruitt blinked, and she could see his mind struggling to compute this.

"It was a ricochet," Jess said. "She caught a chip of rock in her paw, but she's fine."

Pruitt nodded. Inhaled, deep, and closed his eyes, and she thought he might die then and there, but he didn't. "I'm sorry anyway," he said. "All of this."

She believed he was sorry, and she believed it wouldn't do him, or anyone, a lick of good. She was sorry, too, for a lot of things, and none of her apologies would change the plain facts.

"It doesn't matter anymore," she told him. "Just hush."

Pruitt looked at her like maybe he knew she was right, that his own reckoning was coming and soon. He laid his head back and breathed wetly some more, and she listened as each breath seemed to come tougher and tougher, and he didn't say anything else.

And then the mountain was silent again, until gradually it seemed to awaken, the sound of the water and the wind and the birds in the trees, the rainforest coming to life in the aftermath of the violence.

Jess lay there and listened, and wondered how the forest would sound when she, too, was gone.

SEVENTY-THREE

Lucy was barking. Lucy never barked, and that's how Mason knew they'd followed the right path.

The dog had led him through the tunnel, narrow and claustrophobic, and out into a cave beneath a rocky outcrop, hidden amid the forest and likely invisible from above. And where Mason could barely see a trail, the dog had found it instantly, dashing away as Mason caught his breath, turning back to stare at him, whining, yawning, stamping her feet, nervous, her collar jangling as she tried to urge him to keep moving.

He'd never known Lucy to track anything, but it was clear that she and Jess had some kind of connection that trumped anything he could comprehend, and if Lucy was this excited, Mason would trust her without question.

They followed the trail down a ways across the slope of the mountain, Mason carrying the sheriff's rifle and hoping he wouldn't have to use it. He'd never really been trained in shooting—beyond a few hurried practice rounds with Jess before they'd taken on Kirby Harwood and his friends—and he'd come to see pretty quick how he was useless with anything other than a shotgun or pistol at close range. A rifle, a distance shot, he'd be a liability. But at the least, Mason hoped he could scare Logger Fetridge and Dax Pruitt a little bit.

Through the trees, Mason could see the stubby forest thin out and the slope of the mountain steepen, could see how the trail led to the base of a bowl beneath high rocky palisades, where the mountain seemed to drain into the rainforest and drop toward tidewater. He had a suspicion this was the start of the Iron Creek Jess had descended a few days before, and he hoped she'd come up the same way and they'd run into each other, hoped that's what had Lucy so excited.

And then the dog began to bark, and Mason's heart rate quickened. He knew they'd find Jess somewhere down that slide path. What he couldn't know was what shape she'd be in.

———

Somewhere a dog was barking.

Jess opened her eyes and struggled to sit up, blinking in the light that seemed to aim down from above, directly onto her position. From the angle of the light, she could tell it was midafternoon and getting later, the sun beginning its descent toward the west but bathing the slope of the mountain in gold, in the meantime.

Beside the crumbling rock face, out toward the river path, Logger Fetridge lay dead, and Dax Pruitt beside him, still breathing, but faint. Jess's body was sore, but she was alive. And a dog was barking, somewhere.

She'd rarely heard Lucy bark. The dog was mostly quiet, save the odd whimper or whine, but she might join in the chorus if she heard other dogs letting loose. Her bark was distinct, deeper than Jess would have imagined to look at her, to know her; it was a sound of authority that belied her mostly diva personality.

But the bark she was hearing now sounded suspiciously familiar. It came from somewhere above the cliff face, high up the mountain.

Jess lay against the rock, sharp and uncomfortable at her back. She closed her eyes and tried to block out the sound. She'd begun to accept the fact that she might die up here, come to believe it might even make better sense to the world if she did, if she just disappeared and let the man and the dog and the county she loved just evolve to go on without her.

She could die up here, and it would be easy; she would never have to worry about dragging Burke and Lucy into violence again. Wouldn't have to worry that she would hurt Burke someday, that she would let him down and lose him the way she'd lost Ty and Afia.

She wouldn't have to worry. She wouldn't have to work. She could just lie here and wait and just . . . cease to be.

But Lucy was still barking, and that meant Burke was up there too. And as much as Jess wished that things could just be easy for a change, she knew if there was anything worth working for, it was Burke, and Lucy, and the family they'd become.

Jess tried to push herself to her feet, and couldn't. She hurt too bad, her chest where the bullet had found her, and her right leg, which was probably broken. Instead, she made herself crawl, over the dirt and the rock toward the base of the rock face and beyond, past where Logger Fetridge lay dead and Dax Pruitt lay dying.

She crawled, though it hurt, and Lucy kept barking. She crawled and hoped that the dog and the man she loved would find her.

———

He rushed to her. He rushed down the mountain and followed the river chute and followed Lucy to where Jess lay collapsed on the ground. When he reached her he rolled her onto her back and tried to help her, though he didn't know how. He saw she'd been shot and tried to pack the wound with dirt and a strip he'd torn from his T-shirt, and all the while the dog milled about in a panic around them. Jess was breathing, but barely. She'd lost so much blood, and try as Mason might, he couldn't get her to focus her eyes on his own.

He wrapped her up as best he could, feeling helpless and useless and utterly to blame, like she was slipping away and he was letting her go. He tried to prop her up, and she whimpered when he moved her, so he left her with the dog, picked up his rifle and the dead man's rifle and Jess's shotgun, and he went and climbed to the top of the rocky prominence above them and fired the guns, one after the other until they were empty, into the sky, and when they were empty he went down to the men who were dead or dying and dug in their pockets for more shells. And he reloaded the rifles and fired again, over and over, until he heard the roar of the state police helicopter buzzing over the mountainside, until he was sure the men in the machine above had seen them, until he was sure they were coming to help.

EPILOGUE

It was never going to be easy.

She'd imagined, as a little girl, that her life would follow a tidy path. She would marry her high school sweetheart, follow her dad's example and join the Marines, fight and prove herself in service to her country, and come home to Deception Cove to start a family in the place she grew up.

Jess had married Ty Winslow. She'd joined the Marines and fought well in Afghanistan. Then she'd come home broken, and widowed, with no sense of a future.

She'd imagined that life would get easier, after she and Lucy and Mason Burke survived Kirby Harwood and escaped from Dixie Island. She'd dared to believe that though Ty wasn't the man of her dreams, maybe Mason Burke was, and that after all she'd been through, they'd build a nice, tidy life together.

But she'd been silly to believe it would happen that way.

Jess was on crutches, waiting while Lucy nosed around a patch of grass. Burke pulled into the motel lot in the Blazer, now riding on a set of fresh tires.

Lucy looked up from the weeds long enough to wag her tail, then continued her sniffing, secure enough in the relative peace of recent days to treat Burke's arrival as a happy occasion but not an international incident.

There had been no shooting for two weeks, and Lucy, at least, seemed to be adapting just fine.

Burke circled around the front of the Blazer and gave Jess a quick hug around the crutches, taking care not to touch her chest where the wound from Logger Fetridge's rifle was still sore but healing. Burke kissed her on the cheek and then turned and opened the passenger door for her, held her crutches as she climbed into the truck. Then he snapped his fingers and called to Lucy, and the dog, reluctantly, gave up on the weeds and followed him around to the driver's side and jumped into the back seat.

Burke readjusted his seat and climbed behind the wheel, closed his door and turned the key and shifted the truck into gear. It was another beautiful day, warm and sunny, and he had the window rolled down and the radio on, and as they pulled out of the lot, Jess could see how any bystander might see them and feel envious, might imagine that the life they'd built together must be simple and tidy and easy.

But of course it wasn't easy. Burke was still living on Joe Clifford's boat while he and Jess—and the county as a whole—tried to figure out what came next. Tyner Gillies had survived the load of buckshot that Dougie Bealing had put into him, and Dax Pruitt had survived too, despite what Jess had done to him on the mountain. Mitch Derry would keep his foot after all, and the doctors expected both he and Paul Monk would make full recoveries, in time. But there were statements to be made and investigations to complete, endless reams of paperwork, and hours of interviews. Men and women were dead, outlaws and civilians and the law alike.

Burke had been well and truly exonerated, at least. Jana Marsh sat in prison for Boyd, and Dax Pruitt would join her when he'd healed up some, and sooner or later they both would stand trial.

Burke seemed to have made his peace with this, all of it; he held no grudge against Sheriff Hart, or seemingly anyone else in this town. As far as Jess could tell, it was Charlene Todd's murder that had hit him hardest, though they hadn't talked of it much. They hadn't talked of anything.

Burke had saved her life on the mountain, and she'd saved his life on Dixie Island. Maybe they were even now and the accounting was clean. Maybe that was enough.

Burke drove east on the highway for a couple of miles, and then he slowed and signaled and turned north down a road that Jess knew well. He turned again at a sign marking a dead end beyond, and followed that road to about a quarter mile from its end, where on the left-hand side and tucked into the trees was the house Joe Clifford was building for her with Burke's assistance, framed up and walled in now, and waiting for siding.

Burke parked the truck and pulled his seat forward for Lucy to jump out; he was around and holding out Jess's crutches for her by the time she had the door open. Jess took the crutches and stepped down gingerly to the grass below, wincing slightly from the pain in her bullet wound but following Burke up the path to the house nonetheless.

The doctors had wanted her in a wheelchair, but to hell with that.

Burke paused for her at the front stairs, just plywood now and waiting on concrete. This house was much bigger than the one it'd replaced; Joe Clifford had found a way to add a second floor to the equation, a second bedroom and a half bath.

"A place to raise a family," he'd said, winking at Burke, and Jess could still remember how she'd blushed.

There was a door on the house, and a padlock, and Burke unlocked the padlock and swung the door open so that Jess could limp inside. Lucy slipped in ahead of her, tail wagging, looking for

Joe and Rengo. Inside, the house smelled of sawdust and men at work, but the air was still and silent.

"Over here's where the kitchen's going to be," Burke told her, leading her toward the back of the house, walls studded in but not yet drywalled, no cabinets or fixtures but a window overlooking the backyard. "Joe says he can get you a deal on some good appliances, whatever you need. Says they give a pretty decent military discount in Port Angeles."

Jess could feel Burke watching her, waiting for a response, so she forced a smile and met his eyes. "It's nice, Burke," she said. "It's really nice."

Burke smiled back at her. He squinted a little when he did, and there were crow's-feet starting to show around his eyes, and she caught herself wondering what he would look like when he was older, wondering if that was something she would ever get to know.

He walked over to stand beside her, and they stared in together at the empty space that would one day be her kitchen. Then he reached down and found her hand with his, twined his fingers between hers and nudged her back toward the front of the house.

"Come on," he said. "There's something I want to show you."

They took the stairs slowly, Jess leaning on the railing and Burke right beside her, her crutches under his one arm and the other arm held out to catch her.

"Upstairs, see, dead ahead, that's the bathroom," he told her as they climbed. "Joe has the plumbing roughed in, but you still need to figure out how you want it decorated."

She could see the little room at the top of the stairs, facing the rear of the house and the backyard. A doorway on either side.

"Now, to the left, here," Burke said, guiding her at the top of the stairs and holding out her crutches, "we're thinking this will be the second bedroom. You can use it as an office, or if you have guests come to visit. Heck, give Lucy her own bedroom. But this——"

He led her into the opposite bedroom, and it wasn't finished or drywalled yet either, but Jess could see the makings of a walk-in closet, big bright windows overlooking the road out front. "This," Burke said, "is your master bedroom."

He helped her walk into the middle of the room and stood back as she surveyed it, and she could see how it might be nice when it was finished, but it didn't really look like much now.

"Joe says another couple of months," Burke told her. "Then you can move in."

He stepped closer, took her shoulders in his hands. "I'm going to build this house for you, Jess," he said. "Whether it's me you choose to build your life with or somebody else. I'll keep working on this until I'm sure it's a good home, until I'm sure you're going to be okay."

She closed her eyes. "I don't want somebody else."

"Well, good," he replied. "Me either. But as far as I can see, we've got a couple of months yet to try and figure it out."

She opened her eyes and stared up into his, and she could see in his gaze the possibilities he imagined, the way the house would look finished and the two of them in it, and Lucy there too. And she could see, too, an acknowledgment of the work that lay ahead, the kitchen and the bathrooms and the walls, the painting and the furnishing and the landscaping. And the work they would have to do too, the both of them, to build out from the foundation they'd poured together on Dixie Island and the frame of something bigger that they'd pieced together since. She could see how Burke knew it would take time and effort, real effort, to create something together they both would be proud of, something that would last. And she could see in his eyes how he was willing to work for it, how there was nothing else in the world he wanted more.

Jess knew, suddenly and plainly, that she wanted it too.

She leaned up and kissed him and closed her eyes tight, and as he held her and their lips met she could feel the house come alive around her, feel the breeze through the window rustle the curtains they'd pick out, smell Memorial Day hot dogs grilling in the back-yard. She could see the years age Burke's face and how he'd still remain handsome, and how the look in his eyes would never change when he saw her, no matter how the time passed around them.

She could see it, and she could feel it. She kissed Burke some more, and even when she opened her eyes, she could still see what could be, what she knew Burke believed in.

Lucy's collar jangled from downstairs, and Jess could hear the padding of the dog's paws as she climbed steadily to the second floor of the house. Jess pulled back a ways from Burke and the both of them turned toward the doorway as the dog appeared, head cocked and curious.

Her tail wagged when she saw them, but she must have known they were making out; she grumbled to herself and turned around and lay down, heavy, on the landing. Jess and Burke could hear her muttering complaints as she settled herself on the floor.

"You'd better get used to it, dog," Burke called out. "There's going to be a lot more where that came from."

The dog groaned loud, as if she understood what he'd said, and Jess and Burke laughed.

"She'll like it here," Burke said. "When it's all said and done."

"Yes," Jess said. "I think she will."

She was still holding Burke, and Burke was still holding her, and she turned away from the doorway to look into his eyes again.

"I think we all will," she told him. "It's going to be a beautiful home."

ACKNOWLEDGMENTS

It's not always the easiest thing to bring a book into the world. I'm very grateful to my agent, Stacia Decker, for sticking up for me when the chips were down, and to Josh Kendall at Mulholland for his efforts on Jess, Mason, and Lucy's behalf.

Many other fine people at Mulholland and Little, Brown helped to get this story into your hands, including Helen Richard O'Hare, Betsy Uhrig, Sareena Kamath, Shannon Hennessey, Pamela Brown, Emily Giglierano, and Reagan Arthur. Thanks in particular to my wonderful copyeditor, Dianna Stirpe, for saving my bacon over and over again, and for doing so with wit and originality.

Thanks to the many booksellers and librarians who've helped readers find their way to Makah County and back again, and to everyone who's taken that journey, in this book or the last one or both.

I'm grateful to my family—Ethan Laukkanen, Ruth Sellers, Andrew and Terrence Laukkanen, Laura Mustard, and little E—for their wisdom, humor, and love, above all.

And, of course, I'm grateful to my own Lucy, who's in every way as wonderful as the Lucy in these books.

ABOUT THE AUTHOR

A former commercial fisherman and professional poker journalist, Owen Laukkanen is the author of six critically acclaimed Stevens and Windermere FBI thrillers, the nautical adventure *Gale Force,* and *The Wild,* a thriller for young adults. A native of Vancouver, Canada, Laukkanen spends nearly every waking hour with his dog, Lucy, a seven-year-old rescue pit bull whose hobbies include hiking, napping, and squirrels.

MULHOLLAND BOOKS

You won't be able to put down these Mulholland books.

LONE JACK TRAIL *by Owen Laukkanen*

TROUBLED BLOOD *by Robert Galbraith*

THE BOOK OF LAMPS AND BANNERS *by Elizabeth Hand*

BLOOD GROVE *by Walter Mosley*

SMOKE *by Joe Ide*

LIGHTSEEKERS *by Femi Kayode*

YOU'LL THANK ME FOR THIS *by Nina Siegal*

HEAVEN'S A LIE *by Wallace Stroby*

A MAN NAMED DOLL *by Jonathan Ames*

THE OTHERS *by Sarah Blau*

Visit mulhollandbooks.com for
your daily suspense fix.